IT Can Be Dangerous

Ita Ryan

 Published 2013 by PPP Publications

 21-22 Lower Stephen Street, Dublin 2, Ireland. Printed 2013 by createspace

ISBN: 978-0-9562403-5-4

DEDICATION

This book is for my parents and all the rest of my very supportive, encouraging and loving family.

DISCLAIMER

All characters appearing in this work are fictitious (even Harold, unfortunately). Any resemblance to real persons, living or dead, is purely coincidental.

CONTENTS

ACKNOWLEDGMENTS

I would like to thank all of my friends who took the time to read early drafts and supply much-needed criticism. A special thanks to my editor, Amelia Etherton. She had a lot to put up with. All remaining errors are due to my stubborn determination to ruthlessly split infinitives, invent words and smuggle in last-minute typos.

1 — INTRODUCTION

Even though Nathan Boyle's murderer has been tried, convicted and locked up, rumours about Nathan's death are still flying around the City. People are always asking me what 'really' happened. Some internet blogs — the conspiracy-theory type — have suggested that there was a massive cover-up. They can't decide whether it was orchestrated by Airwolfe or by the government. Maybe by terrorists. Whatever, they're certain that someone out there is lying to them.

I was stuck right in the middle of the whole thing. I've been told — though I can't mention any names — that it would be in the public interest to publish an eye-witness account. So I've dug out some personal notes that I took back then, looked over emails and talked to friends and colleagues about what they can remember. This is the result.

By the way, I was startled when I began this project by how much has changed since Nathan Boyle was murdered in 2007. It was only a few years ago, but there was no Twitter, no iPhone and hardly any Facebook. No tablets. It was like some kind of prehistoric age. I've tried to remain true to that time, going back over what I've written to make sure I don't talk about anachronistic stuff like using Google Street View to get around.

Anyway. Everything that happened to me is in this document. But I'll totally understand if you don't believe a word of it.

2 — TROUBLE

At nine o'clock I stretched, yawned, and reluctantly decided to call it a day. My stomach was telling me to go home. I powered down my computer and stood. As I came back to the real world I realised that my eyes were tired, my legs were stiff and my shoulders and neck ached. As usual. I'd be fine tomorrow.

My gym timetable was on my desk but I knew without looking that there'd be no classes on so late. Oh well, I thought, there's always another day. Coat, scarf, hat. The large open-plan office was almost in darkness. The security guard had swung by at some point and turned off all the lights except those in my corner. To my surprise, my boss had left the light on in his office behind me.

Perhaps he was still working too. Yeah right, I thought, I kill myself with my sparkling wit.

The door was open so I stuck my head in and called out to make sure he was definitely gone. No reply. Just as I stabbed at the switch something caught my eye. I turned the light on again. Bizarre. Nathan's chair was turned to the wall, and his hand was visible, dangling at an odd angle. Maybe he'd fallen asleep. I went in, and walked around his desk to wake him up.

Light-heartedness was at an end.

Nathan was motionless, silent. He was slumped in his chair. His head had fallen awkwardly forward. His neck was a bloody, mottled red.

Inappropriate, obscene, a gold handle protruded above the back of his collar.

I couldn't process it. How could someone be alive with that blade in their neck? A thin line of red had trickled downwards and seeped into his shirt. There was an awful stillness about him; an air of finality.

He must, but I couldn't believe it, be dead.

I took a step forward and said 'Nathan?'

He didn't shout at me for being in his office. He didn't make a sarcastic remark. He did nothing.

I reached out and touched his shoulder. He shifted slightly. Thousands of fictional detectives screamed at me: 'Don't touch the body!'

It seemed so ruthless not to give rest to the lolling head, not to close the unseeing eyes.

Murder.

Who did it? I whirled abruptly, terrified. There was no one there. I ran out of his office. No one. Was the killer lurking in the dark shadows of the open-plan space? Behind that palm? God! I grabbed the phone on my desk and dialled '999'. Silence. I slammed down the receiver. Whirled, looked around. Realised: office telephone. '9 999'. Emergency services. Police. Spun to and fro, scanning the dim recesses of the room as I spoke.

'There's been a death, no, a murder, in my office. Airwolfe on City Road. Near the Prêt. No, I don't know the number. I've only been working here a few months. A white concrete building; three stories. Nathan Boyle. My name? Cynthia Hegarty. No, I haven't contacted security. I don't know how to get them. Yes, *I*'m OK. Thank you. Tell them to hurry.'

The woman had sounded quite suspicious. As I hung up I realised why. Only person in the office — finds the body.

Isn't there some proportion of people who find bodies who turn out to be the murderers? What is it? Could google it.

Right. I'm in big big trouble.

I tried to think what Poirot would do. No, he was never a suspect. Hastings. No, he was an idiot. Different writer. Any Dick Francis hero. Better. He'd cover his arse.

OK, I can do this. My mobile. With a deep breath, I slunk in to Nathan's office. Looking firmly away, approached the body. Took photo. Took more photos.

Keep looking at the blank wall. Walk around body. Photograph body. Don't worry. Police on way. Photograph floor. Ceiling. Walls. Other side. Body again. Don't get sick don't get sick don't get sick.

OK leg it.

From my chair I dialled '0' for Reception, far away in the Docklands main building. They connected me to security downstairs.

My mobile beeped while I was talking.

Babes. Up for dinner tmrw @ 8? H

Fantastic. Great. A dinner invite from the victim's son. Suddenly I understood the phrase 'rising hysteria'.

Hugh, the security guard, appeared and made for Nathan's room. He emerged looking shaken.

'Cynthia, what happened? Did you see anyone?' he asked.

'No. I was programming.'

He sank into a chair, staring at me.

'I never notice anything when I'm working.' Even I thought this sounded weak.

'Who could've done it?' he asked.

'I dunno. Anyone in the company,' I said. 'Most of them wanted to.'

Then I felt guilty. After all, Nathan was dead now.

He looked at his pager.

'There's someone outside. Must be the police. We'd

better go down and let them in.'

He opened the door to a uniformed bobby, about twelve years old; skin as smooth as a baby's bottom. He seemed enthusiastic but disbelieving, like a puppy that's had too few walks. His tail would be wagging soon, I thought.

'Good evening.' He drew out his ID card. 'I'm Constable Wilson. We've received information that there's been a murder on these premises.'

'I'll take you up,' said Hugh.

Lift rides at work can be strained when your companions are unfamiliar, but this was a living nightmare. As we reached the second floor I caught Hugh's arm, stumbling. He helped me to my chair. My desk — usually my haven, my refuge — was an alien environment.

I realised that my initial bravado had been the first effect of shock.

Now there was time for all the later effects of shock. Reality was hitting home.

How could I have sat through a murder a few metres behind me? And would anyone believe it?

The puppy took a few steps into Nathan's office. His ears pricked up. He pulled out his walkie-talkie and muttered…'Caucasian male. Mid-fifties. Stabbed in the neck. Weapon present. Definitely dead. *Yes*, bring backup.'

After the call, he turned to us. 'I need some information. Names, dates of birth, where you were for the past few hours, who found the body.'

Hugh and I looked at each other. The policeman fixed on Hugh.

'You, sir. Are you the security guard in this office?'

He got his details, then said:

'Did you find the body?'

'No. Cynthia did,' said Hugh. 'She rang you and then she called me and I came up.'

'Did you touch the body?'

'No. He was obviously dead. I gave a quick look around and then came out and asked Cynthia what had happened.'

'Thank you, sir. Now you, miss. What's your name?'

'Cynthia Hegarty.'

I gave him my details, trying to speak calmly.

'Where have you been for the past few hours?' he asked.

I gestured lamely at my desk. 'I was here.'

His eyebrows rose. 'Here, as in, in the office, or here, as in, at this desk.'

'Here, as in, at this desk,' I said.

'Whoever killed Mr…Boyle, must have walked right behind this desk to reach his office door,' he said. 'Then walked right behind this desk again to leave the building.'

'Yes, I know,' I said.

'Did you see the killer?' he asked.

'No.'

'Did you kill Mr Boyle?'

'No!'

'Miss, I would have thought it was impossible for you to fail to see this killer,' he said. 'They must have passed close behind your chair.'

My hands were trembling. I clasped them.

'Officer,' I said. 'I know it seems unlikely, but I was working. I concentrate very hard when I'm working. I rarely notice people coming and going. And I do have my back to Nathan's office.'

He studied me for a while. He wrote something in his notebook. He said:

'And you're positive you didn't see anyone, notice anything odd? I'll let you think about it for a while.'

'OK. Could I get a cup of tea? It's just over there,' I indicated the coffee station on the other side of the corridor.

He shook his head.

'Contamination of the scene should be minimised. You must stay where you are.'

After a moment I closed my eyes because they were both staring at me. Normal human relations were suspended, I realised. I was the obvious suspect. Who else could it have been? Anyway, who else wanted to kill Nathan?

I couldn't believe how idiotic I'd been over the past weeks. Sending silly emails about the boss. Uh-oh. They'd show up during the investigation. I rested my head in my hands, thinking back. Remembering Friday's staff party, I groaned. In fact, everything that had happened since Thursday morning now seemed fraught with an unanticipated significance.

Oh for a cup of tea.

3 — COUNTDOWN TO MURDER — THURSDAY

Another eight hours plus of soul-destroying wage-slavery ahead, I thought. I went online and read the day's headlines in the *Financial Times* and the *Irish Examiner*. Then I scanned my email for personal messages. There was one from Sparky, my ex. I deleted it.

I'd been at Airwolfe and Co, real-time software developers for the airline industry, for four months. It was starting to feel like home.

Through the glass wall behind me I could hear Nathan shouting at some unfortunate colleague. In a foul mood as usual. Shortly, we were due to explain to him why the AirCross project had missed another milestone. Fun meeting that would be.

To: James
From: Cynthia
Subject: Missed Milestone
Dear Boss,
I'm very sorry we missed another milestone. However, this could not be avoided for the following reasons:
– Management is dysfunctional

– Not enough skilled people
– Disappearance of essential test servers for 'two hours of maintenance' three weeks ago
– Management's goals conflicting, unattainable and subject to constant change
– Everyone so depressed after last round of pay reviews that motivation gone through ground floor and now tunnelling below cellar.
– Management is dysfunctional
Kind Regards,
Cynthia

I hit the 'Send' button, waited for the chuckle from James, who was labouring on the other side of the partition, and felt better. I wished I had the guts to forward the mail to Nathan instead of the standard list of meaningless excuses.

Gloomily, I got stuck into my real meeting notes, designed to spread blame so diffusely that we'd all survive. It was hard work, and a gentle tap on my shoulder made me jump.

'Excuse me?' The voice behind me was quiet and polite.

I swivelled, preparing to blast the intruder.

'Yes?' I snarled, then took in the very, very handsome face smiling sardonically at me. Floppy blond hair. Suited, but suit in disarray with shirt casually untucked. Mm. Not my type, but still…mmm.

'Can I help you?' I asked.

The visitor clocked my rapid attitude change. He seemed amused.

'Do you know where I can find Mr Boyle?'

'That's his office.' I nodded at the door behind me, which bore the legend 'Mr Nathan Boyle'. No surprise that he'd missed it. Everyone did. Sitting in front of the boss's office is a curse if you're a woman who wants to get some work done.

On this occasion it was a blessing though. 'Do you have an appointment?' I asked. Like I cared, but it was a chance to try to get my eyelashes to flutter.

'No, but I don't need one, do I? I'm his son,' he replied. His amusement deepened as I suppressed the instinctive reply ('You poor sod') and managed to force out an insincere 'That's lovely. Nice to meet you.'

'Thanks. I'm Harold.' (You poor sod).

'I'm Cynthia.'

We shook hands. His grip was firm and his eyes seemed to burn straight through me, triggering all sorts of ideas inappropriate to our surroundings. I needed a cold glass of water. He should be out doing a movie launch, I thought. Nathan's son. Extraordinary.

'He seems to be free now,' I said. I couldn't wait for lunch, when I could discuss this Godlike interloper with James, who was popping his head over the partition like a prairie dog every ten seconds.

At 11.30, Nathan was visible through the glass wall of his office, and faintly audible, shouting at Harold. No meeting yet, then. Eventually Harold left, shooting me a grin as he passed. Nathan emerged with a notepad. James and I headed downstairs together. He was looking his best in a bright pink shirt, blond hair spiked with gel. Not the usual geek image, but James isn't the usual geek.

'Nathan's in a good mood.' Liz joined us. She was the most junior of the team. Tall and slim, with wispy strawberry-blonde hair, she had huge eyes that gave her a fragile, waiflike air. It was belied by her sharp coding skills.

'Yeah, maybe we should ask for a pay rise,' said James. We all cackled as we arrived in the comfortably shabby meeting room.

Airwolfe's corporate image was shiny and new, like the flagship headquarters recently erected in the Docklands. The software development office I worked in on City Road was the exception. The PR department hated the thought of our dilapidated, lived-in look. We'd been scheduled to relocate to glass-building-land, but when the time came they had no space left. So we were the company's forgotten outpost. Upper management never crossed the threshold; we had to make do with a relaxed, cosy atmosphere.

Luckily, most of the employees in our building were programmers, and thrilled to be off the corporate radar. But would-be upwardly-mobile management types — like Nathan — hated our isolation.

(I'm sure you're probably dying to hear all the glamorous details of aeroplane software development, but I'm afraid we won't have time to focus on them in this document. A secret: there's not much glamour really, it's much the same as most other software development except there are more rules and the stakes are higher. Don't tell anyone.)

Just as the meeting began, our fourth team-member, Eugene, appeared. He had to conduct the traditional hunt for an extra chair. As always, he looked exhausted.

Nathan went for me first.

'We need to discuss the problems with this project,' he said. 'Cynthia?'

'Well we're not in system testing yet, which puts us five weeks behind our last revised deadline,' I said. 'That's eight months behind altogether.'

'Why not?'

'The test servers are down and we've lost two people from the integration testing team. Also there was a diversion of resources towards doing a demo for higher management. That took a fortnight.'

'Ha! Eugene, you were supposed to do the demo work.'

Eugene — slight, dark-haired and in his early forties — seemed unusually nervous, even for him. He rubbed his neck with a tired hand. There was baby-sick on the sleeve of his nylon jumper.

'Yes, Nathan. Um, we encountered a problem with the night-fly feature,' he said. 'James had to help because he's the only one who's worked on that part of the project.'

'And you couldn't have handled it yourself? You've got, what, twenty years of experience? Surely you can fix a trivial little bug by now.'

James tried to intervene: 'The night-fly software is *very* buggy, Nathan. If you remember, we removed it from the latest version because it's so unstable, and—'

'Don't interrupt, James, you're under contract to write code here, not hide other people's incompetence. Eugene, if you can't solve problems by yourself, maybe you're in the wrong company. You won't always have friends around to hold your hand. Shape up or ship out.'

Eugene, who had been working in Airwolfe for fifteen years as opposed to Nathan's five, looked shocked. He glared at Nathan, who had already turned his attention to Liz. His hand tightened on his pen. For a moment it seemed as though he might stand up for himself. But then he sighed, slumped, and went back to dozing over his notes.

'What about the soak testing?' Nathan had started on Liz. 'Have you managed to finish it yet?'

So poor Liz had to explain why the soak testing was late. A difficult task. She was a shy, polite girl — too polite to mention that it was Nathan's own fault for taking servers out of commission.

When Nathan started shouting I tuned out. I tuned back in after a while to hear:

'...you should do more than sit around waiting for things to happen. We want highly-motivated self-starters on this team. You should have found something else to do. Blue-skies thinking, that's what we need. Have you thought about running a virtual machine over the interweb? There was an article in *The Times Technical Supplement* last week...'

I tried not to meet James's eye. Programmers do their best to keep their bosses away from imperfectly-understood technical articles, but some always slip through.

'What about the user interface?' Nathan snapped at James. 'How's that going?'

'Not too bad. We ran it by a focus group with mixed success. We've tried to apply 'The Principle of Least Astonishment', but they still couldn't figure out what some of the buttons do. We really should employ a user-interface expert to help with the design.'

'Too expensive. Is the database stable?'

'Getting there, but we need more testers.'

'None available. Cynthia, what about the Overflight piece?'

'Under way, making reasonable progress,' I said.

'Will it be on time?'

'No.'

'What a surprise. Time for more dedication here, people. You all seem to be half asleep. No initiative, no vision, no drive. I can't carry you all at once…' And off he went on one of his rants. He lectured on about something or other while his little eyes glittered and the vein in his forehead glistened unpleasantly.

As usual, I spent the time doodling and thinking about getting a new job. Occasionally I varied the routine by calculating how much money I'd earned since the beginning of the meeting. Then I worked out the total cost to the company of the time wasted by Nathan's current speech. The work-foregone cost involved guessing everyone else's salaries, which were supposed to be secret, so it was good fun. The demotivation cost was incalculable.

'…Eugene, you stay behind.'

Meeting over. At last. Nathan wouldn't come near us again for at least a week.

James swung by for lunch shortly afterwards.

'Did you see him?' I asked as soon as we'd settled in Prêt.

'Mm hmm. Hugh Grant without the hesitancy.'

'More *Bridget Jones* than *Four Weddings*,' I nodded. 'He thinks I'm his dad's secretary.'

'Who's this?' asked Liz, approaching with a salad on her tray.

'Nathan's son,' James told her as she sat down. 'He paid Daddy a visit before the meeting. A dreamboat, and lucky

Cynthia got to talk to him. Cynthia, shaggability level please?'

'Oh, a nine,' I replied. 'Would be a ten but he's called Harold. One would have to address him as 'darling' in the throes. We'll probably never see him again, sadly. How did Nathan manage to produce *that*?'

'Wife's by first marriage?' asked James. 'He's clearly not Daddy's favourite little boy today though. Nathan sounded even worse than when he's 'mentoring' Eugene.'

'Yeah, he's horrible to Eugene,' said Liz. 'What's that all about?'

'Oh, Eugene's a COBOL programmer,' James said, 'eminently dispensable.'

'But he's the only person who knows how to maintain the UKIS system,' said Liz. 'Of course, that's been replaced and it's come offline this month…oh.'

'What does UKIS even do, anyway? Eugene is a model employee, dedicated, loyal and hard-working,' James said, 'which makes him exactly the kind of guy who gets pushed around.'

'Yeah, but why?' asked Liz.

'Because the less loyalty you have to a company, the better you're treated,' I said. 'Nathan knows *your* weaknesses as well,Liz, you're far too conscientious and sweet to leave. Speaking of sweet, who fancies some of my amazing chocolate slice?' My addiction to Prêt's chocolate slices was well known to my lunch buddies. I think they were secretly becoming addicted themselves. They always helped me out diet-wise by taking a third each.

'I wouldn't eat that if I were you,' said James.

'Nonsense, it's delicious.'

'OK, don't turn around then.'

Of course I turned, all chocolate and crumbs. Dreamboat was approaching, looking devilish. Harold, as a name, was growing on me. I swallowed hastily and said:

'Can I help you?'

'I hope so,' said Harold. 'I hoped I'd find you here. I'm terribly sorry, and you can tell me to get lost of course if you want to, but I thought you might help me out.'

I raised my eyebrows, attempting to disguise my glee with a faint smile.

'Nathan wants me to come to the company party. It's a crazy idea, I don't know anyone at all, and you seemed friendly, so I wondered if you could possibly, I mean, if I could get you a drink beforehand and accompany you and maybe ask you to hold my hand. Metaphorically. And tell me who everyone is.' He glanced at James and Liz. 'But you'll be with your friends. I don't want to intrude.'

'No intrusion, I assure you,' said James. 'Cynthia would be thrilled, wouldn't you Cynthia?'

'Oh. Yes. Yes, feel free to join us.'

'We usually go to the Lighthouse, off City Road. Just beside the office. It's been dreadfully prettified and they don't sell jugs of beer any more but we still love it. We'll be there about five,' said James. (The Lighthouse had been turned from a dingy brown pub to a less dingy reddish kind of pub. James likes tradition.) 'We'll be happy to see you, won't we Liz? This is Liz. I'm James.'

'Great. Thanks. I'll see you all soon I hope.' With a smile for everyone, he turned and loped off, long coat swinging. He looked even better from the back.

God, if only I hadn't been sweaty, inarticulate and covered in chocolate slice.

'Wow, Cynthia,' said Liz, 'if he'd smiled at me like that I'd've been stuttering and blushing and generally humiliating myself. Then I'd have had to skip the party out of embarrassment. Which would be a pity. He is *gor*geous. Is that a date?'

'I dunno,' I said, 'but I certainly hope so.'

'OhshitI'mlateagain,' said Liz.

Back in the world where Nathan was dead, people bustled. No one approached me. I thought about what I'd done in the past few hours. Had I gone to the loo, seen anyone on the way, or coming back? I didn't think so. I needed to go now. Had I made myself a cup of tea? Probably not. I was fairly sure that I'd been working flat out since five. But I have a goldfish memory while concentrating. Often, I can't remember what I did an hour or even twenty minutes previously.

When the real police appeared, they'd arrest me. They'd have no choice. A dead body in the office. Only me and Hugh in the building. The CCTV would probably show Hugh sitting at his desk until just before his rounds. I was in big, big trouble.

All the same, I still wanted to laugh when I remembered our return to the office on Thursday.

Airwolfe and Co had strict lunch hours that were rigidly supervised in City Road by Vicky, the office manager. An efficient-looking, sharp-suited blonde in her early twenties, she was on a perpetual power trip. The unfortunate Liz, as a junior staff member, bore the full brunt of her wrath.

'It's nearly five past two,' was her friendly greeting. 'You're more than four minutes late. That's your third infringement in the past two weeks. Is there some reason why you can't keep to the hours specificated in your contract?'

'Sorry Vicky. Prêt was busy and I didn't notice the time.'

'One more late in the next fortnight and you're on a reprimand. I don't recommend that you model your time-keeping on senior staff,' this with a glare in our direction.

'Wagon,' I muttered, making my way back to my desk.

To: Cynthia
From: James
Subject: Deviance!
Itt has cum to our attenshun dat sum employyes hav bin enchoying themselves. Dis beehaviour is nott permited.
Yorrs Sinseerly,

The Orfiss Manacher.

To: James
From: Cynthia
Subject: Re: Deviance!
All dose staf memberz hoo hav bin taeking the ful hour for lundge wil be execooted at dawn tommorow.
Yorz Faytfuly,
De Offiss Mandiger

Email acknowledged, I got down to business. Harold's inviting himself to the office party had increased my feeling of anticipation by about a million times. I'd considered skipping it. Now I was definitely going, and I needed a killer outfit.

By a lucky coincidence my fashion-loving sister Alice was arriving from Dublin that afternoon to spend the weekend with me. When she dropped in to Airwolfe for my keys, I put her on red shopping alert.

There's not much choice in the vicinity of Old Street, so we met in Oxford Circus at 6.30. As so often before, I swore I'd stay off the tubes before eight in the evening in future. I'm armpit height to most smelly males.

Early December pre-Christmas exuberance had kicked in. Oxford Street was busy busy busy, with everyone hoping to find those elusive perfect gifts. The Christmas lights brightened the cold dark evening and enhanced the air of expectancy and excitement. I love shopping at that time of year.

'Brilliant flat,' said Alice when we met.

'Apartment,' I corrected her.

'Flat,' she grinned at me. 'You're right about the dodgy carpet, but your rug does the job. The lamps are lovely, and the bookshelf and the posters. Did you raid every stall in Camden? And do you have a cleaner or something? Your kitchen is surprisingly spotless.'

'It is,' I said, not mentioning that I'd been up till the early hours scouring tiles and washing floors. It was Alice's first visit and I wanted her to love the flat like I did. I adored having my own place. Going home in the evenings, I felt like a squirrel returning to its cosy nest.

'Heard from Sparky?' (My ex).

'A bit. Let's not talk about him.'

'So why are you suddenly all interested in this party?' she changed the subject. 'You hate those things. You always say you couldn't care less about whatever poor sods happen to be employing you this time and you don't want to have to socialise with boss type people. You were moaning last week about having to go.'

'Yeah but now they've said there'll be Kris Kindle and fairy lights and everything.'

'Yeah, right. Who is he?'

'You know me so well, Alice. He is divine. And also the boss's son. Is that a bad idea?'

'Do the words 'shit' and 'doorstep' mean anything to you?'

'I could always leave Airwolfe and go write some exciting derivatives software for a bank. Oh wait, there's a recession. Anyway I'm not actually *working* with Harold. He's attractive though. A blond Hugh Grant, with a devilish grin.'

'Oh well, jobs come and go. There's a sale in Whistles.'

Shopping with Alice is fun. She pulls the most unlikely garments off the rack, holds them up, runs an eye over me, and packs me off to the changing room. I emerge looking fabulous — for me — in an outfit I wouldn't have spat on myself.

We got lost in Top Shop, ending up in the maternity section.

'Cool stuff. I wish I was pregnant,' said Alice, fingering a black lace top.

'What a thought.' I tried to imagine her projecting motherly gravitas. I failed.

'You'd be a great Aunty,' she said, making for the exit. She laughed back at me and promptly fell over a buggy.

'If you will wear four-inch heels…' I said, pulling her up.

'Cynthia.'

I turned. Pushing the buggy, and looking unusually relaxed, was Eugene, my permanently harassed colleague. I dropped my gaze. No, they hadn't found a triple buggy.

'What are you doing here, Cynthia? Are you pregnant? Not that, I mean…none of my business…' he trailed off, then gestured to a pretty young woman who had joined him.

'This is Gwyneth. Gwyneth, this is Cynthia, from work. Remember I told you about her? The Irish one.'

Gwyneth smiled.

'Lovely to meet you, Cynthia,' she said. 'This is Colin,' she lifted the hand of the toddler she had in tow, 'this is John, and that's Gary,' indicating the double buggy.

'Great to meet them at last,' I said, 'I've heard so much about them from Eugene. This is my sister, Alice.'

The triplets were adorable — all dark and cute and ruffled-looking. John seemed to be asleep. Gary was relaxing, surveying the world contentedly in comfort.

'Luckily, Colin likes walking,' said Gwyneth, releasing his hand and absently rubbing her stomach. I noticed that it seemed rather large and round, even for a woman who'd had triplets within the past eighteen months. Should I ask? Oh no, I couldn't. Supposing I was wrong?

Gwyneth copped my hesitation.

'You're wondering if I'm pregnant, aren't you? Yes, I am.' She gave a merry laugh. 'Don't worry about looking surprised, I'm surprised myself. We didn't expect to have any more, did we Eugene?'

'No, but the more the merrier,' said Eugene fondly, 'bring 'em on'. Colin grabbed his leg, hiding from me and Alice. Eugene picked him up and kissed him.

'I gave all my maternity things away, didn't think I'd need them, so I have to buy new,' said Gwyneth. 'I'm just getting to that stage now. The stuff here is lovely.' She sounded wistful. 'Bloody expensive though.'

'That top you have on is fabulous,' said Alice, 'where did

you get it?'

Typical Alice, she wasn't even pregnant, but she'd store up the answer and whenever her turn came — even if it was fifteen years later — she'd have an extra destination on her shopping trip.

'**D**oes he work with you?' Alice asked after we'd parted ways.

'Yeah. He's the stressed guy,' I said.

'He doesn't look stressed,' she said.

'I've never seen him so laid-back. He's a home bird, obviously. Isn't Gwyneth lovely?'

'Lovely. Perfect skin. Beautiful hair. You know, I think I *will* get pregnant myself.'

After a satisfyingly long time spent shopping, comparing outfits and drinking tea, we found the perfect black dress. Almost knee-length with a soft ruched effect, it was equally flattering on Alice (tall and willowy) and me (rather less tall, and considerably less willowy). We ended up buying one each. I got a new pair of fabulous black shoes too — just because.

All set.

Activity around Nathan's office was mounting. I wondered how much time had gone by since the tail-wagging PC had arrived. It felt like aeons. Idly, I speculated on what I'd study during my thirty years in the slammer. A life sentence was definitely long enough to encompass a PhD.

'Excuse me, miss.'

A policewoman hovered.

'I believe you found the body. I'm PC Lawson. Superintendent Foster wants to see you immediately.'

'Could I go to the loo first?' I asked.

PC Lawson accompanied me to the toilets. As I washed

my hands I studied myself in the mirror. My face was deathly pale. My occasionally-straightened brown hair had fled back into its natural tight curls. My eyes, normally hazel, shone bright green. They always do when I'm crying. Or trying not to cry.

I blew my nose, which promptly turned red.

I washed my hands again, picked up my make-up bag, then put it back down. Maybe the clown-after-electric-shock look would arouse some much-needed sympathy.

In the mirror my chin wobbled. I clutched the basin and blinked furiously, thinking of the Frenchman who once tried hard to teach me wind-surfing:

'Do not be so afraid. You must 'ave courage!'

'You should bring some tissue,' said PC Lawson.

I went into a cubicle and grabbed some bog-roll, which I stuffed up my sleeve like a child. I straightened my shoulders and smiled tentatively at PC Lawson. To my eternal gratitude, she smiled back.

An office on the floor below had become a makeshift operations room. PC Lawson opened the door.

'Cynthia Hegarty, sir.'

The man behind the desk looked up.

At that first terrifying meeting I noticed nothing about his appearance. Afterwards, the only things I remembered were the friendly wrinkles at the sides of his eyes and a sort of comforting feeling.

'Hello, Ms Hegarty. I'm Superintendent Foster.' he said.

'Please call me Cynthia.' It'd be less scary. I didn't think he would, but he did.

'Cynthia. You're Cynthia Hegarty?'

'Yes.'

He checked my date of birth and so on. Then the nitty-gritty.

'How long have you been working for Airwolfe?'

'Nearly four months. Fifteen weeks today.'

'Where were you working previously?'

'In Australia. I'm just back. I came straight to London

and got this job that week.'

'Have you lived in London before?'

'No, this is my first job here.'

'I gather you live close by.'

'Yes, in Shoreditch off Brick Lane, in a two-bedroom flat over a shop.'

'Alone?'

'Yes.'

'What is your role in Airwolfe?'

'Senior Developer on the AirCross project. I write code and help junior developers. Reporting to Nathan Boyle.'

'I understand you were working near Mr Boyle's office for several hours before, and probably during, the murder.'

'Yes.'

'PC Wilson showed me your desk. The killer must have passed close behind your chair. It's only a few metres from Mr Boyle's office door.'

'Yes.'

'Are you surprised that you didn't see him?'

'No.'

He raised his eyebrows. Encouragingly, not so much sceptical as curious.

'I know it seems unlikely, but I was working. I'm a C++ programmer.' (Reader, this is pronounced 'C plus plus'. That's all you need to know about it, you'll be pleased to hear). 'I concentrate very hard when I'm working. I never do notice anything going on around me. I'm not very observant anyway. And I was testing a particularly tricky piece of code this evening. That's why I stayed late, no interruptions. You could have marched a herd of elephants into Nathan's office and out again, and I wouldn't have known a thing about it.'

'It's very unusual,' he said, but he smiled, and my courage rose.

'Well, you know, I always think those witnesses in detective stories who can tell you exactly what someone was wearing from fifty yards are highly suspect. How the hell would they remember that? How would they even notice?

Why would they care?'

'Indeed. We find that clear, accurate recall is rare. But sitting less than seven metres away from a murder and noticing nothing is even rarer. It's unfortunate for us, but very lucky for the killer.'

'Superintendent. It is Superintendent?'

He nodded.

'I've been thinking about that. I know it looks bad. You probably think I killed Nathan. But everyone in here knows that I never notice a thing when I'm working. So they could have sort of counted on that. Though it would have been risky, of course.'

He looked thoughtful. It would have been risky? It would have been downright insane. But what else could I say?

'Look, Cynthia, you've had a terrible shock and you probably want to go home. We must ask you to give us your fingerprints first. Is there anyone you'd like to call?'

Was he suggesting I get a lawyer? I think I looked shaken because he added:

'I mean, would you like to arrange to stay with someone? You shouldn't be alone tonight. Being in such close proximity to a murder is likely to upset you more than you realise. I suggest you call a friend, then get a taxi straight to their house. PC Lawson will organise one for you.'

'OK.'

'Before you go. Do you know who Nathan's next of kin is?'

'No. But I know his son's name is Harold and I have his mobile number.' I could feel a tell-tale blush flooding my face and neck.

'Do you now?' His attention had sharpened. 'Could you give it to PC Lawson please? Thanks for your co-operation, Cynthia. Naturally, we must ask you not to leave London until we contact you again. I suggest you take a day off work tomorrow. We'll be in touch.'

I felt like bowing as I backed out the door. This man held my entire future in his hands. If he decided I'd done it, I was as good as banged up already. They were bound to be able to come up with a motive. Imagined or real.

The Super's goodwill was the only thing between me and a prolonged sojourn at Her Majesty's pleasure.

By the time I'd done the fingerprints thing and got back to my desk, that whole corner, including Nathan's office, had been cordoned off. For a horrible moment I thought they wouldn't give me my mobile. But they searched my handbag and coat, then handed them over. I took out my phone to get Harold's number. His dinner text, still unanswered, jumped out at me.

I dictated his number to PC Lawson, who escorted me to a taxi. James had been alerted and was waiting at his flat. Agog with curiosity no doubt.

But what should I text back to Harold?

Hi ur dad ded im chief suspect tmrw off

or:

Harold, I'm afraid your father has passed away and I'm suspected of his murder. Are you still free for dinner tomorrow?

I couldn't tell him via text that his father had died, but I wanted to prepare him for bad news, as the police would be contacting him at any moment. I achieved what I thought was a reasonable compromise:

Hi, had very sad news at work. Probably can't make it tomorrow.

Abbreviating 'tomorrow' in the circumstances would, I felt, be in the worst of bad taste.

4 — COUNTDOWN TO MURDER — FRIDAY

As the taxi sped through London to James's house and comfort, I thought back to the day of the party. Had there been any pointers to this evening's grisly find? Maybe, I mused, one or two…

I've never been over-fond of mornings, but on the Friday of the party I wanted to be ready to head pub-wards by five, arrayed in my new finery. Plus my hair needed straightening. So I got up at dawn. I let myself out of the flat to the sound of Alice snoring in the spare room.

I had to do a new 'build' of the latest programming code that morning. It meant gathering together everyone's recent work, then merging and testing it. Although the procedure was automated at Airwolfe, builds were always tedious and time-consuming. Everyone accidentally overwrote one another's work, broke one another's code, failed the automated tests, then blamed someone else. Whenever an error cropped up, a hapless team member had to be 'volunteered' to fix it.

Experience had taught me to allocate several hours to this process. Everything was guaranteed to go wrong if you were in a hurry.

As usual, I tried to mitigate the misery of starting a working day by checking my email.

I had a mail from Ronan, Airwolfe's head of Systems Administration. Ronan mostly hung out with the other SysAdmin guys, but he was Irish so there was a bond. He'd sent me a link to Wikipedia's page on the Football Association of Ireland. We were losing a lot of games at the time, and it had, possibly, been modified by an unfriendly soul:

'The FAI are a bunch of talentless, no-hope f***ers who couldn't manage their way out of a paper bag,' the entry began, and the next few sentences weren't any milder.

As I was reading, my phone rang and Ronan's number flashed up. 'I gather you won't be flying home to watch the next match,' I said.

'No, fuck it, I wouldn't bother my arse. D'ya see Nathan this morning?'

'No.'

'Shout if you do.'

'Sure. Now, Ro, when are we getting the rest of our servers back?'

'Not until you admit the Northside has the best chips in Dublin.'

'Never, then?'

'See ya later,' and he was gone. Called away to some emergency no doubt. According to him, most people in Airwolfe couldn't tell their arse from their elbow. Ronan liked to point out the difference to them in his own inimitable style. I was never sure how he got away with it. Maybe it was his Irish charm.

To: All Staff
From: Vicky
Subject: Office Hygeen
It has come to our attention that cups are been left on the draining board without been dried. Anyone seen leaving cups

in the canteen area will be givn a written warning.
Regards,
The Office Manager

To: Cynthia
From: James
Subject: Re: Office Hygeen
Doo not use de crokerry or yoo wil be kilt!
Yors Taughtfuly,
De Orifice Manger

'Excuse me, is Mr Boyle in?'

I managed not to sigh out loud. I turned. The interrupter was a short, stout, pompous-looking man. Resisting the urge to say 'I don't know, because I can't see through my own skull and his office is behind me', I glanced at Nathan's glass office wall. The blinds were down.

'I'm sorry. I'm not sure.'

'Is he busy?'

'I'm afraid I'm not familiar with his movements. I suggest you knock and go in.'

He did as advised and let himself into Nathan's office, pulling a sheaf of papers out of his briefcase as he went and kicking the door shut behind him.

Back to work. Ton, a Dutchman I'd met in China, had sent round a long email about his travails exploring Vietnam on a motorbike, including photographs of roadside repairs in remote regions. The *Irish Examiner* online had details of another health crisis, queues in A&E and a row between politicians. Ho hum.

While gleaning this useful information, I'd been putting the build together, so around ten o'clock I set it running and started thinking about my cup of tea. A proper hot cup of tea with decent milk, which meant fetching one from a café. Gathering my coat and bag, I heard Nathan yelling 'Get OUT! Don't ever come here again!'

Pompous Man stalked out of Nathan's office, turned, and

said 'You haven't heard the last of this. You'll be hearing from my solicitor.' Unbelievably — so clichéd — he shook his fist.

Nathan, not to be outdone, snarled 'And you'll be hearing from mine!' and slammed his door so hard my monitor buzzed. For a moment I thought Pompous Man would kick the door, but he turned and stomped to the lobby instead. He stood and waited while the lift creaked its way up to our floor.

I arrived and joined him just before the lift descended. He was clearly still furious. He resembled an angry bull. Trying not to check his nostrils for steam, I said:

'Lovely day.'

'Harrumph.'

'How did your meeting with Mr Boyle go?' This with my best winning smile — hopefully conjuring up my own elusive Irish charm. He had no desire to confide his troubles to me, but anger overcame reticence.

'Badly. I wouldn't say anyone's meetings with him go well. He's a most difficult man to deal with.'

'You're telling me. I work for him.'

'I don't want that repeated, of course, although I suppose the fact of our disagreement will be public knowledge by now.'

'Do you mind my asking what you were disagreeing about?'

'Confidential, I'm afraid,' he grunted. 'Please, go ahead. Nice to meet you, goodbye.'

Cagey, but I had got a peek at his visitor's badge. Cecil Howell, from CityRich Properties. What was Nathan up to? None of my business, of course, but curiosity is a besetting sin of mine.

Bharathi the accountant liked Prêt's lattes. I picked one up for her and brought it to her desk when I got back to the office. Bharathi was a Londoner of Indian descent, tiny and feminine, with short spiky black hair. She had an air of tolerant acceptance of absurdity that attracted me as soon as

I met her. As I got to know her, I found that she had as good a sense of humour as I'd suspected.

She seemed happy to see the latte so I ventured to ask her 'Do you know why Nathan had a visitor from CityRich Properties this morning? If you do, will you tell me?'

'I do, but not officially. I probably shouldn't tell anyone,' she said, 'but I don't suppose it matters all that much. You'll keep it to yourself?'

'Oh, yes. Won't let on to a soul,' I told her, 'except James, and maybe Liz.'

'Best I could hope for. Well CityRich is just one guy, Cecil someone-or-other, and he bought the decrepit old building next door to Nathan's house. He bought the whole terrace, in fact. He wants to knock them all down and build a shop or something. Nathan is objecting. I'm not sure on what grounds, but I'd say it's simply his instinctive desire to be as much of a nuisance as he can, as often as he can.'

'He's pretty successful with that.'

'He certainly is.'

The hours flew by until 3.30, when there was a general sense that enough work had been done for one day. The silence of fifty people concentrating became the escalating murmur of fifty people looking forward to a free booze-up. Liz and I made for the Ladies with our bags of goodies, taking turns for mirror-space with the seven or eight other women on our floor. No one went home before going out at Airwolfe because the commute was at least a two-hour round trip for most people. My flat was only a short walk away, but I enjoyed the buzz of getting changed at work, everyone doing their make-up and admiring each other's outfits and exchanging gossip. The heady scents of hair spray and perfume and make-up bags, the laughter, shared mascaras and jokes, built the mood for the night ahead. Being new, I didn't know everyone, but somehow the story of my un-date with Harold had gone round so I got a fair bit of slagging.

The boss's son, I don't need to spell it out.

By four o'clock we were ready. We stuck our work clothes in sports bags under our desks, picked up James and descended to the ground floor. Approaching the door of the Lighthouse I felt the tiniest of little butterflies in my stomach. 'Safety in numbers,' I reassured myself as we entered in a wind of expensive cosmetic products.

The six or seven round wooden tables in the Lighthouse were all standing height, just right for accommodating variable numbers of roving drinkers. I did a quick scan of the few occupied bar stools. He wasn't there. Of course — after all, we'd said five. I felt relieved, and broke my no-drinking-at-office-parties rule with a half of Carlsberg.

Bharathi joined me at the nearest table. She was wearing a simple fitted dress with a black bodice and a dark green flared skirt. It contrasted with her spiky hair, making her look both feminine and sharp.

'So, Cynthia, are you really bringing Nathan's son tonight? What's he like?' she asked, as we climbed up on bar stools, trying not to spill our drinks. I hoped the lights were low enough to disguise my inevitable blush.

'Um, I don't know to be honest. It's not really just me, he kind of invited himself to join myself and James and Liz. He seems nice, but we were only talking for a minute.'

Curses. The lights were low all right, but not that low, and I could see Bharathi trying not to laugh. Right now, I could do without that sense of humour of hers.

'OK the evidence is clearly visible,' I admitted. 'Wait until you see him. He's absolutely yum. But he just wants moral support. Nathan insisted on him coming to the party. I don't think he's interested in me really.'

'But you like him?'

'Oh, I'm madly in love. There's no hope for me at all.'

'Sounds interesting. I'm looking forward to meeting him.'

Meanwhile, Liz was chatting to Peter from SysAdmin. She wore a loose flame-coloured sleeveless dress that emphasised her ethereal air. Peter, a tall, attractive black guy, seemed smitten.

'They're getting on well,' I said, nudging Bharathi.

'Yes, she's lovely isn't she? I'd say she's easy to work with. You're lucky, you have a good team, but do you find Nathan difficult to deal with?'

'He's awful, always bullying people.'

'Yeah, I've worked with him before. Who's he got his knife into this time?'

'Liz, for a start. She's an amazing learner but she's inexperienced and lacks confidence and she gets thrown when he starts hectoring her.'

'Poor thing.'

'Yeah. Mind you, she's single and bright and just out of college. She'll toughen up. Eugene gets the worst of it. He'd be in big trouble if he lost his job, and Nathan has seriously got his knife into him.'

Bharathi nodded. 'The triplets. They're nearly eighteen months now, aren't they? And his wife isn't working?'

'That's right, they're totally dependent on his salary, but his skills are nearly obsolete.'

'Surely he can retrain and move into a more up-to-date area?'

'You would think, but he never gets any free time to learn anything new. Nathan hates him. James said he applied for a Dot Net course but Nathan didn't get around to processing his application. Then, after the training budget had run out, he rejected it. James thinks Nathan's been stopping him up-skilling on purpose, and he'll make him redundant now UKIS is gone.'

'Can he do that?' asked Bharathi.

'He can do anything he likes. Eugene could go to Human Resources but they're paid by Airwolfe. They won't rock the boat. You're always in trouble if your boss hates you. And Nathan's not blatant.'

Bharathi nodded. 'Just never gives him a break.'

'Yep. Everyone makes mistakes but unfortunately, Nathan's blame-focused. He's a classic bully.'

'Eugene is very quiet. I suppose he's easy to push around.'

'Yes, and he's getting quieter and quieter all the time.'

'He's probably getting no sleep either,' said Bharathi, 'poor fellow. I'll try to think of a way to help. Maybe I can find some special COBOL programmer training money in the budget.'

'Another little drinky?' asked James over my shoulder. 'Bharathi, can I tempt you?'

'Never drink at staff parties,' said Bharathi sternly, 'but I suppose I'll need one to survive tonight. Did you hear that Nathan is due to get some award or other? Best Manager or something?'

'Ah. That's probably why he wants his handsome son along,' said James. 'Is there any way we can lodge an objection?'

Bharathi shook her head, smiling.

'How on earth are we going to get through that? OK, ladies, doubles all round.'

The back of my neck started to prickle. I swivelled on my bar-stool. Harold was pushing towards us from the door, looking delicious. Bharathi glanced at me. I nodded.

'Hello, Cynthia. Can I get you a drink?' he asked, giving me a peck on the cheek. I nearly fell off my stool.

'James is at the bar, thanks,' I managed to say. 'This is Bharathi.'

He smiled and I thought, my goodness, if he gave me that smile I'd melt through the floor. Then he turned to me and the smile got smilier. 'Ulp,' I thought, as I melted through the floor.

'All set for the party?' Bharathi asked. 'Did you know your dad is going to get a 'Best Manager' award?'

'Good God. How little one knows one's family. I always assumed he was a dreadful manager. Still, no man is a prophet in his own country, as he keeps telling me.'

'What do you work at?' Bharathi kept the conversational ball rolling, which was just as well because I wanted to curl up under the table and sleep for a year. Very attractive men often have that effect.

'I wouldn't use the term 'work' in connection with my activities. I, shall we say, arrange things.'

'Ah. The old wheeling and dealing, ducking and diving?'

'Something similar, though rather less energetic.'

'Sounds intriguing,' said Bharathi. 'Are you in a relationship? I've often wondered whether Nathan is a grandfather?'

'Go, Bharathi,' I thought.

'Oh, you know. Do people *do* relationships these days?' he replied, somewhat evasively. 'No offspring yet. What about yourself?'

'A boy and a girl,' said Bharathi, smiling. 'Two right little terrors.'

'Keep you busy?'

'Oh yes, we have no time for anything else. I'm looking forward to relaxing tonight. The meal should be good.'

'Aren't they always dreadful?'

'Yes, but,' leaning towards us, she murmured, 'I happen to know that it was unusually expensive. Accountants' gossip.'

'Maybe they'll have champagne.' I had finally recovered my wits.

'Mm,' Harold grinned. 'Are you a champagne fan?'

'I *so* am.'

'I have to get a drink.'

I watched as he made his way to the bar. He was like Moses parting the Red Sea. He radiated confidence. People stepped aside for him, then started queueing again with bemused expressions.

'Gosh, he *is* gorgeous. Are you nervous?' Bharathi asked.

'Terrified,' I told her. 'Thanks for taking the heat off.'

'My pleasure. I think he likes you.'

'Why?'

'His eyes lit up when you spoke. You weren't exactly analysing the finer points of the latest constitutional crisis.

Must be love.'

A hand descended on my shoulder. 'So what's wrong with the loony tune?' Ronan's voice in my ear.

'What?'

'Vicky. The office manager. She Who Must be Obeyed. The wagon who used to be Nathan's PA. What's wrong with her?'

'What do you mean what's wrong with her?'

'Jayziz, did you not see her running out of Boyle's room earlier bawling crying?'

'No.'

'Cynthia, you're a dozy cow. You sit right outside his office. How could you miss her? She was bleedin' sobbing for fuck's sake.'

'Cynthia has her head in the clouds when she's working. She never notices anything. You could play the national anthem behind her with a trumpet and she'd just hunch over her keyboard and type faster,' said James. 'Harold offered to get the drinks in, and he got served straight away so I left him to it. Are you talking about Vicky? What did she say? Anything?'

'Nah. Stomped to her desk and grabbed her stuff and stomped out. And it was two o'clock, her special time for standing at the door with a stopwatch, hassling people who're late back from lunch. She *must* be doing the dirty with Nathan.'

'It's such a cliché though,' I said. 'Would she really do that? He's not attractive and she's not desperate.'

'The power thing. Chicks always fall for it.'

'Power? Nathan? Pur-lease Ro. No, I think he was just being a wanker as usual. She probably mis-spelt an email or something. Not that he'd notice, the illiterate twat.'

'Ahem, here comes his son,' said Bharathi.

Ro glanced at Harold, raised an eyebrow, gave me a broad wink and disappeared back to the huddle of insane SysAdmin people cracking insane SysAdmin jokes.

Harold was carrying a magnum of champagne in one

hand and some glasses in the other. Mm…champagne.

'A small thank you for helping me out this evening,' he said as he deposited the goods on the table. 'I know not everyone likes champagne, but I find a glass or two before a tedious night out gets you going with a buzz.'

He popped the cork and handled the bottle in, I thought, a suspiciously practiced way. He gave the first glass to me with another heart-stopping smile, then turned to pour for Bharathi and James.

The champagne put everyone in a good mood. We laughed as Harold described the blandishments he'd used to get past security that morning. Bharathi and James regaled him with funny stories about the office. Soon it was party time and we wandered outside to get a taxi. No problem with Harold on board. He whistled and waved like someone out of a New York movie and a cab screeched to a halt for us. We were off.

'He likes me, he likes me, he likes me,' I thought. Clearly, for Harold to breathe was to flirt. But I still had a good feeling.

The venue for the Christmas party was an old, beautifully ornate theatre in Camden, recently made available for corporate events. There was a band on the stage, unfortunately. One of the two bars provided a hot Italian buffet, the other Thai. We tried both — they were delicious. With free wine and beer, there weren't many people drinking shorts.

Once we'd eaten we went for a wander, exploring the stalls and circle and the lower boxes. The auditorium had had all the fixed seating removed to create a dance area. Even though the band was so bad that it would have been ejected from any wedding, Airwolfe employees had taken to the floor in droves. They danced as though they'd been locked up for a year. There were tables dotted about the edges at standing height and we clustered round one, resting our drinks on it and bundling coats, handbags etc underneath. Liz joined us with Peter, looking radiant.

The top two tiers of boxes were — symbolically no doubt — reserved for management. Nathan was visible in one of them and seemed to be enjoying himself. He loved hanging out with the big boys.

'Who's that fella he's chatting to?' I asked Liz.

'Tom Archibald, the Technology Director,' she said.

'I suppose I'd better go say hi to Nathan,' said Harold rather glumly after a while.

I stayed where I was, chatting to Liz and Peter and half-watching Nathan's grizzled head in the box above. I saw Harold arrive and knock. Nathan turned and ushered him in. He introduced him to his companions and they chatted for a minute. Then Harold gestured to the door. They left the box together, vanished, then reappeared in the shadows to the side of the stage. They seemed to be arguing. Harold bent forward, his face close to Nathan's, and said something. Nathan flinched and took a step backwards. Harold glared at him, then stalked off. Nathan watched him with an intent expression.

'What's wrong?' asked Liz.

'Nathan and Harold. What's going on between those two?'

'Do you think he's his real son?' Liz asked.

'What, you think he's adopted?'

'No, I mean Nathan's wife's a lot older than him isn't she? Maybe Harold's her son from a previous relationship.'

Before I had time to consider this, Harold was back.

'How was he?' I asked.

'Fine,' he said. 'Excited about this award.'

At last the musicians took off with their instruments and treated us to some delightful silence.

All too brief: then inevitably muzak began. Ronan appeared on stage, fiddling with a laptop. One of the company bigwigs followed — judging by age and sharpness of suit — and launched into a presentation. Turned out he was one of those trophy American CEOs that European companies bag when they go global. They show up at the annual parties and try to make the staff clap and shout and get enthused etc. Goes down like a lead balloon in Ireland, and not much better in London I discovered now. However, the message was clear. Airwolfe was on a roll and it was all down to us! But not so much down to us that we would be getting any more money! Etc! Prosperity! But belt-tightening!

'Are these things always like this?' Harold's warm breath tickled my ear and made the hairs in that vicinity stand on end.

'Yup. I change company every year or two, but they're all much the same. PowerPoint poisoning.'

'God.'

After enough happy-clappiness to make us extremely grateful that there'd been a free bar for the previous few hours, the prize-giving began. One after another, the great and the good were called up. As always, more of the great than the good. Finally the moment we'd all been waiting for arrived — Nathan's prize.

'Managing people is always difficult,' said Bigwig and paused. 'Managing programmers is almost impossible.' Cue laughter, duly supplied by the sycophants in the crowd. 'But one man who's shown he can achieve the impossible is…Mr Nathan Boyle!'

There was a light sprinkling of claps. I looked around. None of Nathan's team, and no one from our floor that I could see, was clapping. Clearly the applause was being supplied by people from other floors and other buildings. Not only had they never experienced Nathan's unique managerial methods, they didn't know who he was.

Then I realised that Harold was quizzically studying me and the rest of the team. I jumped and started clapping madly. The others copped and joined in. The warm breath again: 'He's a shocking manager, isn't he?'

'Well, he can occasionally be a little overbearing in his methods.'

'You mean he's a crass, small-minded bully? It's OK, I know that already, but hey, let's not ruin his special day. Anyway, I don't care about that now.'

He captured one of my clapping hands in his. The theatre disappeared. We studied each other in the hush. His eyes were a glowing brown, like the sunlit depths of a still pool. He had a tiny dusting of freckles across the bridge of his straight nose. I smiled at him, then, feeling overwhelmed by his answering smile, hurriedly looked back up at the stage.

'...challenge of managing a multicultural team...' Nathan was saying. 'I have Nigerian, German, French, Argentinian and Chinese resources all working in perfect harmony. I have several female programmers. I even have an Irishwoman — for my sins.'

Cue laughter — again, not from our team. They knew what was good for them.

'God, I need a drink,' said Harold.

He squeezed my hand and set off for the bar again.

As Nathan blundered on, James muttered a running commentary.

'...I've always found that patience and tolerance are key management virtues...'

('*but you prefer impatience and intolerance*')

'...luckily I seem to have the rare knack of being able to bond a team...'

('*because they all unite to fight the common enemy — you.*')

'...as my team and I continue to work together in a spirit of mutual understanding and support.'

('*as your team continues to work while you play Solitaire on your computer.*')

Nathan finally stopped talking.

''E eez a wonkair,' said Pierre from the MAT team, wandering by.

A few people clapped lethargically and the VP bounded back to the microphone.

James shrugged his shoulders and said 'How the HELL did he get that award?'

'Nearly every single project he's managing at the moment is late,' I agreed. 'The other managers must be absolutely horrendous.'

'Maybe he's not passing all the trivial little details up the line,' said James.

'Yeah, like the fact that the software due to be released next month crashes as soon as you try to process a flight speed of more than two hundred miles an hour,' I laughed. Then we looked at each other. I think a shiver crept up his spine just as it did up mine, as together we realised that we had hit on the truth.

'Shit, what'll happen when they realise?' asked James. 'Work could be considerably more fun in the near future.' He ran a hand through his perfectly-gelled hair — a sure sign that he was too excited to think. 'Should we rat?'

'Nah. It's his business, his job and his problem. Let's just get on with our work and wait for the fireworks.'

'I'm his pet Nigerian,' said Peter, 'do you think I should ask for a bonus? Did you know, when I started he asked me if I find London very cold?'

'What did you say?' asked Liz.

'Said it was an improvement on Bristol. He always trots me out when he wants to look good.'

'I thought Cynthia might jump on stage and kill him after he made that remark about an Irishwoman,' said James. 'So, Harold,' he continued, as Harold reappeared with more champagne, 'what bribes did our glorious leader use to get you along tonight?'

'Didn't need any, once I knew who'd be here,' said Harold, regarding me meaningfully.

When the speeches were finally over, James got back to the topic. 'Why did he want you to come? I mean, you two don't exactly live in each other's pockets.'

That was James's polite way of saying we'd never heard of Harold before.

'I think he feels it's time I settled down,' said Harold. 'He wants me to see the rewards of doing the old nine-to-five in the City. He obviously doesn't know me very well. The only effect has been to make me resolve to continue to avoid work for as long as I possibly can.'

'Does he fund you?' asked James. 'Couldn't he cut you off without a shilling?'

'Fortunately not. He's not my dad, he's my stepfather,' said Harold. 'My mother does try to encourage me towards toil occasionally, but a pithy description of this evening's gaieties and she should lay off for the next ten years or more.'

'I have, of course, enjoyed myself enormously,' he added hastily as James and I exchanged glances, 'but only because you've all been so kind and generous.'

'Not to worry mate, any time,' said James. 'Must go and talk to a man about a horse,' and he wandered off.

'Alone at last,' said Harold, looking deep into my eyes (again). 'Would you like to go somewhere quieter?'

I nodded, keeping my nervousness to myself. He took my hand and led me up the stairs to one of the lower boxes. It was empty. He held the door open for me with a flourish before drawing me to the balcony. The appalling band was back. We watched as my colleagues made eejits of themselves drunkenly trying to do the twist in front of the stage below. Liz seemed to be dancing closer to Peter than to anyone else. I smiled to myself. If there was anything happening, Liz would tell me immediately she got me alone. She was frank, candid and artless to the point of having no instinct for self-preservation at all.

Meanwhile, the sensations flooding through me from Harold's gently stroking my palm were wreaking havoc on my own instinct for self-preservation. He was a flirt through-and-through, it was so obvious, and way too good-looking. Not to mention that I didn't believe in mixing work and fun. But leaping without a look had never been so attractive. After all, what harm could it do? If I had to leave Airwolfe from embarrassment, I could always get a job somewhere else. Or move home and live with my parents. No problem.

'You like them, don't you?' he asked. I realised I was grinning inanely down at the others. 'Are you happy at Airwolfe?'

'Well I'm only there four months and we're always hideously overworked and so on, but yeah, they're a good bunch to work with.'

I steeled myself to turn and look up at him. If he smiled I'd be in trouble. But he was studying me thoughtfully.

'Except my dad.'

'Well, all bosses are fairly alike,' I said.

'But some are more alike than others.'

He released my hand and slid his arm round my waist, pulling me closer.

'Enough about my dad. What about me? Do you like me?'

'Ah, you'll do for the moment, I haven't anyone else coming along this evening.'

He laughed softly.

'I like you too, little Irish girl…'

I practically braced into the kissing position, leaning forward, drawn by the promise in his eyes.

Bang! I leaped backwards as the door of the box was flung open. Vicky the poisonous office manager.

'*Hi* Cynthia. Are you enjoying yourself?' she asked, eyes raking Harold from top to toe. He and I stood side by side, not touching. I ached with disappointment but there was something else. Could it be relief? I had had a reprieve.

It took me a moment to catch up with events.

'Um, yes, great venue. How about you?'

'Oh, these office parties. I don't like socialising with people from work. Still, Christmas comes but once a year.' She continued to stare at Harold. I felt obliged to introduce him.

'Vicky, Harold. Harold, this is Vicky, our office manager,' I said.

'Is it, indeed?' he asked, studying her with detached interest. Neither of them seemed inclined to shake hands. 'I've heard about you from my stepfather, Nathan Boyle. He says you're very…dedicated.'

'That's kind of him. I've heard a lot about you too.' She sounded unusually civil. Maybe she fancied him rotten. Like me.

'Tell me, do you…enjoy working with him?' he asked. Vicky seemed to catch the bite in his tone. She edged back towards the door.

'He's very fair. Nice meeting you. Bye Cynthia.' She turned and fled.

The music had stopped.

'I'd better go downstairs. Liz is staying at my place and she'll be wondering where I am,' I said. I felt as though someone had thrown a bucket of cold water at me, bucket and all. My reckless mood had vanished, and the reasons I shouldn't get involved with Harold were clamouring for attention. I needed a break. I sensed that Harold had lost focus too.

'OK,' Harold replied, 'I'll join you in a bit.'

I glanced back at him as I left the box. He was looking over the balcony again, his expression grim. I wanted to stay. But Harold was much deeper hot water than I could easily climb out of.

I took a detour to the Ladies on the way down. My face in the mirror was flushed and my eyes were sparkling. I was humming an old Horslips song as I reached the dance-floor: 'Trouble, trouble, trouble with a capital "T"…'

The lights were up. People stood around, mildly lost, wondering where their coats were. Bharathi had gone. Nathan had joined Liz, James and the lads and was complacently accepting congratulations. He was swaying slightly, not unusual for that hour of the evening.

'You deserve it, Nathan,' said Vicky.

'Thanks, love. About time they gave me something for all my hard work. The wankers should've done it years ago,' he replied. Charming.

'What's it like? Can I see?' asked Liz. He showed her the little statuette, obviously modelled on an Oscar. The Human Resources department's creative team must have needed lots of extra meetings to come up with that one.

'Like an Oscar, but got no dick though. That's not right for me, is it, love?' Nathan was leering at Liz, who was blinking uncomprehendingly back at him.

'You shocked are you? Right little virgin aren't you? Wouldn't be a bad ride though, if you had any tits.' He peered drunkenly at Liz's upper half. Liz, after a frozen second, turned away and ran for the Ladies.

'What did you say that for, you stupid fucker,' said Sam, Nathan's chief drinking cohort. 'She'll do you for sexual discrimination and you'll be fucked. You'd better go and grovel quick.'

'Ah, she'll be OK,' said Nathan with a nasty grin. 'Just wants attention, that's all that's wrong with Little Miss Prissy.'

'I think it's time to leave,' said James disdainfully. 'Sam, get him his coat before he falls over.'

'We're off to Indiana's. See you there.' said Nathan. He and Sam lurched away. Vicky followed them, looking upset and anxious. I turned towards the loos and saw Peter watching Nathan and Sam contemptuously as they back-slapped their way to the cloakroom. Nathan had made himself yet another new friend.

It wasn't hard to figure out which cubicle Liz was in. The sobs were audible, particularly heart-rending because she was obviously trying to smother them. My heart went out to her. Stupid, drunken, thicko Nathan. Why couldn't he have picked on me, or on James? Of course no one would say anything like that to James. He could give as good as he got.

'Liz?'

A sniff.

'Liz, don't worry about it, it's the drink talking, he didn't mean to insult you. He'll have forgotten all about it by Monday, or else he'll be apologising like mad.'

No let-up with the sobs.

'He's a tosser, always was, you know that, don't let him ruin your night.'

'It's not locked.'

I pushed the door open slowly. Liz sat slumped on the closed toilet lid, her head in her hands. A picture of despair, she wouldn't even raise her eyes.

'Liz? You're not too upset are you? You know what he's like.'

'I thought I looked OK tonight.'

'What? You do. Of course you do.'

'I never did have anything on top but I got a Wonderbra and a tight-fitting lacy thing and I hoped no one would notice. God, everyone was probably laughing at me all night.'

'Liz, you're not taking that eejit seriously are you?'

'Cynthia, you *know* he's right. It's just, most people are too polite to say anything.'

'Liz, you could take him to court for a comment like that. It's illegal. It's harassment, not just rudeness. And you're even more beautiful than usual tonight. All the AIK team were flocking round you.'

'And Peter was there and I thought he might like me but he's probably laughing at me too and it's so *humiliating*!'

'Liz, honestly. You look fabulous. Bharathi was even saying it earlier. You know we'd all give our eye-teeth to be as beautiful as you. You can't let a drunken fool like Nathan ruin a great night on you. *I* noticed that Peter likes you too, I think he's really interested. He's furious with Nathan.'

I got the ghost of a smile but her heart wasn't in it. It took me another ten minutes to convince her to leave the loos. Even then, she'd only agree to go when I loaned her my shawl to drape over her shoulders and cover her cleavage. She thought everyone would be checking out her assets or lack of them as soon as she reappeared. She was probably right. I felt like punching Nathan.

When we emerged, James descended on Liz and gave her a big hug, saying 'I hear it's you that Nathan took his insecurities out on this time, my darling. Don't worry, I've seen him in the little boys' room and he won't be going to the big boys' room any time soon. I'm not surprised he feels the need to vent.'

Liz smiled. After some more of James at his adorable best she began to perk up, but she didn't want to go on to a nightclub, even though Nathan wouldn't be there.

Peter offered to take her home. She smiled at him but said she was tired and turned to me saying 'Cynthia, I'd love to go to bed. Would you mind coming back with me?'

'Course I'll come with you,' I said, just as Harold rejoined us. He glanced at Liz and asked me 'What's up?'

'Nothing.' I drew him aside. 'Only the usual end-of-night drama. Somebody always gets drunk and insults someone else. This time the insultee was Liz and the insulter was particularly rude. She's staying with me so I'm taking her home.'

'Poor girl. She looks tired. But do you have to go with her?'

'Yes, we're giving the club a miss. I don't want her going home on her own. Plus, my sister's getting back around now and they've never even met.'

'You're not responsible for her, outside work,' he glinted down at me. 'Can't you let James or someone take her? I'd hoped to spend more time with you.'

'Yeah, me too, but I'll have to go, I'm afraid.'

'If you must, you must. I'd like to see you again though. Would you come out with me this weekend?'

Curses.

'I'd love to, but my sister is over from Dublin. We have a full weekend planned and I can't really get out of it…'

Damn, I was over-explaining. Where was my cool?

'…I'm sorry. Maybe we could do something next week?'

'Perhaps. I'll get your number from James.'

James had a spotless white handkerchief out and was gently drying Liz's tears. Coats had been collected, everyone was leaving. We headed towards the door. Peter walked beside me.

'Is Liz OK?'

'Yep,' I shot him a warning glance, not wanting Harold to realise that his dad was the evil nasty person responsible for ruining our night.

'God, he's a tosser isn't he?' said Peter.

'Yep. I could kill him.'

''E eez a wonkair,' said Pierre, joining us.

James had flagged down a taxi and Liz was climbing in.

'Take it easy, babes,' said Harold, bending to kiss my cheek. His floppy soft blond hair brushed my forehead, causing a definite chain reaction which ended up somewhere in the tips of my toes. God. Fun *and* sexy.

As I shut the door I heard him continue:

'James, my dear chap, are you going on to frequent a nightclub? Do you need some help?'

'Take me to your dealer,' said James.

I sat back with a sigh, telling myself that an early night was the best possible outcome of the day's adventures. My mum says that people only get the chance to miss you if you occasionally go away. Perhaps the night would now turn to ashes for Harold. Very likely.

Stupid Nathan getting drunk and ruining everyone's evening. Liz was still upset. I put my arm around her. She subsided and cried on my shoulder for most of the twenty-minute taxi ride. When we got back to my place, she went straight to bed. I dropped in to check on her before climbing into my new fold-up bed in the living-room. She was fast asleep, curled up with her head resting on her hand, tears drying on her cheek.

The toughening up process I'd predicted to Bharathi had begun.

By the time I'd finished telling him about the murder, James was in almost as much shock as me.

'How could that have happened without you noticing?' he kept saying. 'Cynthia, I never realised you were *that* bad.'

I didn't mention the photographs. I felt ashamed at having been so calculating in the presence of death. All the same, I was happy to have them. My defence lawyer might need them. Eventually, I told James what was on my mind:

'James, they're going to think I did it. Who else could it have been? You can't get into the building without ID. The security people will know exactly who was in there. They'll make a list and it'll say: 'Cynthia'. Full stop. I'm amazed the police let me go. Maybe I should clear out my savings account and fly straight to one of those countries that don't extradite people.'

'God,' was his inspiring reply. Followed by: 'Blimey, that's a point.' Even better: 'It *wasn't* you was it? No,' (seeing my expression), 'only joking, of course I know it wasn't. You hardly knew him.'

'And plus I wouldn't murder anyone.'

'Well, of course not. I suppose. Although, Cynthia, I don't actually know you all that well, do I? It's not like we've been mates for years. Potentially you could be a member of MI5, come to Airwolfe undercover to eliminate arseholes. Oh, don't look so serious. I know murder's not your style. You'd be far more likely to pin some vicious satire to the office drawing board, then go merrily off to a new job. Happy-go-lucky, that's you.'

'I hope the Super agrees with you,' I muttered.

'Is he really cute?'

'You'll probably meet him. You can decide for yourself. I thought he was *very* cute, in a reassuring, pipe-and-slippers-in-front-of-the-fire kind of way.'

'Mm, just my type. Not. He must be fairly decent if he told you not to go home alone though. You must be in shock, my poor petal. Someone gave me a Goofy hot-water-bottle for Christmas. Let me root it out and then put you into bed with the best fresh linen and some flowers.'

I must have looked surprised because he grinned and said, 'Oh well, clean sheets and an open window anyway. It's the thought that counts. I'll pour you a bath and you can recline in suds while I get everything ready.'

Darling James. He topped up my red wine and went off. I looked around. I'd never been in his flat before; an entire floor in an old house in Stamford Hill. The living room was clean and cheerful, with wood floors and tall windows. I grinned. He had a flat-screen TV and the latest in gaming technology. He wasn't as retro as he pretended then. Morcheeba played quietly in the background, soothing my jangled nerves.

James reappeared and sent me into the bathroom. Soon I was stepping into an old-fashioned claw-foot bath, with towels and a bathrobe waiting on the towel rail. I reclined in the steaming bubbles. I tried to relax.

I couldn't. Nathan's pale and lifeless face was difficult to forget. Then I found myself thinking that James didn't like Nathan any more than I did. Stupid. I gave myself a mental shake. No sense in getting paranoid.

But eventually, guiltily, I climbed out and, as quietly as possible, naked and dripping, locked the bathroom door.

5 — COUNTDOWN TO MURDER — THE FATAL MONDAY

The morning of the Monday Nathan was to die dawned grey and grizzly.

I hadn't heard anything from Harold.

The weekend had had its compensations. Alice had never visited me in London before and we had big plans. Liz was subdued over Saturday breakfast. I invited her to join us for the day, though I wasn't keen to share my sister, but she felt too down to go anywhere. I suggested she chill in my flat instead, and post the keys when she left. She brightened. She lived with her mother and couldn't face her yet.

I introduced Alice to Brick Lane. I love the market on a weekend morning, with its jostling, good-humoured mix of well-heeled Londoners, artists, hippies and hawkers. This is the heart of the East End, I explained to Alice, although it's being rapidly gentrified. I told her how, over centuries, the area has absorbed wave after wave of immigrants and refugees, including Huguenots fleeing religious persecution in France, Irish people escaping poverty and famine and Jews from all over Europe. Today, the population is largely Bangladeshi.

'Look at the beautiful Huguenot architecture of the buildings,' I said.

'Did you swallow an encyclopaedia or something?' Alice asked.

'No. I just love this area.'

'I can see that, and I can understand why — it's so exciting,' she said, clocking a tall, dreadlocked apple-seller wearing multi-coloured stripy leg-warmers and a matching hat.

We wandered towards Spitalfields. I showed her the pink graffiti-covered car that, for me, embodied London's lovable eccentricity. When I saw it first I assumed it would soon be clamped, towed away, stolen or set on fire. Four months later, to my continuing astonishment, it was still there.

At Spitalfields we stopped at a permanent stall for some posh wine and cheese.

'I hate the way it's getting so up-market here,' I moaned when we got the eye-watering bill.

'Best move out then, hadn't you?' said Alice, expertly spearing an olive.

'What do you mean?'

'Well, are you Bangladeshi?'

'No.'

'Are you a cockney?'

'No.'

'Are you a poverty-stricken artist?'

'I know where you're going with this.'

'Do you have a ridiculously overpaid job in the City, enabling you to pay this bill with ease?'

'Yes.'

'You're ruining the area. Best move out.'

I made a rude face.

In the afternoon we checked out the Tate Modern and ambled through the South Bank.

On Sunday morning we lounged around the flat eating bagels and reading the papers. In the evening we had a meal in Chinatown. The intriguing ingredient 'one hundred year old egg' was advertised, but neither of was brave enough to experiment. After dinner we went to a show in Covent Garden, finishing with cocktails in a seedy Soho bar.

So, I told myself, I haven't been sitting hunched over a silent mobile for the weekend.

All the same, I wished Harold had called.

Monday morning dragged even more than usual. Liz had shadows round her eyes. I dreaded lunch time and the inevitable party post-mortem with her and James. I soon realised he did too.

To: Cynthia
From: James
Subject: Manners
Zere wil b know morr slaggink of innosent C plus-minus programerz at ofiss partys. Ze ofender in qweschun wil be torcherred.
Yors Optmistcally,
The Orfiss Mancher
P.S. Yeah we wish!

Sitting down for lunch, Liz was distraught and apologetic.

'I'm so sorry, Cynthia. I'm sure you wanted to go clubbing with Harold. Thanks for giving me your key on Saturday. I didn't leave the flat till tea-time. It was such a relief not to have to go home. My mum would've realised something was wrong, and she'd have been so upset. I told her we spent the day drinking tea and watching old movies. Anyway that's what I did do. I watched all your Poirot movies. Your flat is so comfortable, and thanks for lending me your bed.'

'You're welcome. Don't worry, nothing like absence to make the heart grow fonder. I'm sure Harold had a terrible night without me.'

Glancing at James, I caught a sceptical expression.

'So, James,' I said casually, 'what did he get up to? Did he ask you for my phone number? He said he would.'

'No, sorry, Cynthia. He told me he'd realised just in time that you're totally not his type,' said James.

'Oh.'

'Ha, ha, only joking. You always fall for it, don't you? Yes, he took your number, and he said he thought you were delectable. He asked me to give you his. He did enjoy himself at the nightclub though.'

Darn.

'But he wasn't chatting up anyone in particular, just drinking and dancing. We fell out the door at three am. I think he's right about champagne. It is the best high out there, and the most expensive, these days.'

Harold counted as hot gossip, but we couldn't distract Liz from the Nathan episode for long.

'He looked straight through me this morning,' she said miserably.

'Hungover again,' said James.

'Liz, he probably doesn't remember a thing about it,' I said.

'How could he forget something like that?' Liz asked, wide-eyed.

'Because he's a prick. As far as he's concerned it was friendly banter. And he was so drunk he probably forgot what he said the second he left the theatre,' said James.

'It was just so awful. Peter says I should go to Human Resources.'

'Are you going to?' I asked.

'I haven't decided. What do you think?'

'What would you be looking for if you went to HR? Would you want him to be fired?'

'Oh, no. Just, you know, an apology.'

'You'd be putting your head above the parapet,' said James.

'What do you mean?' she asked.

'The word troublemaker mean anything to you?'

'I know. I didn't cause any trouble. But if I went to HR, I would be.'

'Up to you,' I said, 'but you might get more satisfaction from mentally writing him off and forgetting about it. Wait a day or two, and see how you feel.'

'Yeah, good idea.' She still looked troubled.

'Don't worry, Liz,' I said, 'if you do go to HR, we'll back you up. Won't we, James?'

'Absolutely,' he said, 'I was going to look for a new job soon anyway.'

After lunch, Bharathi told us that Harold and his mother Laura had been in to visit Nathan. Laura and Nathan had gone off somewhere, while Harold waited in Nathan's office. I wondered if he'd been expecting (hoping?) to meet me. I gave myself a mental shake. He had my number. Time to get down to some work.

The office was immersed in the silence of post-lunch slumber. Then, from the other side of the partition, came the infuriating sound of James whistling. Beethoven or something. He only ever whistled when his work was going well. Unfortunately, the immediate effect was to cause everyone else's work to go badly.

But as soon as I started concentrating, James — and everything else — went away.

I was looking forward to getting stuck in to the afternoon's work. The particular task I had planned was testing an implementation of 'placement new'. If you're a C++ programmer you'll know that I was in for some fun. If not, I'll simply say that I was doing something the hard way. No, not just because there is a hard way! I'm not that much of a geek.

Writing code is difficult, but the real challenge lies in making sure it works afterwards. I had to write a series of tests to run my new stuff and tell me whether it behaved correctly. Over and over again I pressed F5 to run the tests and got the 'TEST FAILED' message. (That's the killer about being conscientious. A less scrupulous programmer could get the screen to display 'TEST SUCCEEDED' and go home, postponing the problems for days or even weeks).

This sort of testing, called unit testing, is like playing a game of chess with yourself, trying to make yourself lose. You have to guess where you're likely to have messed up, then devise a way to expose your possible error. Sometimes a test failure reveals that a basic assumption is wrong, and weeks of work have to be discarded and redesigned.

It's engrossing. There are worse ways to serve your nine-to-five, forty-plus year sentence.

The hours flew by as I devised tests, watched them fail, and fixed the problem. The reasons for some failures were easily found. Others were bizarre, apparently unrelated to any possible scenario. They had to be due to one or more logical errors in my code, but the error(s) could take hours to track down and fix.

All my powers of deduction were pushed to the limit. The initial tests are always the most difficult. As each one passed, I 'committed' the test and the bug fixes to the master source code on a central server. (This useful precaution makes your work available to everyone else on the team, and it won't be lost if your personal machine crashes and dies forever.)

As such sessions go, this one was very productive.

At nine o'clock I stretched, yawned, and reluctantly decided to call it a day. My stomach was telling me to go home. I powered down my computer and stood. As I came back to the real world I realised that my eyes were tired, my legs were stiff and my shoulders and neck ached. As usual. I'd be fine tomorrow.

You know what happened next.

6 — THE MORNING AFTER

When I woke in James's flat it took me a second to remember where I was and why. Then there was no hope of going back to sleep. I couldn't stop myself going over and over the awful experience of finding Nathan. I felt tense and on edge. When James started to move about, I got up and joined him in his tiny kitchen. He grinned, endearingly tousled and barely awake. He gave me a big hug and said 'Better?'

'Much, thanks. I don't know what to do about work though.'

'I've got a plan. Want to hear it?'

'Yes, please.'

'I'll go in to work as normal. Suss out what's going on, whether the office is still open, what they're doing with our beloved AirCross project. Meanwhile, you lounge about on the sofa watching breakfast TV. I'll text you as soon as I have any news, and you can decide whether to come in. OK?'

'James, that'd be wonderful. You're so right, I couldn't face the place this morning, but I'm dying to find out what's happening. Maybe the killer's on the CCTV tape and they've already arrested them and I'm in the clear. Hey, there might be something on the radio.'

We turned on Radio Four and the TV too. There was nothing on the news. James checked the Internet. Although this was only a few years ago, Twitter was still just a twinkle in Jack Dorsey's eye. Some newspapers didn't even have a website. We couldn't find anything about the murder. I ran out for the morning papers while James got ready for work. The *Telegraph* had a short article on an inside page — 'Man Found Dead in City Office'. That was it.

'No news is good news,' said James, but actually no news is scary. The only bright spot was that the police knew my location and hadn't arrested me yet.

James set off, promising to fill me in as soon as possible. He'd been so good to me. I tried not to think about the fact that, as I'd been dropping off the night before, I'd heard a key turn quietly in his bedroom door.

Just after eleven he sent a text.

Big boss here, furious re AirCross. Now in basement. Full steam ahead. Overtime! All v curious. Come in no sign bodies/blood u'll be OK.

It had to be done eventually. Whatever the Super had said about a day off, I couldn't stay at James's feeling like a cat on hot bricks. Slowly, tentatively, I locked up and found myself walking to the tube. I got out at Moorgate and dropped into Marks on the way up to the office. I needed new underwear and a blouse.

If there's ever a good excuse for being ridiculously late, I reflected, the discovery the previous evening of your undesirable boss's murdered body has to qualify. So it was almost two by the time I approached Airwolfe. My phone bleeped as I walked the final few yards:

Babes, got news. You poor thing. Still come to dinner? Need to talk. Good food, champ, feel better. H x

Replied:

Can you make it tomorrow? Head wrecked.

Meeting Harold and being spoiled sounded tempting, although in the circumstances the conversation was likely to be a trifle stilted at first. But I had plans for the evening.

Harold's reply arrived immediately:

OK 8 tmrw. Stay cool.

Arriving at the office was like going in the day after you got drunk and sang karaoke, or were spotted in a corner of the pub snogging the slutty guy from Accounts. The stares — and glares — had to be braved on entry. It would have been easier with a partition to hide behind, but the police had cordoned off the whole of the murder floor. We'd been relocated to the basement. There we sat around a huge oval mahogany meeting-room table, with less privacy than laboratory rats. We all had to share the single phone. Deprivation indeed, especially as our mobile signals didn't work underground. I don't think it was damp, exactly, but it smelled stale and there were no windows to open.

Someone asked me if I'd really been on the spot the night before, and what had happened. James had obviously kept his mouth shut. I decided not to tell the whole story, implying that I hadn't seen the body and didn't know the cause of death. Someone else suggested a heart-attack. Blanching inwardly at the memory of the implacable metal and the shock of red blood on a white collar, I shrugged.

The police wouldn't thank me for giving every detail away. I kept my little handbag close by me on the desk, with its mobile photos of a very dead Nathan. I wondered, if I sent them to anyone, would they end up doing the Internet rounds? I'd have to be careful. He might have been an arsehole, but even Nathan didn't deserve that.

Ronan's lads dug out an old laptop for me to use, my usual computer being cordoned off outside Nathan's office. Luckily, I was able to copy all my work down on to the laptop from source control because I'd been so careful to update it the evening before. Nothing was missing. The laptop was pretty creaky though.

Shortly after my arrival, Big Boss Tom Archibald called myself and James in to a meeting. Archibald was a large man in a white shirt and tie and a tweed jacket. I put him in his fifties. He had succumbed to baldness on top, but bushy grey hair sprang out with triumphant vigour just above his ears and over his collar. His face was red and he seemed to be in a bad mood.

'Sorry about your unpleasant experience yesterday,' he said. 'Nathan will be sorely missed. James here tells me that integration testing on AirCross won't be finished for another few weeks.'

'We're making progress, but yes, we're behind schedule,' I replied.

'I was under the impression that this software was in acceptance testing, and that it was definitely on target for release next month. That's what we've told our customers. Some of them are only still customers because they're waiting for AirCross. Now you two are telling me it won't be ready for months.'

He sounded like he was having difficulty keeping his voice down. Oh dear.

'Afraid so. The schedule has been slipping for ages,' I said.

'Why? And why wasn't I told?'

'The original estimates seemed wildly optimistic to me,' I said.

'They sure were,' said James. 'The team have been working their…very hard. But they can't do the impossible. For example, integration testing on a project of this size was never going to be finished in three weeks.'

'A few new features were requested at the last minute,' I added, 'by the Marketing Department. And some unexpected bugs came up. They always do.'

'Right, but again, why wasn't I told?'

His voice was definitely rising now. Even his ears seemed

to bristle. I wondered if a toupee would improve or disimprove his appearance. His hair was so energetic that the wig might seem exhausted by comparison.

James studied the ceiling. I shrugged. What were we supposed to say?

'Maybe there was a hiccup in communications? James and I kept Nathan informed OK. Perhaps his line manager forgot to update you.' I felt this was reasonably diplomatic.

'I *am* his line manager.'

'Oh. Really? Well, em, maybe Nathan was waiting for a specific meeting, or hoping we'd meet the next milestone.'

'Miss Hegarty, I was under the impression that all milestones had been met. James, is it true that you kept him up-to-date about the slippage?'

'Yes. We expected more overtime to be authorised soon. We assumed Nathan was negotiating it.'

Archibald made an angry note on his A4 pad.

'Nathan didn't flag the problem with me. He must have had his reasons. I'll be reviewing his email Inbox and may get some hint from that.'

'You should see emails about this from both of us.' Thank goodness. Our backsides were covered. I wondered if the project would be cancelled, being so overdue. I could be searching for work again very soon.

'In the meantime,' said Archibald, placing his palms on the table, leaning forward and looking almost as though he was about to take flight himself, 'we need to speed up. The UK development office will look bad if AirCross is delayed. The whole company will suffer. James, you're in charge; Cynthia, you're his deputy, and subject to authorisation we'll give you whatever you need to deliver in a month. So what do you need? More resources? How many? Ten? Twenty?'

James and I exchanged a look. Archibald sat back again, waiting.

'If you give us too many people it'll take us forever to teach them what to do and the finish date will be pushed back even further,' said James. 'If they're new it takes a week just to get desks organised and phones and network access set up. Can we have Adel and Pierre from the MAT team instead? They'll slot in fast because they've worked with us before. And at least two more decent servers and some good testers. Best give us people who already work here. Then hire new people to do their old jobs. That way, the training hit is spread over other teams.'

Archibald nodded, writing.

'Also,' I said, 'someone will have to co-ordinate all the new people. Up to now we've collaborated, but with a bigger team we'll need top-down direction. James and I won't both have the time to write code.'

'You're still *writing code*?' Archibald looked up, appalled.

'Ohhhh-kay. Let's meet later and discuss which features we can forget about for this release,' said James.

'What are the chances we'll get the servers?' I asked, crossing my fingers under the desk. They would make my life so much easier.

'I'll tell Ronan to get on it immediately. Do we already have any that you could take?'

'The MAT test boxes. The MAT team wouldn't be too happy though.'

'Ha, they'll all be on our team now so they won't care,' said James.

'OK.' Archibald stood. 'Put everything in writing and mail it to me straight away. I'll get it organised as soon as possible. Tell the team that overtime is authorised from now. Also, ordering in pizza, and taxis home. Send me a mail about that separately. But extra resources first. Within the next hour if you can.'

He held open the door. We left. Shell-shocked.

'A boss who's giving us what we want!' said James.

'And understands that quicker means more expensive!'

'I suppose I'll have to start doing overtime now,' said James gloomily. 'There'll be no getting out of it.'

I rattled off the mail — I'm a fast typist — and then we took Liz out for a coffee, away from prying eyes and ears.

She too marvelled over our efficient new manager, for about five seconds. Then she wanted to discuss Nathan's death. She'd only heard when she arrived at work. I think we both felt mildly guilty. She was speculating on the chances of a heart attack when James broke it to her: 'Cynthia thinks it's murder, Liz.'

'Murder?'

'He was stabbed in the back of the neck,' I said. 'Definitely not natural.'

'I don't believe it. People don't get murdered these days. I mean, not in offices. Why would you murder anyone?'

'Why, indeed?' said James.

'She's right,' I said. 'What on earth would it take to make you want to kill someone in today's world? If you're in an unhappy marriage, you can get a divorce. If you're bullied at work you can get a new job. (Reader, this was 2007). If you're being blackmailed you can make a fortune selling your sordid story to *The Sun*.'

'Anyway, weren't you sitting outside his office, Cynthia? No one would murder him with you only a few metres away. Are you sure he didn't just collapse or something?' said Liz.

'Liz, I saw the dagger,' I said. 'And the killer must have been insane because you're right, I was just outside. I'm totally freaked out. The police are bound to arrest me if they can't find anyone else. I'm in big trouble. The only chance I've got is if I find the murderer myself.'

'What? How can you do that?' Liz asked.

'I don't know. But the police aren't going to look hard, are they? Unless the killer shows up on CCTV, waving and brandishing a knife, they're going to assume Nathan pushed me a little bit too far and I snapped.'

James laughed, then straightened up when he realised how serious I was.

'I have to find out who did it, but I'm totally stuck for motives. Any ideas?'

'Money,' said James.

'Passion,' said Liz.

'Jealousy.'

'Lust. Eeww not Nathan.'

'Revenge.'

'Slow down, slow down,' I said, laboriously typing them into my iMate (a smartphone precursor).

'Anger,' said James, 'which is kind of the opposite to revenge. If someone lost their temper then it was probably unpremeditated, so that'd be manslaughter, wouldn't it? Was the murderer angry? Where did the murder weapon come from? Did they bring it with them? Was there any sign of a struggle?'

'Wouldn't Cynthia have heard, if there was?' Liz looked at me. 'And wouldn't you have heard any raised voices, any shouting?'

Pathetically, I shrugged. 'Liz, I just don't know. I hear nothing when I'm concentrating. A circus troupe complete with orchestra could have gone in to visit Nathan and I probably wouldn't have noticed.'

There was a silence. Then I said, 'So will you two help me?'

'Of course,' said Liz.

'I'm in,' said James. 'We need to get together and make a plan, figure out what to do. What about after work?'

'It'll have to be tomorrow,' I said, 'We're working late tonight and I can't do it after.'

'Why not?' asked Liz.

'I have to go and play poker.'

James, after a thoughtful pause, tapped the side of his nose. 'I see,' he said. 'Contacts. Zorr?'

'Zorr,' I confirmed.

A mail from Archibald was waiting when we got back to the office, confirming that we could take over two of the MAT team's test servers. I headed up to where Ronan presided over his SysAdmin empire. As usual, all the SysAdmin boys were sitting around with their feet up, giving the impression of geniuses in full control of their obscure (to other people) but simple (to them) tasks.

Ronan loves gossip so he was thrilled to see me. I gave everyone the edited version of my evening's adventures. They were sarcastically sympathetic. The unmistakable impression was given that if I'd been a SysAdmin head rather than a programmer I'd never have found myself in such an awkward position.

I asked Ro for a quick meeting. One or two meeting rooms were still available in spite of Plod taking over the whole third floor (it's possible that rather less work was being done than usual). It only took a couple of minutes to explain to him about the MAT servers. My personal request needed more finesse.

'OK Ronan,' I said, 'there's something else I wanted to ask you. I need a favour, just between you and me.'

'What kind of favour? It's that laptop, isn't it? I know, it's a piece of shit. Can't get anything better with the third floor closed off, though. I could find you some extra RAM? It'll never be a good machine but it might crawl faster.'

'Cheers, Ro, but the laptop's the least of my worries at the moment. It's Nathan.'

'What about him? He's gone now, no more trouble to anyone.'

'I wish. Ronan, don't you get it? I was right there. Outside the *door*. I'm going to be arrested any minute.'

'Jayz. You could be. Shit, man, could be dodgy.' He looked thoughtful. 'Are you *sure* you didn't hear anything? You must've heard *something*.'

'I was implementing 'placement new' Ro. I'm a *programmer*. I wouldn't have heard the Messiah proclaiming the end of the world and the Second Coming.'

'What's 'placement new' when it's at home? No, no, don't tell me. You programmers and your gobbledygook. I suppose you were really stuck into it? And everyone was gone. I bet you save the interesting work for when they all piss off and leave you in peace.'

'Yep.'

'So did the police question you? What did they say?'

'They didn't say much, Ro. They weren't too happy with my alibi. "Oh I was right here guv but it's OK I'm a programmer, we never interact with humans even to kill them. Especially not managers." I can't believe they're going to look any further. In fact, I can't believe they haven't banged me up already.'

'Yeah, but why would you want to kill Nathan?'

'Why would *anyone* want to kill him? I mean *really* kill him, not just fantasise about it? But someone did. It wasn't me but if I don't figure out who it was, I'll be in a Black Maria before you can say "Police are under Pressure to Make an Arrest".'

'OK. I get your point. But what do you want me to do?'

'His Inbox.'

'What?'

'His email Inbox. I want it. I want his Sent box as well, and his stored messages. Don't pretend to be shocked, Ro. You could easily get them. If I had his emails they might give me a clue as to who had it in for him. Really had it in for him, I mean. Who was actually prepared to actually KILL him.'

'OK. Cynthia. Are you *crazy*? I can't give you his emails. All right, yes, I *could* do it. The police have asked already, as I'm sure you've guessed. But I can't just hand them over to a random contractor. That'd be highly illegal and totally against all the stuff they make you sign when you start working here.'

'Yeah, Ro, but I wouldn't tell anyone.'

'Cynthia, if they found out they would String me Up by the Balls. Individually. I'm sorry. Can't do it. Out of the question.'

'I'm in big trouble, Ro. You must see I'm the obvious suspect. Another day or two and I'll be locked up, with no chance of clearing my name.'

'Well that's the police's job and I'm sure if you're innocent you've got nothing to fear. OK, OK, it's no time to crack jokes. But I'm sorry, no can do.'

'I suppose I can't blame you,' I said. 'I knew it was a long shot. You can still help me out, though. Will you tell me if you hear anything?'

'Yeah. Did you know the Superintendent is questioning everyone who works in the building? Starting around now.'

'Have you met him?'

'I have.'

'What do you think?'

'He could be worse. You might get away with it. I don't think he's made his mind up yet. He asked me if Nathan had any enemies. He asked me something else too.'

'What?'

'He wanted to know if you'd be likely to murder your boss.'

'Really?'

'Nah, only messing. He asked me how long you'd been here and if you were well liked.'

'What did you say?'

'What d'you think, missus? I said the sun shines out of your arse and we all love you.'

To: Cynthia
From: James
Subject: Killink!
I haff bin infoarmed that sum memberz of staf haf bin kilt.
This iss unacccetpable.
Yorrs Grayshussly,
The Orfull Mancher.

To: James
From: Cynthia
Subject: Re: Killink!
A hollyday haz bin deklared as Mr Boyll is no longerr wiz us.
Yourrs aptly,
The Offiss Manger.

After pressing 'Send' I spent a paranoid hour wondering what the Super would make of that little morsel if (when) Ronan was asked for my own emails. Meanwhile, Adel and Pierre joined our team. I started assigning work to them. James took himself off to meet Archibald and discuss which incomplete features to remove from the upcoming release.

The day passed swiftly. At nearly seven o'clock I was summoned back to the police presence.

The Superintendent was beginning to look at home at his commandeered desk. Heaps of files had appeared on it since the day before. (Had it only been a day?) He looked grave and tired.

Liz and James had given me a hard time about my failure to remember anything about him, so now I tried to focus. He was younger than I'd have expected, clean-shaven, though with a hint of five o'clock shadow. His eyebrows and hair were a nondescript reddish brown. His hair was cut short at the sides and longer at the front. He wore a white shirt. There was a tie on the coat stand in the corner. I wondered if it was his.

He radiated solid reliability, but his sleepy eyes held a sharp gleam and a pronounced dimple in his chin hinted at a sense of humour.

He certainly seemed to find me amusing. He sat back and surveyed me thoughtfully.

'Have you remembered any more about what happened last night?' he asked, raising an eyebrow.

'No, I've been racking my brains, but I haven't been able to remember a thing. No one believes I didn't hear anything.'

'Is that right? I thought your powers of concentration were well-known.'

If his eyebrow got any higher it would hit the ceiling.

'Yeah, but…a murder? I can hardly believe it myself.'

'There may not have been any noise involved.' He paused, as if considering, then continued. 'The initial medical assessment indicates that death was instantaneous. It's unlikely that Mr Boyle had time to cry out. Sometimes things come back to people later on, when they think over an event. Please keep trying.'

'I don't think I'm going to remember anything now, though,' I said.

'I suggest you try to reconstruct your activities for the few hours in which the murder occurred,' he said. 'It might jog your memory. At the moment we have very little to go on. Any extra clues would be welcome.'

'OK. Thanks. Will do.'

I could read between the lines. 'Give us someone, or we'll take you.'

'Thank you, Hegarty. Please don't repeat what I told you. We're trying to release as little information as possible.'

A smile (that set some flutters going, definitely not related to the imminent danger of being arrested) and that was it, my interrogation over for now. I walked out of his temporary office still uncuffed. The day was looking up.

Shortly before eight I donned my coat and hat, bade farewell to our dedicated team, and joined the trickle of City workers heading through the graveyard to the *King's Legs*. There was a poker tournament in its old-style upstairs function room every Tuesday. Everyone was welcome. Most participants worked in nearby offices. It cost a fiver to enter. The prizes were rubbish but it was fun.

A few of my colleagues had brought me along soon after I joined Airwolfe. Since then I'd tried to go most weeks. Poker is a game I've always enjoyed, and it's a good way to get to know fellow workers. It's a fast-track to people's virtues and failings.

It was at these tournaments that I'd met and struck up a friendship with Zorr. He was the enigmatic head of SwordBlade, the company that took care of security in our office building. He had long, luxuriant black hair and wore a swashbuckling, complicated belt in which he slung walkie-talkies, phones and intriguing unidentified devices. He sometimes enlivened the time between games by imparting the precepts and wisdom he'd gleaned from his decades in the apparently sinister underworld of office security.

There was a full house that night, with all twelve tables occupied. I was definitely the card player *du jour*. Just as at work, everyone wanted to know the details of Nathan's death. He had been a frequenter of the tournament, but had won few friends there. His bullying play, boastful wins and sulky losses put people off. However, now that he'd been fatally stabbed at his desk in a City office his popularity had rocketed.

The game was Texas hold 'em. Each initial table had four players. Only one would go through to the second round. I was too late to join Zorr's table, so I joined a table where I'd meet him in the next round if I got through. That would save waiting for him all night — he almost invariably reached the final game. I got good cards, and soon took my place beside Zorr, setting up for the second game.

'Cynthia,' he said, pushing back his flamboyant black hair. 'Was hoping to meet you.'

'Me too,' I replied frankly.

'This murder.' His beetle brows drew together and he shot me a piercing dark-eyed look from beneath them. 'I don't like it. Were you frightened?'

'I suppose I was. Hugh came up though. You train them well, Zorr, he knew exactly what to do.'

'Not afraid he might've done it?'

'Perceptive of you. You're right, just for one second I wondered.'

'He probably thought it was you.'

Adam, from the first floor of Airwolfe, and a banker named Sarah completed our foursome. They couldn't hear our muttered conversation and were getting restive, so we played a few hands. Adam was quickly eliminated. Zorr was doing well. He usually did. He always bet early and high. He must have bluffed sometimes, but I'd never caught him at it yet.

On the next hand, Sarah started the betting. She went in high, unusual for her. We all stayed in for the three cards called the 'river'. No one raised the betting, not even Zorr. Two Aces and a Jack lay on the table. I had a pair of Queens in my hand. Not much, unless Sarah and Zorr were doing very badly.

'Zorr,' I said, 'It's not looking good for me. The police are breathing down my neck because I was on the spot. I suppose Hugh filled you in. I'm hoping you'll be able to help me out with some information.'

Zorr looked at me, then down at his hand, then at the three exposed cards.

'All in,' he said calmly, pushing his entire pile of chips into the centre of the table.

'Gotta finish this,' he added in an aside to me.

I gulped. 'All in.' I followed his lead. The chances of my winning were infinitesimal, and like Zorr, if I lost this hand I'd be out of the tournament. But if we didn't finish soon I'd be waiting around all night.

Sarah looked from one to the other of us. She was intimidated, but she'd opened with good cards and she stuck to her guns. She pushed her chips in to the middle of the table and grinned.

She laid her hand down first. Two Jacks, giving her a Full House.

'You have me.' I showed her my paltry two pairs.

'It's mine,' said Zorr, displaying the two missing Aces.

'Buy us a few minutes before the next round. Have a drink. Thanks,' he nodded at Sarah as we left the table. 'What you want to know?' he asked, when we'd been served, and were propping up the bar a good distance from potential eavesdroppers.

'Did they get the killer on CCTV? Am I off the hook? I'm sure you're probably not supposed to tell me but I hoped you could give me a hint.'

'Do more than that. Tell you everything. Wouldn't like to be in your shoes, you'll need all the help you can get.'

'That good, eh?' I stared bleakly down into my drink.

'Two things. They didn't get the killer. No CCTV indoors except on the ground floor and in the lift lobbies. The one by the lifts should catch people coming from other floors, but if they use the stairs there's a blind spot.'

'OK. So it's down to the people in the building. Do you know who was there? Was there anyone apart from me and Hugh?'

'A few. The office manager. A bloke down in the server room. One or two others. I'll get you a list. But it's more complicated.'

'Why?'

'Don't tell anyone I told you this. Top secret. The back door used for deliveries, you know it takes a code number?'

'Yes. I don't have the code though. Why?'

'Could've been used. The camera over it's been broken for three days. Due to be replaced tomorrow.'

'Wow. But anyone coming in that way would have to know the code, wouldn't they?'

'Yeah. Except there was a stationery delivery yesterday evening. Someone could've slipped in. Might not have been noticed.'

'OK, so it's wide open. Anyone could have come in, sneaked up to Nathan's office and done the deed.'

'Would've had to get past you, though.'

'Yep, that's the trouble. Thanks Zorr, much appreciated.'

'No worries. Wish you the best of luck. Never could stand Nathan.' He went off to join his table for the next round.

Time to leave. My heart sank. I'd told James I'd be OK going back to the flat. But Nathan's dreadful stillness remained with me. I'd be checking behind all the doors and in the bathroom for knife-wielding maniacs if I went home.

I had a battle with myself. A pretty short one. Then I walked down the road to the Holiday Inn and checked in. After all, what's the point in earning wads of cash if you don't use it to buy a good night's sleep?

I'd planned to load the photographs I'd taken of the crime scene on to my work laptop and study them before going to bed. They might contain a clue. But now that the moment was here there was no way I could do it. I was missing my cosy, Cynthia-optimised flat. The unfamiliar Holiday Inn room was clean and comfortable. I had twin beds to choose from, and nothing to do but lie around watching TV. All the same, compared to home it was barren, bare and uninviting.

Even thinking about the photos creeped me out. They would have to wait till morning, till there was daylight coming through the window, and sunshine, and the possibility of cute puppies and kittens and flowers.

I'd been reading the latest Marian Keyes, but that was in my flat. I switched on the TV and wrapped myself in the bed-covers, shivering although it wasn't cold. I had forgotten to have dinner but I was too tired to go looking for food. I didn't feel very hungry anyway. I lay awake for a long time, channel-surfing. Eventually I fell asleep, to a soporific repeat of *Keeping Up Appearances.*

7 — THE INVESTIGATION BEGINS

My phone alarm woke me at eight. I stumbled into the shower to get my head together, then wrapped myself in a towel and sat down to look at the Nathan photos. Lacking the proper connector, I had to laboriously upload them one-by-one onto my laptop via infra-red. During upload, each photo flashed by in miniature, a grisly foretaste of what was to come.

This done, I reluctantly opened them at full-screen size.

Which didn't get me far. Looking at the murder scene told me nothing new. The floor was clear. The ceiling remained just a ceiling. No murderer lurked behind the coat stand, fatally revealed by the camera flash.

There was just dead Nathan being dead.

My stomach rumbled. I needed breakfast. I flicked to a close-up of the body and forced myself to examine it properly. A good way to kill my appetite. The ornate handle of the murder weapon caught my eye. Liz or James might recognise it. Personally I found it vaguely familiar but, as I'm not terribly observant, this didn't help much.

After some thought, I drew its distinctive pattern on the back of a copy of the AirCross functional spec. I could tell James and Liz that I'd sketched it from memory.

Or I could just tell them about the photos, I reflected as I dressed in my office uniform of jeans, t-shirt and trainers, but if I did they'd want to see them. And nobody should have to look at dead Nathan, no matter how much they had disliked him. These photos would confront them with the irrelevance of personal animus in the face of the mortality of all humankind, which might freak them out.

So I deleted the photos from the laptop, leaving them on the phone. Then I went looking for food. It took me a moment to find the breakfast room. Subconsciously I had been expecting a delicious smell of frying bacon, eggs and sausages to beckon me in the right direction — boy was I hungry — but it turned out the Holiday Inn only did a buffet in the mornings. Ah well, I reflected, piling a plate with croissants, toast and jam, it's good for the figure anyway.

After breakfast I extended my Holiday Inn booking for a week. The deep sleep I'd had was worth any amount of money. Then, feeling a little like Sid Halley but less hungry and without the nerves of steel, I set off for work.

I dropped in to Oasis on the way, for a few changes of clothes and underwear.

Text from Harold:

Looking forward to tonite pick you up at 8 where from?

I considered the office but thought it might have bad associations for him.

Pret OK?

OK l8r

James spent the morning organising the next few days' work. Archibald had scrapped every single piece of new code except the Overflight add-on I'd been working on during the evening Nathan died. Apparently that was essential. Archibald thought it'd been finished months ago. Sheesh.

Who was to blame? I wouldn't even know where to start.

So I got to code blissfully while James did the management grunt work. Long may it last, I thought.

At lunch time, Liz, James and I headed out for our murder meeting.

'One good thing about this murder,' James commented, 'usually during an overtime drive they expect us to eat sandwiches at our desks. But as long as you keep looking pale and interesting, Cynthia, we can claim you need a refreshing hour off each day.'

'Are there any bad things about this murder?' joked Liz, then looked self-conscious and guilty.

'Is that the first even faintly cruel remark you've ever made?' asked James.

'You are coming on,' I said. 'Don't worry. If we couldn't laugh etc etc.'

'Well it *was* cruel,' said Liz. 'Poor Nathan, but I don't seem able to take it in. I keep expecting him to turn up and say it was all a joke.'

Definitely not a good idea, I thought, to show the photographs to this girl.

'Better not go to Prêt today. There's a quiet place off Old Street.' James brought us to a hideously modern bar, The Odeon. Oceans of low, cheap imitation-wood plastic tables were surrounded by flimsy metal chairs that screeched when moved. Several televisions broadcast whatever mindless dross is on TV at that hour of the day (sofas and racecourses seemed to feature heavily). Floor to ceiling glass walls faced out on to the street — a busy road near a junction, with a constant flow of traffic. I didn't find the flimsy laminated menu inspiring. But the vast emptiness was ideal for privacy. We got a table miles away from the few other customers.

There was no visible staff.

'Good choice, James. I think the best thing to do is make a list of all the possible suspects and then figure out what motive they might have,' I said as we sat down. 'Motive, means and opportunity are the three things required in court, right? I've brought my iMate so I can take notes.'

'Um, Cynthia I brought a notepad and a pen,' said James. He's such a technophobe.

'Right. Let's begin with some names. Who had a motive for killing Nathan?'

Silence. Then James: 'let's start from the other end. Who didn't have a motive?'

'Ha ha. Seriously though, he wasn't that bad,' I said. 'Mind you, what about Eugene?'

'Horribly bullied, being set up to be fired, now might hang on to his job?' asked James after a pause.

'Yes, that sort of thing.' I typed it all in on the tiny iMate keyboard.

A blue-haired waitress appeared, yawning, and ambled over to us with a pad and pen.

'Vicky,' said James, when we'd ordered.

'What?' Liz asked, round-eyed.

'Didn't you hear she ran out of his office crying on Friday? Cynthia, put "love, lust or jealousy",' said James.

'And there's his wife,' Liz said. 'If Vicky was having an affair with him, the wife would have a motive too, wouldn't she? When I googled murders yesterday, it said domestic strife is statistically the most common motive in solved killings.'

'Jayziz give me a minute. I can't type that fast.'

James smirked at his notepad but said nothing.

'Who else?' I asked.

'Um,' said Liz. 'There's me.'

'Did *you* want to kill him? Amazing. Oh, yes, of course you did.'

'Revenge,' Liz hissed evilly, giving me a fright.

'Peter,' said James. 'He was there, and it's obvious he fancies you something rotten.'

'Ah, leave her alone, James,' I said, but he wrote 'Peter' down all the same. I'd given up somewhat on my iMate.

'You and James had motives too, didn't you?' asked Liz.

'Did we? What did you have in mind?'

'You were always saying you'd never had such a terrible boss, and the project wouldn't survive unless he was taken out.'

'That's true,' I admitted.

'I don't care about the project enough to kill him myself, but of course you only have my word for that,' added James, grinning at her. 'If incompetence were a motive for murder, it would depopulate the Square Mile faster than you could say "The Peter Principle".'

The blue-haired waitress appeared, carrying three plates with surprising aplomb. I was side-tracked by the smell of basil and parmesan from my creamy mushroom tagliatelle. I twisted some onto my fork and tasted it. Yum.

James and Liz were served too. There was a long pause.

Eventually I wiped my mouth with a napkin and pushed my plate aside.

'What about Cecil Howell?'

'Who's he?' asked James.

'He's a property developer or something. He came to Nathan's office on the day of the party and they had a full-on row.'

'OK, we'll put him in. I can't think of any more,' said Liz.

'Me neither. What have we got now?'

James read aloud:

'Eugene — Bullied
Vicky — Love, Lust or Jealousy
Wife — As Vicky
Liz — Revenge
Peter — Liz's Protector
Cecil Howell — Building Issue
Cynthia — Project
James — Project'

We all laughed.

'But really, all we have is Eugene, Mr Howell, Vicky and Mrs Boyle,' said James. 'Even Eugene is looking shaky. And would the ladies really kill him just for having an affair? It seems terribly uncivilised.'

I thought of Nathan, slumped in a chair in his own office.

'There must be a reason,' I said. 'I don't see how Mrs Boyle could've done it, though. The killer needed to have access to the building, and an idea how to get in unnoticed. If Mrs Boyle had signed in through security she'd have been arrested and charged by now. Same goes for Cecil Howell. The back door was unlocked for a short time during the evening, but they wouldn't know that.'

'Ah. Zorr,' said James unerringly. 'What about the CCTV?'

'Zorr would never tell me anything like that, James. He's very discreet. Coincidentally, though, I did hear a rumour…'

'Yes?'

'Apparently, the back door CCTV has been broken for a few days — it's due to be replaced today — and there's a blind spot on the stairs. In theory, anyone could've come in from outside.'

'But wouldn't they need to know about the CCTV and stuff?' Liz asked.

'You'd think so. Otherwise they'd've been spotted. And who'd know that kind of thing?'

'Security,' said Liz.

'Management,' said James.

'Yeah, or any of their friends,' I said. 'Talk about muddying the waters. It literally could have been anyone at all.'

I'd been trying to catch the blue-haired waitress's eye. She spotted me and came over to clear. We ordered coffees. Liz glanced at her watch.

'This is hopeless,' she said. 'By the way, Cynthia, did Nathan have a Facebook account?'

Liz was always trying to get myself and James to sign up to a new website called Facebook. She said it was a way to keep in touch with your friends. So far I hadn't bothered — I had my friends' phone numbers and email addresses.

'I don't know. I'll ask Ronan,' I said.

'I don't see how we'd get into it even if he did,' said Liz.

'He might have had a blog though. I'll google him later. Can't believe I didn't think of it before.'

'Good idea. It might help,' said James. 'We're never going to get anywhere unless we think of some new angles.'

'I've been thinking,' I said. 'In a lot of detective stories—'

'Oh, here we go,' said James.

'Leave her alone, she's an expert,' said Liz, laughing at me.

'Yep, world expert on detective fiction, that's me. Anyway, sometimes when they're stuck like we are, they try to find a way to stir things up. I'm thinking of telling everyone I'm investigating the murder. Then if anyone has a clue they might tell me about it. I could even frighten the killer into accidentally revealing themselves.'

'Yeah, by killing you too,' said Liz. 'I've read those books. The person who stirs things up always becomes the bait. But you don't have Miss Marple hiding in a cupboard, or an eighty-year-old baker hovering next door. I don't think you should take the risk, Cynthia, I really don't.'

'I've taken my own precautions to ensure my safety,' I said. (Moving to a hotel was a precaution, wasn't it?) 'I might as well be dead as arrested for this murder, Liz. I'd be old by the time they let me out. Don't forget I'm probably their only suspect. I have to try it.'

'I think it's a good idea,' said James. 'We'll cover your back. We'll keep an eye on you. Whenever you're poking a stick into a hornet's nest, shout.'

'Thanks. If the three of us act together, we can do anything.'

'Except deliver AirCross on time,' said Liz.

'Except that. Another thing I wanted to ask you two. You know the premeditated versus crime-of-passion question? We might be able to tell from the murder weapon. If the killer brought it to the scene then it's more likely that they planned the murder, right?' I laid my drawing on the table, but just then the waitress arrived with the coffees. I picked it up to clear some space, and handed it to James.

'Is that it?' said James.

'As far as I recollect,' I lied.

'Very detailed,' Liz remarked, 'but I suppose you'd seen it so often.'

'What?'

'It hung on the wall of his office. Don't you remember?'

'Um, no. I did find it vaguely familiar all right.'

'Pretty good drawing,' said James with faint surprise.

'I'll never forget that scene. It's burned into my retinas.' I played the sympathy card.

'You poor thing.' Liz put a hand on my arm. 'Cynthia, I keep forgetting what you've been through. It's not even been two days. Are you OK?'

Weird; I could feel heavy tears behind my eyelids. Must be getting soft.

'I'm fine. But, thanks.' I patted her hand and smiled at her.

I think we'd all had enough of the murder. We talked about work while we finished our coffees and paid the bill. It was great.

My murder-free interlude didn't last long. The first thing I saw when we came in from lunch was a post-it, bang in the middle of my laptop screen.

'Police — Meeting Room 4 — 3rd floor when you get back pronto!'

Lovely. There's nothing like a bit of tact and consideration from one's workmates. Whoever wrote that note would have been in my bad books, if I'd known who it was. Everyone around the oval table was either engrossed in work or hiding behind their screens. With a sigh, I set off.

The journey up in the lift seemed even more interminable than usual. It never broke down when you wanted it to. What now? Was it game over?

As always, a note-taker sat in the corner of the interview room. My comfy Superintendent had been replaced by a rather stern-looking older man. He had a long, narrow, humourless face and short greying hair. He introduced himself, but I was too busy assessing his expression and looking for handcuffs to listen.

He asked me to sit down.

'Superintendent Foster tells me that you seem to be a reliable witness.'

'Does he? I don't know why. I didn't see anything and I didn't hear anything.'

'That's why.' He smiled thinly. 'He said nine people out of ten would have had a funny feeling, or been sure there was a noise, or have caught a glimpse of a masked man. He said the fact that you didn't is interesting.'

'Interesting?'

'Yes. You are, as you probably realise, a suspect in this murder. He's interested in the fact that you didn't make anything up. Unless, of course, you did see or hear something, and you're pretending you didn't.'

'No. I was too scared to invent anything. I knew I'd be a suspect the minute I found the body. May I ask you something?'

'Certainly.'

'Are there any other suspects? Do you know what time he died? Do you know who was in the building? Are you planning an arrest?'

'I'm sorry, Ms Hegarty. I'm afraid we can't release any information.' He steepled his narrow fingers. 'We would, however, like some information from you.'

'OK. What's that?'

'You gave your address as Flat 1, 20 Cray St., E1?'

'Yes.'

'We visited this location yesterday evening, and again this morning. There didn't appear to be anyone present. Are you residing elsewhere at the moment?'

'Not residing exactly. More staying. Yes. I'm staying at a hotel.'

He picked up a pen.

'Which hotel?'

'Do I have to tell you?'

'I'm afraid so. You are an essential witness. We need to be aware of your whereabouts. We could, of course, ensure that your whereabouts are known to us at all times.' This with an even thinner smile, which I didn't like one bit.

'OK. I'm staying at the Holiday Inn on Old Street. I don't want anyone to know, though.'

'Why not?'

'Like you said, I'm an essential witness. I don't want anyone to get any ideas about removing me. If they do, I want to be hard to find.'

'Are you afraid of an attack, Miss Hegarty?'

'Wouldn't you be? Someone committed a murder right behind me. *I* know I didn't see or hear anything. *You* know it because I told you. But whoever the killer was, they're taking a risk assuming they're safe. They can't be sure. I could've seen them reflected in my monitor, or heard their voice through the door. If they're paranoid — and they'd be mad not to be — then they might consider ensuring that whatever I have to tell, I have no way of telling it.'

'Would you like police protection?'

'I wouldn't say no. Can I have some?'

'I doubt it. We're already overstretched. However, I'll put the word out to keep an eye on you.'

Great.

'Will you keep the hotel to yourself?'

'We will divulge your whereabouts on a need-to-know basis only.'

'OK, but please remember that nobody needs to know. Anyway, why did you visit my house? Did you want to search it or something?'

'Not at this juncture. We were merely confirming your residency at that location.' Raising his eyebrows, he added, 'It's just as well we did, isn't it?'

What did it matter to the police where I lived, if they weren't going to search it? What a lot of unnecessary fuss.

Probably best not to mention it, though.

'Am I going to be arrested?'

'Now? No. And I've been informed that you're essential to the success of the AirCross project. So we must hope that you're not arrested at all.'

'Thanks.' I smiled sweetly. 'Do you mind my asking, where's the Super?'

'Superintendent Foster is currently off duty. Getting some sleep if he has any sense. He asked me to check if you've remembered anything more?'

'No. I haven't tried yet though.'

'Thank you, Ms Hegarty,' he said, pulling a thick file towards him. 'You're free to go. For the moment. Please keep us informed of your whereabouts in future.'

He didn't look up as I let myself out the door. Bring back Superintendent Foster, I thought resentfully. This guy wasn't half as cuddly. No reassuring air about him. In fact, he gave the impression that he itched to arrest me.

'What did the police want?' asked Eugene, when I got back to our meeting-room fish tank.

'To ask me stupid questions,' I said, sitting down. The room was still. Everyone was listening. I swung my chair towards him and continued. 'They think I did it. I'm expecting to be arrested at any moment. But I have a plan.'

'What's that?'

'I'm going to track down the murderer myself.' I looked from him to the others squeezed around the conference table. Bharathi, Pierre, Adel. No one gave a guilty start, or jumped out of their chair. Damn it, I thought, another plan bites the dust.

'How will you do that?' Bharathi asked.

'I'm glad you asked me. I'm going to try to remember what happened on the night of the murder. I'm going to ask questions and annoy people. Starting with you.'

'Really?' She looked taken aback.

'Yes. Sorry, I didn't mean that in an accusatory way. What I mean is, you might be able to help me on one or two things.'

'What would you like to know?'

'It's complicated. Come for a coffee?'

'Don't you ever do any work?' But she picked up her handbag and we headed out to Prêt. It was quiet and private — at three o'clock, the lunchtime hordes were back at the office. I bought a cup of tea and sat at the most remote table.

'Do you really think I'll be able to help you? Why, what did you want to ask me?' Bharathi asked, joining me with her latte.

'Yes, I do. You see, Bharathi, I've only been in Airwolfe a few months and I don't know anything about the corporate history, or people's personal history. I think that kind of thing could be relevant.'

'Like how?' she asked.

'Like with the murder weapon, for example,' I said. 'Liz says it was hanging on Nathan's wall, but I don't remember seeing it. I wondered if you had, and if you knew why it was there.'

'It was a knife, wasn't it?' said Bharathi. 'What did it look like?'

'A type of dagger — a stiletto. I drew a picture. As far as I remember, it looked kind of like this.'

She took the sketch for a minute, then gave it back to me.

'It brings it home to me, that you were there,' she said. Her laughing eyes were sombre. 'It must have been a terrible experience. And terrifying. Do you really think the police suspect you?'

'I don't think they have any choice. They have to. I was on the spot and it's hard to believe I didn't notice anything.'

'Yes. Maybe you're right to start investigating for yourself. If they arrest you, it'll be too late.' She picked up the drawing. 'I recognise it. That's the stiletto Nathan brought back from the outsourcing meetings in China.'

'Outsourcing meetings?'

Outsourcing is a dirty word for programmers, as it is for everyone else. No one wants their job to move half-way across the planet, there to be done by someone with twice their IQ on half their salary. I hadn't heard that Airwolfe was considering outsourcing any work so this came as a nasty surprise.

'Yes. At one time Nathan was considering outsourcing the Systems Administration Department. He took several trips to China to review companies there that might take over this functionality.'

'God. What did Ronan think?'

'Ronan wasn't impressed. He made representations to senior management about why SysAdmin should remain in-company. He had a number of objections, but I think the telling one was on security. He said that handing systems security over to a third party didn't make any sense, considering the commercial sensitivity of some of our internal communications.'

'They fell for that one?'

'I believe so.' She chuckled. 'Nathan was disappointed, but not too much so because he'd had a couple of very enjoyable holidays in China at Airwolfe's expense. He was there as one of a delegation of Western firms, and one of the companies he visited presented him with the dagger as a gift. Vicky accompanied him to take notes.'

'I'll bet she did. Bharathi, do you believe the rumours about Vicky and Nathan?'

'I'm afraid so. I wish I didn't. Do you?'

'I'm not here long enough to say. He wasn't very attractive, to put it mildly. But she's looked terrible since he died — really shaken.'

'Yes,' said Bharathi. 'She started at Airwolfe as his PA, before she was promoted to office manager. I don't know about an affair, but they were definitely very friendly. No wonder she's upset. I feel sorry for her.'

'Nathan seems to have had quite a penchant for foreign travel at Airwolfe's expense. Didn't he go to Egypt on that company bash a few years ago?'

'Yes, he did,' said Bharathi. 'He started thinking he was an unlucky traveller, though. Tom Archibald's wife died on the Egypt trip. Then in China one of Nathan's group drowned in the Yangtze. Nathan said he wasn't going to go travelling again for a while.'

'Well, that was true, as it turned out.'

Bharathi had been fiddling with a sugar packet as we spoke. Now she put it down and looked at me.

'You know, I wasn't fond of Nathan but we worked together for a long time. He didn't deserve to be murdered. I hope you find out who did it. You, or the police, or both.'

'So do I, Bharathi. I appreciate your help. I've one more question for you.'

'Yes?'

'Do you have any idea who might have killed him? Who had a motive, or maybe the best opportunity?'

'I'm sorry, Cynthia. If I knew, I'd tell you, but I haven't got any real information. I don't want to start spreading stories about someone who's probably innocent.'

'Oh, Bharathi. That's so tantalising.'

To: All Staff
From: Vicky
Subject: Recent Events
Management has requested me to convey there thanks for your help during recent sad events. The working envirinment will return to normal as soon as possible.
Regards,
The Office Manager

To: Cynthia
From: James
Subject: Re: Recent Events
I don't have the heart to slag her off. What's happening to me?
Regards,
The Ex Awrfuss Mancher

To: James
From: Cynthia
Subject: Re: Recent Events
Real life.

Our dislike of Vicky seemed petty and small-minded in light of what had happened over the previous few days. Maybe she wasn't all that bad, I reflected. Perhaps her lack of management skills was a result of being promoted out of her league without the proper training. She had started her career in Airwolfe as Nathan's assistant. Airwolfe had probably wanted to get an office manager on the cheap. I decided to go and have a chat with her.

I might as well jump in feet first.

'Vicky,' I said, drawing a chair up to her desk, 'I'm so sorry about Nathan. I believe you used to work closely with him. You must be devastated by his death.'

'What do you care? You hardly knew him.' She swivelled away from me, reaching for a large box of tissues that stood on her desk.

'I haven't been here long, no. But I found the body. It was awful.'

'I heard that. Odd that you didn't see or hear anything, isn't it? Are you sure you didn't kill him yourself?'

'I'm sure, but the police keep hauling me in for questioning. I think they might arrest me if they don't find some other suspects soon. I'm trying to investigate his death myself before they do.'

'You shouldn't have too much trouble,' she said nastily.

'What do you mean?'

'You hang out with James and Ronan don't you? It's probably one of them. They both hated Nathan.'

'I don't think either of *them* would have done it,' I protested.

'Yeah well who did, then? Not you, not any of your buddies. Are you going to find the nearest person you don't get on with and frame them? You don't want to think they're killers because you like them, but you've only been here five minutes. How the hell can you tell who it was?'

'You're right, it'll be very difficult. I'll need a lot of help. That's why I came to talk to you. You know everything that goes on in Airwolfe. You've worked here for years. Plus you used to be Nathan's assistant. You must have known him very well. I'm hoping you'll tell me a bit about him. Maybe you even have an idea who could hate him enough to murder him in his own office.'

'If I did I'd tell the police, not you. No one hated him. He was a good boss. He listened to those whining programmers moaning all the time. I don't know how he put up with them. They were always late with their projects and he did his best to cover for them. Always late and always moaning; not enough pay, not enough servers, not enough desk space, not enough silence, not enough noise, not enough free KitKats in the canteen. You programmers think the whole company revolves around you.'

She stopped talking to wipe her eyes and blow her nose. She threw the tissue into her bin, where it joined a large pile of its friends, and pulled another one from the box. I couldn't think of anything to say.

'Cynthia, you're new so I don't know, maybe you weren't going to join the moan-athon. But no one on his team appreciated Nathan. It's like they said at the party, managing programmers is a thankless task. I used to be in meetings with him where he'd be covering his staff's arses big time. Then they'd wander in to his office and tell him it was all his fault the project was overdue.'

'Vicky, you're upset. I'm sorry I bothered you—'

'It's impossible to get them to come in on time. They won't do nine to five, they won't take lunch at the proper lunch hour, they forget their security cards, they're always looking for notepads and Biros, they go through blank DVDs like there's no tomorrow—'

'We are a pretty disorganised lot, I must admit.'

'He finally gets some recognition, a tiny nod from above.

A stupid little statue. Big blooming deal. Before he has a chance to even put it on a shelf someone comes into his office and just murders him.'

'So you think it was one of his team?'

'I wouldn't be surprised. Programmers would kill their grannies for a faster computer. But I can't see what they'd get out of it, except maybe they thought they could stop him outsourcing. But that'd be stupid, because it's in fashion now and the next boss will do it anyway.'

'Was he still planning on outsourcing?'

'I don't know. Maybe he'd given it up.' She seemed deflated suddenly. She looked down at her hands, twisting her tissue round and round.

'You said you thought Ronan or James might have hated him enough to murder him?' I asked tentatively.

'Oh, bugger. I'm sure they didn't hate him. But they were the most annoyed about the outsourcing thing. And they moaned the most in general. Ronan's not a programmer but those SysAdmin guys are nearly worse. They think the whole planet revolves around them, not just Airwolfe. I don't really think they did it, Cynthia, but who did? I can't believe it happened at all. No one in here seems like a murderer. Maybe a lunatic came in from the street.'

'Yeah, maybe it was a passing tramp. Someone always suggests that in detective stories, then someone says "but it looks like an inside job", and they're always right.'

'This isn't a detective story, Cynthia.'

'No, but how else can I think about it? I've never done a course on dealing with murder in the office, but I have read every detective story I ever got my hands on. I'm practically a world detection expert.'

'You really are going to try to find his killer? That's insane. Be careful they don't find you first.'

There was another problem on my mind when I got back to our overcrowded hothouse of a basement meeting room. I had nothing to read that night. Remembering the misery of trying to sleep in the Holiday Inn the evening before, I knew I needed something to take my mind off Nathan's body. But my Marian Keyes novel was in my flat. I thought about buying another copy of it but I didn't have time to drop down to the little bookshop in Old Street tube.

Maybe I could find something on the web, from one of those free book project thingies. Something light and frivolous.

An Agatha Christie? No. Too close to the bone.

A Georgette Heyer? Ah. I could lose myself in witty period romance. I've read most of her books to shreds, but I should be able to find one I hadn't read more than once or twice.

A visit to Google turned up *The Black Moth*, her first novel. Not one of my favourites, but entertaining, and I hadn't come across it for years. I opened it, clicked 'Print' on the first hundred pages and made for the printer outside in the corridor.

Which had a paper jam. A few printed sheets lay neatly in place. But pages 8-100 were somewhere in the bowels of the machine.

The printer was an antique — a mammoth, unloved creature, once top-of-the-range, which presumably had been relegated to the basement years before. A flashing red light on the display indicated the paper jam location, behind the second door on the right-hand panel. I opened the door, pulled a few levers and things, found the jammed paper and yanked it out too hard.

Damn.

I had to crouch, reach in and fumble the last few pieces free. I compared them with the main sheet — still some fragments missing.

At last I'd got them all. I straightened up, shut the door and waited for the print job to finish.

A light came on. Another paper jam.

I sighed, and got to work lifting doors and opening side-flaps.

I fixed five more jams before I got stuck.

The last light indicated a flap at the bottom of the left-hand front of the machine. I'd opened it, poked around and closed it again about fifty times. Just as I was about to resort to kicking, James came past.

'Need a hand?' he asked.

I was about to say yes. Then I imagined James copping an eyeful of *The Black Moth*.

'No. No, I'm fine,' I replied, casually picking up the pages that had printed successfully and folding them.

'Sure?'

'Yep. It's just something behind this door here,' I told him.

He went on his way.

The seriousness of the situation was beginning to dawn on me.

I opened my printout and glanced at the first page.

'He wore no rouge on his face, the almost unnatural pallor of which seemed designedly enhanced by a patch set beneath his right eye. Brows and lashes were black, the former slanting slightly up at the corners, but his narrow, heavy-lidded eyes were green and strangely piercing. The thin lips curled a little, sneering, as one dead-white hand travelled to and fro across the paper.'

Cripes. I should get Ronan or one of his minions down to sort the printer out. But if they saw *The Black Moth* they would be merciless. I couldn't let that happen.

I worked frenziedly for another ten minutes. Then I had to give up. I couldn't get the stupid thing sorted. Shit, shit, shit. By now I'd broken out in a cold sweat. OK, I could leave and pretend to know nothing about it, but when someone reported the printer was broken Ronan would come and fix it and the rest of my print job would appear. He'd die laughing when he encountered *The Black Moth*. When he'd recovered, he'd check the print records to find the culprit. Then he'd track me down so he could laugh at me again, in person.

Maybe one of his SysAdmin guys would come instead.

That'd probably be worse.

It might not be that bad, I told myself, slinking back into my seat at the meeting room table.

I flicked over a page or two.

'The lawyer found himself gazing at a slight, rather tall gentleman who swept him a profound bow, gracefully flourishing his smart three-cornered hat with one hand and delicately clasping cane and perfumed handkerchief with the other. He was dressed in the height of the Versailles fashion, with full-skirted coat of palest lilac laced with silver, small-clothes and stockings of white, and waistcoat of flowered satin. On his feet he wore shoes with high red heels and silver buckles, while a wig of the latest mode, marvellously powdered and curled and smacking greatly of Paris, adorned his shapely head. In the foaming lace of his cravat reposed a diamond pin, and on the slim hand, half covered by drooping lace, glowed and flashed a huge emerald.'

Feck.

I would never live this down.

Ronan would sweep me a profound bow on sight for the next ten years or more.

'What's up?' asked Liz.

'Nothing!' I said, hastily stuffing the evidence into my tiny handbag.

I'm worried about the Overflight piece,' I told James later. 'There's only another couple of weeks' work, but I'm getting side-tracked by the Nathan thing.'

'Hmm. Perhaps you should get Overflight into a state where you could hand it over to someone else,' he said. 'Just in case you want some time off.'

'Or in case I'm arrested?'

He looked embarrassed. I relented.

'OK, that makes sense. I can't apply myself at the

moment. I'll try to finish the unit tests as soon as I can and hand over the integration to Adel or Pierre.'

'Me,' said Pierre. 'All I am doing ees system testing. You 'ave zat and I weel integrate Overflight.'

'All right.' I didn't like saying goodbye to the Overflight module. I had a horrible feeling that it would be my last interesting technical challenge for a while. But I couldn't do everything. Catching Nathan's killer took priority.

I sat down and started in to some real work. The time flew by and Overflight stabilised magically under my fingers. Programming at its best.

'Cynthia!' I came back to earth with a bang as James poked me in the shoulder. 'God, you really do concentrate, don't you? Come on, we have to see Archibald.'

As we passed the printer, I noticed it was still broken. Good.

Ronan was already lounging in the meeting room when we arrived, making small-talk with Archibald. He had the two MAT servers ready for us. That was record time. Two more pairs of servers were due to arrive within a couple of days. Archibald had diverted three testers from other teams to us, to start tomorrow. He was hiring new people to replace them.

All great news, but I was thinking about my heavy workload and time-consuming investigation, and formulating a plan.

'I'm finding it difficult to do enough overtime,' I told Archibald bluntly. 'Nathan's death has affected me more than I'd realised. Also, the police keep questioning me and there's always the possibility that they'll think I had something to do with it.'

He looked concerned. 'Surely not, Cynthia. You haven't been with Airwolfe long, have you? What possible motive could you have?'

'None, obviously, and I didn't do it. But you never know what they'll come up with. They might decide I'm psychotic or something. Either way, I think I should hand over the builds to someone. No one else knows the procedure, it's a risk.'

(I knew the word 'risk' would hoist the red flag. Managers hate risk.)

'But, Cynthia, I can't do everything,' said James. 'I'll have enough to do co-ordinating the new testers and the rest of the team. I can't maintain the server environments and run builds and integration tests and do whatever else you do all evening as well.'

'I think we should ask Eugene to do it,' I said. 'He knows the environment and we could ease him in to the C++ side of things that way. Why don't I get him in and ask him if he's up for it?'

'Eugene. Hmm. What do you think, James?' asked Archibald.

'Not a bad idea. Let's do it,' said James.

Archibald picked up the phone. Eugene joined us a few minutes later. As I'd expected, having been bullied and side-lined for so long he jumped at the chance to become an integral part of the team.

'No problem, Tom. Actually, I have some ideas on how the build process could be improved,' he said. 'It's a bit messy at the moment…' And he went on to expound on some article he'd come across.

How annoying. But I kept my mouth shut. I like to maintain harmony in the workplace at all costs. Usually.

Meanwhile, Ronan was kicking his feet.

'Do you mind if I leave, Tom? You don't need me for this piece,' he said abruptly.

'No, fine, Ronan,' said Archibald, waving vaguely in his direction, still listening to Eugene.

'Cheers. Here, Cynthia, you dropped this,' said Ro. He slipped a tiny memory stick into my palm. I looked up to say 'It's not mine.' He winked at me.

'Oh, really, great, thanks Ronan,' I said. 'God, thanks a million, I'd have been lost without that.'

He flashed me a sardonic look and left.

I had no pockets so I clutched the little device until the meeting came to an end. Back in the basement, I stowed it carefully in my handbag. I didn't know what was on it, but I could guess, so I jumped about five feet when I got yet another summons to the police presence. My favourite Super this time. I made my way wearily back to the lift.

'My colleague Inspector Gadget, I mean Inspector Gannon, tells me that you're not residing at your home at present. He says you're afraid of being attacked by the murderer.'

'Yes.'

'Don't you think that's a little fanciful?'

'I do, but I'm an awful coward, Superintendent. I wouldn't get a wink of sleep if I thought the killer knew where I was. Obviously I won't really be attacked, but knowing that wouldn't help at three o'clock in the morning when the stairs creaked.'

'You must have plenty of money.'

'Yes. I'm a C++ contractor.' I smiled sweetly. Why shouldn't I have plenty of money? The Holiday Inn was some of the most sensible spending I'd done in ages.

'That's frank, at any rate. Ms Hegarty, if you're genuinely worried about an attack, let me assure you that the multiple murders that enliven Agatha Christie novels and regularly decimate the population of Midsomer rarely occur in real life. However, if you wish to reside in a Holiday Inn you are of course perfectly entitled to do so.'

'Thanks.' I knew I should be angry but couldn't help responding to his twitching lip. I got up to go. As I put my hand on the door handle he added 'Cynthia?'

'Yes?' I turned. He smiled quite kindly at me, and I suddenly felt warmer and safer than I had in days.

'All the same, be careful. Multiple murders are rare, but they do occur. I wouldn't like you, of all people, to be a victim.'

Back at my desk, I checked my handbag. Thank goodness. The little memory stick was still there.

So were pages 1-7 of *The Black Moth.*

'Bloody printer,' I thought, before diving back into the compelling world of Overflight.

When I surfaced at 7.30 I had a message from Harold.

See you soon!

Yep b there

I hadn't been home since before the murder. God, how I missed my warm, cosy flat. Not to mention my hair-straightener. On the other hand, I was acquiring a whole new wardrobe. One of the outfits I'd bought on my way to work that morning was a sheer green dress from Oasis, with a pair of silver heels. Anxiety seemed to have flattened my stomach — one good thing. I'd grabbed a silver and green necklace and earring set from the jewellery stand, and a silver barrette to put up my now unmistakably curly hair. I had enough make-up in my locker to do a reasonable job. So I was good to go.

The rest of the team were still hard at work when I came back from the loos all poshed up. There was a wolf whistle as I deposited a bag of clothes under my chair and put on my coat. The whistle was from Liz — the lads wouldn't dare.

Liz came out to the lift with me.

The printer was still jammed.

'You look fabulous, Cynthia,' she said.

'Thanks, Liz. Wish me luck.'

'You won't need it though. Oh yeah, his dad has just been murdered. Well OK, maybe you will. Good luck.'

Usually an undemonstrative girl, she gave me an enthusiastic hug. I hugged her back gratefully.

'See you tomorrow. Don't work too hard.'

'Take care of yourself,' she said, and she returned to our 90-degree hell-hole. I hoped they were ordering a very large pizza for their dinner.

Within a couple of minutes I was standing outside City Road Prêt. Suddenly it seemed like a terrible place to meet. I felt conspicuous and cold, and couldn't even go inside for a cup of tea as it was closed. My throat was dry and my palms moist. I realised that I felt nervous about seeing Harold. After thirty seconds or so, a black cab pulled to a halt.

'Miss Cynthia Hegarty?'

'Yes?' I advanced cautiously towards the cab. Don't forget, I told myself, black-cab drivers spend years acquiring 'The Knowledge'. They're unlikely to risk all that by kidnapping innocent Irish women whose bosses they've murdered.

'I've been asked to pick you up, miss. A Mr Harold Mansfield sends his compliments and asks if you'd be kind enough to accompany me to your destination.'

I'd never heard of a cab picking anyone up before. Crikey. Harold must have given him fifty quid at least.

I hopped in. 'Where are we going?'

'That's a secret, miss, but between you and me it's not very far.' He did a quick u-turn while the lights were red. In seconds we were through the roundabout and heading up City Road towards Angel.

Then we veered right and the cab pulled up outside a red-brick building that looked like a fire station. A red-brick building I recognised. 'Fifteen!'

'That's right, miss,' said the driver, who'd jumped out and was holding the door open before I'd time to find the handle.

'Um, do I owe you anything?' I asked him.

'Not a thing, miss. Mr Harold told me not to accept a tip.'

'Mr Harold?' Hilarious.

'Thanks,' I called as he sped off.

Tentatively, I pushed open the door. A gust of warm air spilled out, carrying a heavenly smell of garlic, olive oil and coffee. I stepped into the murmur of conversation and the clink of glasses. Harold jumped down from a bar stool at the counter, all floppy blond hair and apologies. He pecked me on the cheek. He smelled heavenly too.

'I'm sorry I didn't pick you up myself,' he said, putting a hand under my elbow to help me on to a stool beside his, 'but I thought you'd prefer me to come in and vet the table and the menu. I've been vetting the champagne too, but only a very little bit. I was waiting for you to help me.'

My nerves disappeared. Champagne-swilling desirable blond men I could deal with. It was newly-orphaned men, whose father's body I'd found, who caused goose-pimples.

'We're having a drink up here before we go downstairs,' he said. He filled a glass from a bottle in an ice bucket and handed it to me. Then he lifted his own.

'Here's to us,' he said.

The champagne was delicious — sharp and cold — and Harold in a flirtatious mood. After a few minutes we were ushered downstairs to a table for two in a discreet corner, with a good view of Jamie's counter. I beamed at him.

'Well vetted.'

'Thanks.'

'I've been meaning to come to Fifteen since I got to London. Do you think we'll see Jamie?'

'Possibly. It's not all hype, he does work here quite often.'

I glanced at the famous counter again and crossed my fingers.

When the waiters had left us alone with the menus, Harold said 'How are you? The police told me you found Nathan's body. That must have been awful for you.'

'I'm OK, Harold. How are you?'

'Oh, fine. He was my stepfather and we didn't get on. It hasn't exactly been a crushing blow on a personal level. It's just that I'm upset for my mother's sake.'

'Is she devastated?'

'Yes. Frankly, I never had any idea what she saw in him. He was ignorant, crass and stupid. And I suspect he was unfaithful. So does she, and yet she's — amazingly — upset.'

'Funny what love does to people,' I said.

'Oh, love.' He made a dismissive gesture. 'I doubt it's

anything so melodramatic. But she invested a lot of time and effort in the chap and now that's gone to waste. She'll have to start all over again with some other misfit. She collects them, you know. Anyway, never mind about that. What else shall we drink to?'

'To finding your dad's killer,' I said.

'Why?'

'Why? He was stabbed in cold blood. Don't you want to know who did it?'

'Not especially. They probably did me a favour. Now I won't have to support my mother through the long-drawn-out, ultra-emotional divorce that I always suspected was inevitable. I can't imagine who'd kill him — in his own office, so crass — but I suppose it could've been almost anyone. He made enemies wherever he went.'

'Yes, but, Harold, what about me?'

'You? What have you got to do with it?'

'I'm a suspect. I might get done for it. Even if I'm not, there'll be a cloud of suspicion hanging over me for the rest of my life unless his killer is found.'

'A suspect? You?' He started to laugh. 'You're so sweet, no one could possibly think you killed Nathan.'

'Yes they could.' I felt quite indignant. 'I was sitting right outside his office at the time.'

'Were you?' He looked at me thoughtfully.

'Yes. I was working really hard and I didn't see a thing. But I don't think the police believe I'm innocent, so I've decided to find the murderer myself.'

He choked on his drink. Slowly, he put it down.

'You have? How enterprising. Can you?'

'I hope so. Liz and James are helping me.'

'Suppose one of them murdered him?'

'Of course they didn't. They wouldn't kill anyone.'

'Oh? Did you know them before you started in Airwolfe?'

'No.'

'So you only met them a few months ago. How can you possibly be sure that they're not killers underneath?'

'The same way I know you're not.'

'Because you like me? Cynthia, murderers can be very likeable. If you're serious about this, don't trust me. Don't trust them. Don't trust anyone. But anyway I don't think you should interfere. Let the police do their jobs. They have the experience and the resources.'

'Oh, come on. They're understaffed and under-resourced. It's always in the papers. And how many crimes are committed every year in the UK? They've probably already had dozens more killings since your dad. The easiest thing for them to do is arrest me, make up some insane motive and lock me up.'

'It's not a police state yet though, is it? They'd have to send you to trial?'

'Yeah, eventually, but most people assume the police are usually right. Even if I was acquitted everyone would think that I did it but they just couldn't get me. Either way my life would be over. At least the fun part.'

'That's true. Perhaps it's too late already for the fun part. Whoever did it, you probably know them. They may even be a friend of yours. Have you thought of that?'

'Yes. Maybe you're right and I should stay away from it, but I don't think I have any choice now. Everyone at work knows I'm investigating. Bits and pieces of information are going to start finding me whether I want them to or not.'

'You mean your investigation will develop its own momentum? Interesting idea. Hmm, let's see if I can supply you with any info. His stepson cordially disliked him. His wife distrusted him. He was certainly unfaithful and almost certainly heading for divorce. He was an unsavoury character altogether. Let's change the subject.'

'OK. Tell me about your mum. How come she has all the money? How did she meet Nathan?'

'Completely different topic, eh?' He caught the waiter's eye. 'Let's order first. What would you like?'

When we'd ordered from the intriguing and varied menu, he picked up his champagne, swilling it and watching me, brooding. He seemed to make up his mind. He put down his glass and said:

'Prison.'

'What?'

'Prison. Where my mum met my dad. Or step-dad rather. Romantic, isn't it?'

'Wow, yeah, could be. Why was your mum in prison?'

'She wasn't in prison exactly. She's on the visiting committee. It's one of her good works. She likes to feel she's doing her bit for society. Guilt about the money, probably. She inherited pots from my grandparents — she's always felt like rather a lily of the field.'

'So Nathan was in prison and she met him there?'

'Not exactly. He was one of the guards. Well, more a manager. He used to show the do-gooders round and they struck up a friendship. He must have had his eye on her cash from day one. He spouted all the liberal crim-loving hogwash that she always falls for, poor darling.'

'Doesn't sound like Nathan.'

'No, though he kept that stuff up till the very end with my mum. His inner lout comes out when he's drunk, but he takes care to stay sober around her. I mean, took care. He was nearly as scared of losing her approval as of losing her money, I thought. I don't know,' he added, watching his champagne. 'Maybe he did love her in some ways. He was certainly a lot nicer to her than to anyone else. Not hard, of course.'

'Were they happy?'

'Seemed to be. I never thought it would last. There's one big difference between them: she's honourable to the core; he isn't. Sooner or later when he ripped someone off or pulled a fast one she would have heard. She could never bear dishonesty or subterfuge. She would have felt contaminated by association. She'd have been heartbroken.'

'Did you fight with him?' I ventured to ask.

'No. We were on amicable terms, able to have a chat. Cricket, football, who'll win the National. That sort of thing.

But I cordially despised him and he disapproved of me. I was twenty when they got together, wreaking havoc out on the town. Causing trouble whenever and wherever possible. He was a respectable career man with an MBA, already a few rungs up the greasy pole. Well, you know what I mean. Already in middle-management, about to make the jump into the private sector. I never had any time for arselickers, and that's what he was. And we weren't that far apart in age. He probably found me embarrassing.'

'Ten years?'

'Close. Twelve.'

'What about your dad? Did he get on with him?'

'Oh no. My mum's not divorced. My dad died when I was a kid.'

'Oh. I'm sorry.'

'Don't be. I barely remember him. Sounds like a nice guy though, not like the idiots mum has gone for since.'

The waiter arrived with our starters. My organic smoked salmon tasted divine and I love rocket. I was too interested in Harold to concentrate on the food, though.

'What about recently? Was there any particular trouble between you?' I asked as the waiter topped up my glass.

'No, except I guessed he was having an affair so I tackled him in his office. He denied everything and wouldn't discuss it, said he'd kill me if I said anything to my mother.' He smiled. 'You may have heard some of that conversation.'

I nodded. 'I heard him shouting. Couldn't hear the details, though. What made you think he was having an affair?'

'I borrowed his mobile and saw a text. Hey, you're questioning me, aren't you? That's cheating, taking advantage of our special relationship. You'll have to cut that out.'

Special relationship? Yee-haw. I was in.

'Sorry. Not really though. I'd probably be asking you all this anyway. It seems so odd, you and Nathan being related, naturally I'm curious about how it happened.'

'I'm glad you think we're different. Now it's my turn.

What are you doing working in Airwolfe? What brought you to London?'

'My curiosity again, I suppose. I loved Sydney but didn't want to stay there forever. But the idea of just slotting back into the old groove in Dublin didn't appeal either. London seemed like a good compromise. Abroad. Not too far. Easy to get home. Plus, I've always liked London.'

'Do you have any friends here?'

'No. Only the people I've met in Airwolfe. I thought I'd be lonely, but the Airwolfe crowd go out a lot and I often nip home for the weekend. And I'm footloose and fancy-free — it suits me for the moment.'

'Single, then? I assumed you were.'

'Thanks,' I grinned.

'No, I didn't mean it like that. Just, you're here now aren't you? You seem pretty straight-talking, so I figured if you had someone special you'd have let me know. I can't imagine why you haven't been snapped up, though.'

'You're a right flatterer,' I said. He laughed. 'There was someone, but we split up in Oz.'

'Was it hard?'

'No. The travelling together thing just didn't work. By the end of the first month I couldn't wait to get rid of him.'

That was the story I gave everyone. It was easier than the truth, which was less clear-cut, and messier. I didn't want to think about it.

Maybe my discomfort showed. Harold tactfully changed the subject to a new cinema release. As we discussed our favourite movies something was bothering me. When the waiters had brought our main courses and left, I decided to bring it up.

'In that text after your dad died, you said you needed to talk to me.'

'So I did.'

'What about? Or have you changed your mind?'

He grinned. 'Curiosity killed the little programming girl. It was just my way of saying I'd like to see you.'

'Oh.'

'So no clues there, Cynthia.'

I sighed, and concentrated on dinner. I'd passed on the vegetarian pasta dish because I'd had tagliatelle for lunch. Instead I'd chosen a goat's cheese tartlet with mouth-watering red onion sauce. A good choice, as it turned out. Like a symphony to goat's cheese, onions and peppers.

We didn't discuss the murder for the rest of the meal. He kept me entertained with ridiculous and almost certainly untrue stories about himself and his friends. I told him about my travels in Oz. I tried to keep it brief at first. Everyone has done Oz now, it's not exactly a polar expedition. But Harold was a good listener. I found myself describing the pure terror of my one and only scuba dive, when I was so frightened that the instructor had to hold my hand the whole time but it was worth it because I got to touch a giant manta ray.

'We're in luck,' Harold nodded towards the kitchen. Following his gaze, I saw Jamie standing casually at the counter, looking through the orders. He's just as cute in real life.

Dessert was the most meltingly delicious, perfect chocolate pudding I've ever encountered. It would have been criminal not to follow it with an Irish coffee. I sighed, thinking about work in the morning.

'You were right,' I said. 'Good food and champagne *have* made me feel better.'

'See?' he said. 'Have you started looking for a new job yet?'

'No. I'm still working for Airwolfe.'

'You're staying? I didn't think you would.'

'I couldn't stay away. I don't know anyone else in London, for a start. I'd be sitting at home staring at the wall if I wasn't working. Our project is late too, they need me. And I want to be on site for my investigation. Not to mention to get all the latest gossip.'

'Ah yes, your investigation. Are you really going to keep it up?'

'Yep. Harold, will you help me?'

'What can I do?'

'Arrange for me to have coffee with your mum. She might be able to tell me who his enemies were. I don't know her and I can't just ring her up and invite her out.'

'It's only our first date and already you want to meet my mother? Sorry, that was facetious. Laura and I are having dinner tomorrow evening. You could come along. But I wish you'd let this drop. I'm worried.'

'Why?'

'Why do you think? There's a murderer running around on the loose. You're in danger. I wouldn't like anything to happen to you. I've only just met you.'

He took my hand across the table. 'The police will find the killer soon and you can forget about it.'

'I hope so.' His firm clasp was distracting, spreading a warmth through my system that had nothing to do with alcohol. 'It's not as much fun as it seems in books.'

'I know. The Bill have been on to me already, asking how I got on with him. Whatever you decide, I'll introduce you to my mum tomorrow anyway. It's a perfect excuse to meet you two nights in a row.'

I looked into his eyes. He gazed soulfully back at me, but was there a hint of laughter in those glowing depths?

'Indeed.' I released his hand and stood up. 'Time to hit the sack, I guess.'

'Tomorrow night?'

'Tomorrow night. Probably. Unless I've been arrested by then. I'll let you know.'

'I'll drop you home,' he said.

When the taxi arrived, I considered telling him about the Holiday Inn but it was just too embarrassing. Besides, I thought, surely the flat will be safe enough by now. The shock of the murder had receded, and with a lively Harold by my side it seemed silly to live in a hotel.

He asked the driver to wait and came to the door with me. As I fished nervously through my tiny red bag for my keys he took my shoulders and turned me to face him.

'Good night,' he said. He gave me a peck on the cheek, hesitated, then kissed me softly on the mouth. We smiled at each other. He jumped into the taxi, which sped off as I closed the downstairs door.

I felt warm and tingly as I mounted the narrow stairs to my beloved flat. I hugged my coat around me, imagining our next meeting. Maybe he'd come in for coffee, I thought. Why had he disappeared so fast tonight? Either he didn't fancy me, or he respected me. Hopefully, it was respect. I sighed as I opened the flat door and surveyed my living-room. Either way, I couldn't have invited him in because the place was just too untidy. There were clothes strewn on the backs of the sofas, books all over the floor…books all over the floor?

I looked around, horrified. The room had been trashed.

I listened intently but could hear no one.

The lights went out.

I nearly fainted. Then I remembered the hall light was on a timer.

I flicked the switch in the living-room and waited for an age. There was no movement in the flat. I thought about turning around and going straight back down those stairs. But then I got angry. How dare someone trash my gaff?

So I checked out the damage. The kitchen was destroyed. Smashed crockery everywhere. The cutlery drawers had been emptied all over the floor.

The tiny spare room was bare. I'd taken the bedclothes off for washing after Alice's visit. Still, the intruder had found a way to vent, pulling the mattress off the bed and knocking over the cheap chest of drawers.

The bathroom was ankle-deep in bath salts, perfumes, make-up, moisturisers, cotton-wool and broken glass. It stank.

This didn't look like a search. It looked like a rage.

Tentatively I prodded the door to my bedroom. It swung

open. I stuck my head in. The curtain had been torn down. Shattered glass glinted on the window-sill. The metal anti-burglar shutter had been bent right back, far enough for an invader to squeeze in. The flat roof outside gleamed wet, naked and threatening in the cold night air.

The bed had been disturbed. As I got nearer, I realised that the duvet cover was in shreds, slashed. They must have used a knife. I faltered. Drawers had been pulled out and thrown around. Ripped, torn clothes were scattered over the floor.

A smashed photo frame lay by the window. On top of it…I gulped…on top of it was the photo. It was one of myself taken in Oz, showing me tanned and happy after a skydive, tangled hair blowing in the wind. I loved it. It represented freedom and excitement and independence.

Or it had. Now it was in two pieces, violently ripped apart.

I didn't like to think what that represented.

I couldn't stop shaking. Berating myself for nerves and stupidity, I opened the wardrobe and checked behind the door. No one. Whoever had done this, they had gone.

Even though I knew it was foolish, I still hoped that the Super would respond to my 999 call and come to the flat. His comforting bulk would be so welcome. I waited, shivering, sitting at the kitchen counter, door open so I could monitor the broken bedroom window. It seemed lazy to sit still in the midst of chaos. My all-but-dormant housewifely instincts were telling me to get out the Cif and cloth — well maybe first the hoover — well maybe first the sweeping brush. But I wanted to leave things untouched for the police. And anyway, I was too frightened to take my eyes off that window. I had an escape route to the door well planned out.

Two young policemen arrived, neither a familiar face. They glanced through the rooms and quickly identified the bedroom as the point of entry. I could have done that myself. Then they asked me a few desultory questions. The implied message I got was 'If you will insist on living in Shoreditch, what do you expect?'

'I was wondering…' I said tentatively.

'Yes, miss?'

'I've been involved in a murder investigation recently. In fact, I'm a suspect. Is there any chance that this could be related?'

'Come back to haunt you, you mean? Poltergeist?'

'No. I didn't commit the murder! I mean, maybe the real culprit has done this because he thinks I know something. Or to scare me off investigating.'

They exchanged a look. New psychic powers told me they were thinking 'Nutter'.

'Could you contact the Superintendent in charge of the Nathan Boyle murder case,' I suggested, 'and tell him what's happened?'

'We'll make sure that's done, miss. Now, we'd advise you to get that window fixed before you stay here again. Please contact us if any further intrusion occurs.' They made to leave.

'Wait!' I said. They turned to look at me. Still shaking, I said helplessly, 'could you give me a lift to Old Street?'

My Holiday Inn room had become a haven of security. As I added an unaccustomed sachet of sugar to my tea, I reflected that if I hadn't been staying there I might have been at home when the burglary happened. Paranoia definitely seemed like the way forward.

Every time I tried to process the destruction of my flat I came up against the same questions. If I'd been there, would I have been killed? Was the burglar the murderer? Quiet Eugene? I couldn't imagine him stabbing anyone, and thinking of his tenderness to his pretty wife I couldn't envisage him wreaking spiteful havoc in my flat either. Light-hearted Harold? Was it possible to rip my duvet to shreds, then sit down and flirt with me over a glass of champagne?

The police hadn't seemed surprised by the viciousness of the burglary. Was it just a coincidence? I shuddered. Why would a stranger be so destructive? And why would they rip up the photo? I was sure that was significant. I'd slipped it into an envelope and taken it with me, along with my Marian Keyes. At least I'd got that back.

I sighed and decided to ring my sister Alice. I'd texted her about the murder from James's flat, and she'd rung me straight back, but I hadn't spoken to her since. Her sense of fun would cheer me up. She'd probably tell me I was making a mountain out of a molehill.

'Cynthia! Hand in your notice and come home,' she said.

'What? I can't do that, I have to give a month,' I replied.

'Sod that. Half the company will be leaving, wait and see. But you don't have a month to hang around. Someone's out to get you. Someone who's slashing your duvet, Cynthia, for fuck's sake. How much of a clue do you need to tell you to get the hell out of there?'

'But I can't leave. I have to figure out who the killer is, and I've only just met Harold—'

'Feckless. Unreliable, Cynthia. Sending a taxi to meet you — he must be very lazy. And that cynical remark he made about love. He's obviously not looking for anything serious. You shouldn't either, after Sparky. Forget him. Come home.'

'I can't,' I said.

'Why not?'

'I don't know. I just can't. People will think I'm running away.'

'Well, you will be running away. Running away is the sensible option for you right now. Run away, run away quickly.'

'Yeah, but, Alice, I really do think they might arrest me. It'll look bad if I leg it before I get arrested, and I won't have any chance to find the real killer. And why is the murderer after me, anyway? Suppose he follows me to Dublin and tops me there? No. I have to stay and investigate.'

'What if it was Harold? Hey, maybe you *should* go to dinner with him and his mum — suss him out.'

'Alice! Of course it wasn't him.'

'He told you not to trust him, didn't he? He got one thing right at least. God almighty, girl, you only met him a few days ago. You don't know anything about him. He could be a serial killer for all you know.'

'I don't think he'd have been able to get into the building. Maybe I should ask him what he was doing at the time. But then how would I check? That's the trouble with not being the police. Impossible to verify alibis.'

'Any chance you could get them to pool information with you?'

'About as much chance as there is of Harold becoming an accountant. This isn't a nineteenth-century detective story. The police over here are super-efficient these days, especially since the terrorism stuff started.'

'But didn't you say the Superintendent was flirting with you?'

'I said he was cute, and nice to me. Not the same thing. Unfortunately.'

'Hmm. I still think you should try to get some info out of him. Can't do any harm. And pump the office manager for gossip. If she was having an affair with your boss she might know a few secrets.'

'She goes to my gym. Maybe I can build a rapport over the cross-trainer.'

'Exactly. But first of all you have to read his emails. My God, I can't believe you haven't done that yet.'

'Read obnoxious murdered boss's horrible emails, or fill my sister in on my scary burglary and my hot date. Which would you choose?'

'I see your point. If you're not coming home, be careful. Tell me if anything comes up. You can ring me any time.'

'Thanks Alice, that's good to know.'

'I'll just put my phone on silent if I'm asleep or busy. 'Night sis. Love you. Don't do anything stupid.'

'Thanks. 'Night.'

I hung up, feeling lonely and frightened.

I thought about Sparky. Once I would have turned to him with this or any other problem. Not any more. I looked at my phone. I'd deleted his number. I'd deleted it from my memory as well, by learning lots of similar phone numbers and allowing myself to mix them up.

I gave myself a shake. Sparky complications were the last thing I needed now.

I pondered the shattered glass on my bedroom windowsill, the assault on my flat, my shredded duvet cover. Someone had it in for me, and Alice was so far away.

There were hundreds of people all around me in the hotel, talking and sleeping, scheming and drinking, flirting, getting ready for bed. There were millions of people all around me in the ancient bustling city of London.

But was there anyone I could trust?

8 — SUSPECTS ACCUMULATE

Aren't mornings wonderful? At night everything gets out of proportion. You spend hours tossing and turning in the dark, playing worst-case-scenarios over and over in your mind. Then morning comes, the sun shines through the window (if you're lucky) and everything seems achievable again.

On Wednesday night, frightened and alone, I hadn't been able to face Nathan's emails. The only thing that had kept me sane was finishing my Marian Keyes. On Thursday morning I made myself a cup of tea in my hotel room. Then I retrieved Ronan's memory stick from my handbag and slid it into the laptop. Nice one Ro. Nathan's Inbox and Sent messages, plus his appointments, tasks and reminders. Copying them to my hard drive, I took a deep breath and opened the Inbox.

The top ten or so mails were unread.

Creepy.

One from Sam, Nathan's drinking buddy, just said 'Check this out'. It had a cryptically-named attachment. A functional spec for a new project, probably, or maybe the technical details for something in the pipeline. I double-clicked on it.

'Jesus!' I leaped backwards, spilling my tea, as an enormous naked pair of breasts jumped out at me. There was no context — like a head. Even a pair of arms would've been reassuring. It was very disconcerting.

I began to realise what a horrible job I had ahead. Although you should be discreet when sending emails from work — from anywhere, in fact — most people aren't. And remember this happened a few years ago, before anyone had been publicly fired for abuse of their company's Internet resources. So opening Nathan's mailbox felt like reading his diary and all his private letters whilst simultaneously browsing through his porn stash.

I'd expected to feel guilty for violating his privacy, but I hadn't been prepared for the sheer crudeness of much of his correspondence. A lot of the personal messages were just nude or semi-nude pictures, with accompanying crass comments. Most of the rest were chain letters or jokes.

It looked as though he'd never deleted or filed anything. His Inbox was jammed and the mails seemed to go back ages — presumably to the last time he'd run out of space. Hundreds of them every day. Crikey. I'd have to read every single one of these tedious messages, and read them slowly or I might miss something. How would I spot clues in this morass of detail?

I spent a few minutes opening them at random, sometimes blenching, sometimes laughing. James's emails and mine seemed rather unloved. Detailed descriptions of solutions I was implementing and problems James was tackling languished in bold, unread. Meanwhile the dozens of bulletins Nathan had received from Sam each day had all been opened. No doubt they were the electronic equivalent of well-thumbed.

My old irritation with Nathan resurfaced, but died as I remembered his awful stillness and the dreadful reality of the gold hilt protruding from his neck. He'd been an idiot. He hadn't deserved that though.

The enormous quantity of mails was going to bury anything useful. I only had half an hour or so before leaving for the office. Even then I wouldn't be in until ten. I needed a plan.

I decided to start on the day of his death and work backwards.

He had got, as usual, roughly twenty emails from Sam containing crude jokes and pictures and nasty remarks about assorted bosses and women. I speed-read them and filed them under delete. There were a few meetings in his calendar, some with associated documents — functional specifications, technical specs etc. No way could I get through all these but technical documentation was unlikely to hold any clues anyway. I opened Notepad and started making a list of people Nathan had been scheduled to meet on his last day. When I got to three o'clock, I came across a half-hour one-on-one with Eugene.

Intriguing. No performance reviews were due as far as I knew. Nathan wasn't a hands-on manager. He tended to avoid his staff, particularly people he was trying to shaft.

I had a look for Eugene in the Inbox. Nothing. I opened up the Sent folder.

Bingo!

To: Eugene
From: Nathan Boyle
Re: Today's Meeting
Dear Eugene,
With reference to our discussion today, I am sorry to confirm that I have been forced to take the decision to terminate your position.
This termination takes place with effect from Friday.
Your years of service in Airwolfe are appreciated.
Regards,
Nathan Boyle

I sat clutching the table in disbelief. Eugene fired? He hadn't said a thing. He was still in the office. He had practically been promoted.

So Eugene had a cast-iron motive. Presumably Nathan had died before doing the paperwork. Anyway, his vendetta against Eugene had always been obviously personal. Eugene probably thought that with Nathan gone the whole thing would fizzle out.

I couldn't believe it.

If Eugene was arrested, what would happen to those cute kids? And Gwyneth? And the new baby?

My head was reeling, but it was time for work. I saved Nathan's semi-processed mailbox back to the memory stick with a new name. Then I copied the murder photos onto it too, deleting them from my phone. I double-deleted Nathan's Inbox from the laptop. Ronan had stuck his neck out giving me Nathan's mail. I didn't want to land him in trouble.

Now I had the photos and Nathan's mails all on Ronan's memory stick. I roamed the room in search of a hiding-place. Eventually I sellotaped the stick underneath the fold-out ironing board. It was undetectable unless you pulled out the board and felt for it.

Hey ho. Off to the office.

Excerpt from the *Financial Times*, Thursday

To date, no one has been arrested for the murder at Airwolfe and Co of Mr Nathan Boyle, a manager at the company, last Monday night. One of Mr Boyle's colleagues is said to have found the body. It is thought the death was caused by a knife wound to the neck. Mr Boyle is survived by his wife, Laura Mansfield, the well-known philanthropist.

Detective Superintendent Stephen Foster, of the Metropolitan Police, said that several different avenues are being explored. Pressed, he added that no more details can be released at this time.

The murder took place at the Airwolfe offices on City Road. An Airwolfe spokesperson stated that the building holds fewer than 200 staff, all of whom are due to be relocated to Airwolfe Head Office in the Docklands at a future date. We contacted Mr Eric Zappatone of SwordBlade, the company that handles security at the site. He insisted that the building's protection is top of the range and has not been compromised.

While no motive has yet been found for the murder, a source tells us that the police are examining unexplained lodgements to one of Mr Boyle's bank accounts.

Arriving at work I discovered that the third floor had been reopened and we were back at our own desks. Thank goodness.

'I don't believe it,' said Liz, when I'd dragged her to the Ladies and given her the low-down on recent events.

'No honestly. He kissed me,' I said. 'Only a peck though.'

'I mean about the burglary,' she said. 'Did they really wreck the place? You must be devastated. Your lovely flat — it was so comfortable.'

'Yeah, I am,' I said, 'and I'm worried. Why did it happen? And I'm bloody terrified. I could have been there. They ripped up the sheets, Liz! It has to have something to do with the murder. Suppose they come after me again?'

'Have you talked to the police?'

'Yeah, but not the Super. I'm going up to him now.'

The Super frowned.

'No, I wasn't told,' he said.

'They probably didn't think it was high priority. Maybe they thought I was a crazy lady,' I said.

'Are you all right, Miss Hegarty?'

'Yes. Never better.' I forced a smile. 'Luckily, I'm used to the Holiday Inn now. I felt quite at home going back there.'

'Fortunate.'

'Yes. Superintendent?'

'Yes.'

'Will you go and have a look? Take a few fingerprints? Just in case, you know, in case someone's out to get me.' I laughed nervously. It sounded fantastic even to me. Yeah, like he was going to believe there was a maniac killer on the loose and I was a target.

Hang on, there *was* a killer on the loose.

'We certainly shall, Cynthia,' he said. 'You're lucky you moved to a hotel. The burglary probably had nothing to do with the murder, but you may have avoided a nasty attack. When were you last at your flat?'

'The morning Nathan was killed.' (Was that only three days ago?)

'Several days. A large time-frame. Still.' He stood up. 'I'll check it out.'

He looked down at me. I'd only seen him sitting before. He was tall. 'You're sure you didn't just leave the place more untidy than usual?'

A sardonic, searching look, and he was gone.

'**H**ave you heard?' asked James, when I finally got to my desk. 'The police are questioning everyone in turn. Anyone who's been in is looking stressed. No one's talking about it, though.'

'Who's gone in?'

'Eugene. Pierre. Adel. Vicky.'

'Any arrests?'

'Not yet. I'm next. Wish me luck.'

'Are you going to tell them about my investigation?'

'Don't know. Do you want us to keep quiet?'

'Not fair on you. Say whatever you want. Anyway, we're not doing anything illegal. Probably.'

'Thanks, Cynthia,' he said, looking more cheerful.

Oh, the joy of being back at my own desk. I switched on my machine and went to fetch a cup of inferior office tea while it booted up. Then I sank into my luxurious chair with a little sigh. Over the months, I'd adjusted it to the max — my height, correct arms, good slant to the back, perfectly Cynthia-shaped.

I took a sip of tea, opened my email and prepared to zone out.

I couldn't settle.

I tried to concentrate, but each time work drew me in I felt an uncontrollable urge to turn and look behind me.

I gave up and went to talk to Liz. She'd just come out of her police grilling.

'Do they think I did it?' I asked her.

'I'm sorry, Cynthia. They asked me not to discuss the interview.'

'Fair enough, Liz. I won't ask you any questions. To totally change the subject, I'm thinking of fleeing the country. What do you think?'

She looked puzzled, then laughed. 'Oh. I see. No, I'd say you can probably stay here for the moment.'

I wanted to talk to Eugene. His new role working with the build gave me cover.

'It's going very well, Cynthia,' he said. 'I've already cut build time by five per cent. I changed a parameter on the Subversion automatic check-out command.'

'That's great, Eugene.' Had this guy never heard of tact? 'So, I hear you got questioned by the police this morning?'

'Yes.' He pushed a piece of paper away and straightened his back before looking up at me.

'What's it about?' I sat on his desk. 'They want me in again later. I'm a bit nervous.'

'Just crossing me off the list, I suppose. They asked me where I was between five and nine on the evening Nathan was killed.'

'Oh. Well, that was probably easy enough to answer. Where were you?'

'At my desk until seven. Then I went home. Alone, but I

was there by eight thirty and no one could get out of London much faster than that.'

'You stayed here till seven?'

'Yeah. Don't you remember me saying good night to you? No, I suppose you don't.' He grinned. 'I probably shouldn't tell you this, but the Superintendent asked me if you seemed engrossed in your work when I left.'

'What did you say?'

'I said, yes, you did. As usual. I called good night and you glanced up at me but I don't think you saw me at all, you smiled vaguely and then started typing like mad. You looked pretty pleased with yourself. I suppose you'd just figured something out.'

None of this rang any bells, but Eugene said goodbye to me every single day. It'd be most unlike me to specifically remember one occasion several days ago.

'The Superintendent didn't tell me what time Nathan was killed,' he continued. 'It must've been after five o'clock. He probably had meetings and things before that.'

'Yes.' I needed to know about the email. From my perch on his desk I could see over the adjacent partitions. Eugene had a window seat and there was no one nearby. I lowered my voice. 'Actually, you had a meeting with Nathan on Monday yourself, didn't you?'

'Yes.'

'What was that about?'

'Oh, just a pre-performance-review performance review. He felt that there were aspects of the project I might need some help with.'

He couldn't meet my eye. Not a surprise — he didn't strike me as one of nature's liars. I forced myself to stay quiet, hoping he'd elaborate. It worked.

'You know, Cynthia, I was going to talk to you about it, but then Nathan was killed anyway. He actually gave me a really hard time. He said my ignorance would drag AirCross down, he'd been wasting resources on me that could be used to support someone who knew what they were doing.'

Eugene's voice got quieter and quieter. 'He said he'd no choice but to consider terminating my employment. Now UKIS is gone he said I no longer have anything to contribute and I've shown I'm not capable of moving with the times.'

By this stage he was mumbling into his jumper. I felt sorry for him. Nathan had bullied and humiliated him. Now he was reliving the experience. Slowly he raised his eyes and looked up at me.

'Do you think he was right, Cynthia? Should I tell Tom?'

'Who's Tom?'

'Tom Archibald.'

'Eugene. Don't you dare. We really need you on the project. Nathan was just a pillock with a grudge. It was obvious. A bit of retraining and you'll be grand.'

'D'you think so?' He sighed. 'I don't seem to have achieved anything for such a long time. UKIS is really all I know, and that's gone now. I find the C++ code hard to follow, I'm not used to it, it seems more difficult than COBOL.'

I did some COBOL in college. He wasn't wrong.

'Yes, but you're a subject-matter expert. You know everyone in Airwolfe, you know how to get things done and who to go to to make stuff happen. And you know everything about how real-time air industry software should work.'

'Mm. I've been working here for over fifteen years. There aren't many surprises these days.'

'Exactly. We have plenty of C++ nerds. If you're building a bridge, you need someone who knows the river. Nathan was an idiot.' I glanced around again. Still quiet. 'Did he fire you, Eugene?'

He looked at me, surprised, then shrugged.

'Yes. It was awful. I thought I'd collapse. And I had to go home and tell Gwyneth. But I couldn't tell her, so I just didn't.' He paused. 'And then, next day, he was dead.'

He straightened his shoulders, looking more determined.

'The killer did me a favour, but anyway I'd decided to go

to HR. Nathan had some sort of problem. He's had something against me ever since the Egypt trip, when Tom's wife Janet died. Gwyneth was so good that time, so kind to Tom. Tom's always been friendly to me since. He even asks us out to dinner occasionally. I sometimes wonder if Nathan is jealous of that. Wondered, I mean.'

'He had the knife out for you all right.' I winced at my choice of words, but Eugene didn't seem to notice.

'And, you know Tom's wife died of food poisoning? At first we all thought she'd be fine. All the same, Gwyneth wanted to call a doctor but Nathan said there was no need, everyone always gets sick on holidays, she'd be right as rain in the morning. We were in Sharm el-Sheikh, it would've been easy to get a doctor, everything is laid on for tourists. But Tom took Nathan's advice, and by morning it was too late. I've wondered if Nathan suffered from some sort of guilt syndrome. Maybe he blamed me because it was easier than confronting his own mistake.'

I thought about that.

'Nah, he was just an arsehole,' I said. 'What were you all in Egypt for anyway? Some kind of junket?'

'A developers' conference for Airwolfe worldwide.' He smiled. 'But yeah, it was a junket really — most of the delegates were managers, not developers. I was one of the few actual programmers there. That was back when UKIS was still up and running, and I was the only person who knew how to maintain it. I was a lynch-pin of the department. They'd have given anything to keep me on board then. But shortly after the conference Nathan commissioned the UKIS replacement, and it's been downhill ever since. From my point of view, I mean. And there's the triplets.'

I nodded, smiling at the memory of his cute little toddlers.

'They're wonderful, but a lot of work for Gwyneth, and we've a baby coming, and everything costs so much. I have to have a job. *Have* to.'

'Things should improve for you now, though,' I said. 'James will be hassling Archibald to get you on to a few courses. And you'll be a central part of the AirCross effort once you've got the hang of co-ordinating builds and testing and all that.'

'How about you?'

'I don't know. But I'd say no matter what happens, my days in Airwolfe are numbered. It's just not the same, I haven't been able to relax since I found the body.'

'Don't blame you. It was right behind you.'

'Yep. Eugene, do the police know that Nathan fired you?' I was wondering whether they'd checked Nathan's emails. Surely they had?

'Yes. They saw an email he sent to me. They asked me to explain.' He looked strained. 'I told them that Nathan had had personal issues with me and that I'd planned to take my redundancy up with the Human Resources department.'

'And what did the Super say to that? Did he seem suspicious?'

'I don't know. He said "I see" or something. But at the end of the day, Cynthia, people don't murder other people just because they've been fired. He'd have a hard time pinning it on me. Typical Nathan, though. Getting me into trouble even after he's dead.'

On balance, I believed Eugene's assertion that he'd planned to attack Nathan via the Human Resources department rather than with a dagger. I found it easier to relax now that we'd discussed the firing email. The Overflight unit tests still weren't finished, but I had other plans for the morning. I'd started those unit tests on the murder night, and because the work was so intensive I'd saved it to source control every few minutes.

Source control is an essential part of the computer programmer's armoury. It allows you to store as many versions as you like of the program you're working on. This is useful when things go wrong.

Suppose your program worked perfectly yesterday, but something in it is broken today. You made eight changes in the meantime, and you're not sure which one caused the problem. Plus some of the changes were so trivial that you've forgotten about them.

If you saved your work to source control yesterday when it was running well, then you can get back that exact version. You then do a 'diff' (difference) between that working version and the one you have now. This highlights all the eight changes you made. Now you start with the good version and reintroduce the eight changes, testing after each one. When you test and the program is broken, the last change you made is the culprit.

The Superintendent had asked me to reconstruct my actions on the night of the murder. I figured I could use Subversion, our source control tool. All I had to do was get the code as it had been at five o'clock, then run it and see what was broken. The errors that came up would pitchfork me straight back to Monday night, when I had seen them first. As I remembered how I'd dealt with each problem, I might be reminded of what had been happening around me when I'd done the work the first time.

Then I would get the next version, which I could see I'd saved at five fifteen, and do the same thing.

I'd saved nearly twenty versions between five o'clock and nine o'clock, when I'd wrapped up for the day. Going through them would be a tortuous task, but not as bad as weaving endless baskets or whatever it is they do in prison.

Boy, was it boring. As I slowly stepped through line after line of tests and code it began to seem futile. Gradually, some memories returned. At one point I'd been about to make tea but then a test had broken and I'd sunk back into my chair to fix it. A while later I remembered checking my gym timetable, toying with the idea of going to Step class, then getting drawn back in by a memory leak.

Then I found a comment. (I always comment my code

thoroughly, so that when people break it they know who to come to and blame.)

// You'll have to if you want to keep me quiet! — Cynthia

Needless to say, that was an unusual comment. It catapulted me back in time to three days earlier. Nathan had shouted it at someone and I'd absently typed it, vaguely planning to ask James about it next day. (I can touch-type faster than I can think). I tried to remember if I'd turned around to see who Nathan was shouting at. Probably, but of course the blinds had been shut behind his glass office walls. That's why I'd had to open the door to look in, on my way home when I'd seen the light on.

Yipp-a-dee-doo-da! I went back into Subversion and checked the timestamp on this section of code. The previous 'commit' had been at 6:59. This 'commit' was at 7:05. That pinned it down nicely — sometime during those six minutes Nathan had shouted at someone, loud enough that I had half noticed. Well done me.

I went through the rest of my work with no more revelations. As I finished up, I got a summons to the Police Presence. I delayed to print out the relevant code. Thank goodness we were back on our own floor. I wondered whether the basement printer was still jammed. Ronan hadn't stopped by to bow at me yet, so it probably was.

'You look like the cat that got the cream,' said Superintendent Foster, regarding me over a huge mass of paperwork.

'Thanks. I mean, great. I've remembered something,' I said, waving my printout at him.

'That's good,' he said, but his face remained stern. 'Please, enlighten me.'

I started babbling, explaining the source control process, the frequent 'commits' and the way a whole evening's work can be retrieved bit by bit, assuming you've saved often. I stood beside his desk and showed him the printout, pointing out the comment. I explained the flashback it had triggered, and how I was certain that Nathan had been speaking to the murderer. Finally I told him about the six-minute time-frame, and stood back waiting for praise. I'm not sure that I wasn't expecting him to pat me and feed me kitten treats.

'Very interesting,' he said.

'Yes.' The atmosphere was, I began to realise, less convivial than usual. Almost frosty. He waved me to the interview chair. I retreated and sat down.

'You've just remembered this now?'

'Yes. I went over Monday night's work, like you suggested, and found it.'

'I see. You had no opportunity to observe the visitor in Mr Boyle's office?'

'No.'

'Didn't you watch them come out?'

'No. The change I'd just made to fix the test I was working on broke an earlier test. It didn't make any sense and I spent forty minutes figuring it out. That must be why I forgot all about the comment till now.'

'Interesting.'

'What's the matter? I thought you'd be pleased. Doesn't this fix the time of the murder?'

'No, since we have no way of determining how long the meeting you describe lasted, if it occurred at all. We now know that Boyle was killed between seven and eight, so the conversation may have been with the perpetrator. However, if you don't mind my saying so, your story is frankly incredible.'

'What do you mean?'

'You type a whole sentence because it's so dramatic, then immediately forget all about it for three days? Both actions are unlikely. Put together, they are downright unbelievable. One of the interesting features of this case has been your blank refusal to admit that you saw or heard anything on the night. Now you've changed that story. I'm wondering why.'

'Because it *wasn't* a 'story'. It's the truth. Everything I've told you is true.'

'Let me ask you something, Ms Hegarty. During interviews today, several people mentioned that you're investigating this murder on your own account. Apparently, you're afraid of being—' He glanced down, then back up at me, "—stitched up" by the police. Is that true too?'

Oops. I stared out of the window for a minute before replying. The sun flashed from the glass office block across the road. I looked him in the eye.

'Yes, it's true. Sort of. It's not that I don't trust you, but I know I look really suspicious. I thought I'd better try to find some evidence to clear myself.' I smiled weakly.

'And have you?'

'No. Eugene told me he was fired, but I can't imagine Eugene killing anyone. Anyway, losing a job isn't really a reason for murder is it?'

'No, and especially not for a programmer. I believe there's no shortage of work available,' he said. 'Anything else?'

'No.'

The Super made a note, then put down his pen, pushed back his chair and relaxed. A smile quivered behind his eyes.

'You shouldn't be nosing around this murder, Cynthia. You're interfering in police business.'

'No I amn't. I haven't done anything to interfere.'

'Nevertheless. You would be better off leaving the investigation to my colleagues and myself. We have the resources, and we are also less likely to be…er…bumped off. Let me tell you that if you become aware of any facts related to the murder, and you fail to inform the police, then you'll be guilty of a criminal offence.'

'Oh.' What did he think I was, an idiot? 'And if I do tell you?'

'Then we will, of course, be grateful. But I would prefer you to desist.'

I remembered Alice's suggestion.

'Superintendent, hasn't it occurred to you that we could help each other? I could find out things you'd never hear about.'

'Such as?'

'Um…I don't know yet. I'm due to have dinner with Mrs Boyle and her son Harold this evening, though. I might pick up something useful.'

The Super looked sceptical.

'And in return, you could tell me who has a cast-iron alibi for the murder. That'd help me to limit the scope of the investigation I won't be undertaking.'

I beamed guilelessly at him. Would he go with it, or would he lose the rag? Did I detect a hastily-suppressed chuckle?

'Hegarty, I appear to be making no impression on you. Let me reiterate that we advise you to terminate your investigation. We are following a number of lines of enquiry. If we'd been lucky enough to find someone with a cast-iron alibi, it would be absolutely against procedure for me to tell you so.'

Score! No one had an alibi. I kept a straight face, conscious of Constable Lawson taking notes in the corner.

'OK, Superintendent. I'm sorry if I've caused problems with my investigation. Everyone's heard about it now, though, so I think people might come to me with information. Obviously I don't want to shop my friends or colleagues, but whoever killed Nathan is a dangerous nutter. I'll actually be happy to hand them over if I find them.'

'How gratifying, Cynthia. You may go. Please ask Peter Eneduwa to come up.'

The interview had eaten into my lunch break. By the time I'd found Peter and passed on the Super's message, James and Liz had already gone. About to join them, I remembered Nathan's drinking and emailing cohort, Sam. I sighed. He was the last person I wanted to see, but it was the perfect time to catch him.

Sure enough, I found him plonked on the games-room

sofa, eating an enormous roll, reading *The Sun* and watching sport on the telly. I dropped into an armchair beside him. He didn't seem to mind being questioned.

'Nathan wasn't happy at Airwolfe,' he said. 'Felt he wasn't appreciated. He had to kowtow to that Archibald tosser who'd only been here about five minutes.'

'He got a 'Best Manager' award.'

'Ha. They hand those out in strict rotation. Today Nathan, tomorrow some other poor fucker. You get one to keep you happy when they don't want to give you a pay-rise. Or when they're gearing up to shaft you.'

'What was Nathan's problem with Archibald? He's not a very hands-on manager, is he? I never even met him until after Nathan died.'

'Didn't matter. It's not *having* a boss that bothered Nathan. It's *not being* the boss. He wanted that promotion, he wanted the money, he wanted the power. He would've been in charge of some of the arseholes who've been out to get him since he started here. Could've had a bit of fun winding them up. Then Archibald breezes in. No experience, no business nous; his degree is in herbology or tree-hugging or something for fuck's sake. But he went to the right school and he's in the same golf club as the IT VP and — wahey! — he gets the job.'

'So you think Nathan actively disliked him?'

'Hated him.' Sam took a huge bite of his roll. We watched the racing until he swallowed. 'Bloody Microsoft Project and Excel spreadsheets. Archibald's addicted to them. Everything had to be recorded, and in fifty different places. Surprised he didn't have the staff logging how long they spent having a shit. It wasn't just at work, though. Nathan used to say Tom So-Damn-Professional Archibald was an arsehole in his spare time too. They went on some junkets together, so I figured he knew what he was talking about.'

'Can you think of any reason why Nathan might be killed?'

'Everyone knows he'd been having an affair. Nothing

serious, but wives don't like that sort of thing. And Laura's the jealous type. Course, you'd expect her to stab him in the bedroom or at the kitchen sink, not in the office. But maybe she wanted camouflage. Get one of his co-workers done for it.'

'What about his mistress?'

He lowered his Coke bottle and gave me a sharp look.

'You know who that is, don't you? Pretty little thing, but it wouldn't have gone anywhere. He planned to finish it. She was getting too demanding. That's what he told me anyway.'

'Maybe he did, and she killed him?'

'Possible. Nasty way to go, stabbed in the back of the neck.' He shook his head and took a slug of Coke. 'Someone had it in for him all right.'

'Anyone else in here who could've done it?'

'He didn't make too many friends. Couldn't stand slackers, and never learned to be diplomatic about it. He wouldn't hold people's hands and tell them how fabulous they were. He even fired a few of them in his time — total losers who shouldn't have been here in the first place, but some of them took it personally. People hold grudges.'

I said nothing, remembering Nathan's treatment of Eugene. Maybe they'd been dead right to take it personally.

'Poor fucker.' Sam looked thoughtful. 'He knew a secret about someone in here and he loved gloating over it. Something they'd done. When he got pissed he'd try to wind me up, put a finger to his lips and make a shushing noise. Wink at me. Fall over. He thought I was dying to know. Kept him happy, poor sod.'

'And were you dying to know?'

'Nah. He told me fairly early on, one night when he was hammered. He couldn't hold his booze. He didn't remember that he told me, but I did. It's some story all right.'

'Really? What is it?'

'Do you know how to keep a secret?'

He gestured me closer, glancing around the empty room.

'Yes, of course,' I said, leaning towards him.

'Well, so do I.'

He guffawed and took a bite of his roll, wiping mayo from his mouth with the back of his hand.

Git.

'Did you ever have any disagreements with him yourself?'

He chewed then swallowed, looking at me indulgently. 'Trying to fit me up for it, love? No chance, I'm afraid. I have an alibi. And no motive either. Nah, I wouldn't have killed him. He was a tosser, but he was always good for a few beers watching the footy. Knew how to have a laugh, not like most of the pricks in here. Pokers up their arses.'

Passing through reception I saw Hugh, and realised it was the first time I'd seen him since the fatal night. I stopped to say hello and ask how he was doing.

'Fine. The day after it happened I nearly booked a plane home to Oz. But I'm over it now. How are you, Cynthia?'

'Not too bad. Still slightly jumpy when I'm sitting at my desk.'

'I don't blame you. Oh, here.' He produced a small brown envelope from under the counter. 'Zorr asked me to give you this.'

'Cheers,' I said. 'See you later.'

Once on City Road I stopped to examine the contents of the envelope. One slim sheet of paper.

Cynthia. As promised, list of people in the building after five. Confidential — please destroy once read. Z

Eugene Reaney — left 18:59
Elizabeth Simpson — left 19:30
James Garber — left 19:31
Sam Babcock — left 19:34
Peter Eneduwa — left 19:50
Ronan O'Brian — left 20:58
Vicky Hubbell — still in building when body found

A couple of people I didn't recognise had left before six-thirty. According to the Super, the murderer struck between seven and eight. So either the culprit was on the list or they'd sneaked in with the stationery and taken advantage of the CCTV blind spots. Not much help, then.

James? Liz? What was the story? Until this week Liz hadn't been paid for overtime and never did any. James was paid by the hour, like me, but he worked nine-to-five on principle. He didn't believe in burning himself out for his capitalist overlords.

I slipped the paper into my handbag as I arrived at the empty, TV-afflicted pub we used as our investigation headquarters. Being so late, I was too hungry to sit and wait for the waitress. Anyway I was meeting Harold for dinner later, so there was no need for a big meal now. I went straight to the counter and bought leek and potato soup and a roll. The soup looked hot and smelled delicious.

'Hi, Cynthia,' Liz looked up as I carried my tray to our table. 'How did your interview with the handsome Superintendent go?'

'Do you think he's attractive?' I was startled. I'd thought his bulky, rough-cut charm was visible only to me.

'Smokin'! He's an irresistible mixture of hunky and reassuring. James doesn't agree though, do you, James?'

'Not my type, but I can understand the appeal. Did he give you a hard time, Cynthia?'

Shaking my head, I blew on my soup spoon and had a taste. It was as good as it smelled.

'No. Well, sort of. He was fairly OK. He's heard about my investigation.'

'Yeah, he mentioned it,' said James. 'I said you're just asking around.'

'Did you tell him we're helping you?' asked Liz.

'No. Implied I'd scale it back. Didn't say I'd stop though — not really a lie.'

'Oh, are we keeping it up? Good,' said Liz. 'Let's go over our list of suspects. I thought of a new one — Archibald because Nathan never told him about the AirCross missed milestones. He'll look like a right idiot for nominating Nathan for that award.'

'OK.' I put down my spoon, pulled out my phone and added:

'Archibald. Reputation damaged.'

'We'd best add Ronan too,' I said. 'Apparently Nathan was trying to push outsourcing of the SysAdmin Department, and Ronan knew. Oh, and we'll keep Eugene. He told me that Nathan fired him. That's confidential, of course. It gives him a motive.'

'*Fired* him? What an arsehole,' said James. 'Do the police know?'

'Yes, but they think all programmers are the same. They don't realise that COBOL developers who haven't retrained are close to unemployable. Dunno if they know about the triplets either. I don't think he did it, anyway, so I'm not going to tell them.'

I was breaking open my roll as I spoke. It was fresh and soft. This place was growing on me.

'No, it'd be awful if he was arrested.' said Liz. 'What would happen to those poor little kids? I'm glad you said nothing.'

'Yeah. Although if I'm charged I'll throw everyone to the lions,' I said. 'More news. Both Ronan and Vicky were in the building during the time when the murder occurred.'

'How do you know?' James asked.

'I have my sources.'

Liz looked away. James shifted on his seat. I wanted to ask them why they'd been at work until half seven. And why hadn't they told me?

I drank some more soup instead.

'Have you talked to Vicky?' Liz asked after a moment.

'Yes. Not about running out of Nathan's office on Friday though. She goes to Step class on Thursdays after work. I might go along today, hang out at the gym, suggest a coffee. Maybe she'll be more talkative if we're not in the office.'

'Good plan,' said James. 'I hope she tells you about the Friday crying thing. I'm dying to know what happened.'

'I'm conducting a serious murder investigation, James, not digging up scandal for your vicarious enjoyment,' I said, pushing my bowl and plate away.

'Yeah. Be sure you tell me, though,' said James.

The blue-haired waitress wandered by. I called her over. I needed a cup of tea.

'I'm going out for dinner with Harold and his mum later,' I said, when we'd ordered teas and coffees. 'I wonder if I'll learn anything. Liz, do you remember he seemed to be fighting with Nathan at the party? Probably nothing, but I'd like to rule him out.'

'Unless he did actually kill him,' said James, 'although he seems way too laid back to bother.'

'I can't believe anyone we work with would do it, though,' said Liz. 'I know you like Harold, Cynthia, but I'd prefer it to be him. Or his mum. Or any outsider.'

'I understand,' I said. 'I hate suspecting people in Airwolfe. It makes it hard to concentrate on work. Maybe it was the bloke from CityRich properties. Cecil Howell.'

'Oh, I forgot to tell you, I googled him,' said Liz. 'I didn't find out anything we don't already know though. He's a big property developer, apparently. We should go and talk to him.'

'I'm going to ask Harold if he knows any more about Nathan's issue with him than we do,' I said. 'You were going to google Nathan too, weren't you, Liz? Did you find anything on him?'

'No,' said Liz. 'He might as well not exist. If he had an Internet presence it was anonymous.'

'Thanks for trying, anyway,' I said, smiling at her. 'Now, about the dagger. Bharathi told me that Nathan was given it as a gift, at an outsourcing event in China. Liz, you were right. It's been hanging in his office ever since. So does that mean that the murder was an opportunistic crime? Unpremeditated?'

'Maybe the murderer knew about it, and planned to use it? He could have brought another weapon along just in case,' said James.

'True. Bummer. Not much help there then. Unless it was Ronan, and using the dagger was symbolic.'

We laughed.

'I don't think Ronan would stab him in the back of the neck though,' said Liz. 'He'd be more likely to beat him up and leave him with a bloody nose.'

'That's an interesting point,' I looked up from pouring milk into my tea. 'Ronan's no coward. Whoever stabbed Nathan from behind must have been trying to avoid a fight.'

'Yeah, and they definitely wanted to kill him, not just give him a fright,' said James. 'So what does that tell us?'

'According to most detective fiction, the murderer must be someone he knew, because he turned his back on them. Although I'd much rather turn my back on a stranger than on some of the people I know,' I said. 'So. Either a cold premeditated killing by a murderer who knew the dagger was there, or an unplanned passionate attack by an enemy or a lover who lost their temper.'

'But,' said Liz, 'if someone lost their temper during an argument and snatched the dagger down, he'd hardly turn his back.'

'True. He died sitting down, turned away from the room. Not likely if he was having a full-on row. Liz, where exactly was the dagger?'

'On the right, just inside the door. I suppose they could've pretended to leave, then snatched it and gone back to kill him. The carpet would've muffled their footsteps. But he'd have seen them coming, unless he'd already turned away from his desk. Doesn't seem likely.'

'Could someone have taken it down on the way in, if he was too busy to notice?' asked James.

'Yes but that'd be premeditated, and they couldn't rely on him not noticing. Would it have been hard to get? Was it in a frame?' I asked.

Liz shook her head. 'No, it was resting on a couple of nails. And even you could probably reach it, Cynthia — it wasn't that high.'

'The most practical approach would be to take the dagger beforehand and hide it in your clothes,' said James.

'True. So it was probably premeditated murder, with the weapon obtained in advance,' I said, 'although it could have been a crime of passion where the murderer sprang when Nathan turned his back. God. We need a profiler.'

'Anything else?' said James. 'Hang on, Cynthia, did you say you know when the murder took place?'

'Kind of.' I told them about the code comment, and that the killer had apparently struck between seven and eight. 'Don't tell anyone though, maybe it was a secret,' I added a little guiltily. 'The timing doesn't make any difference to me, of course, cos I never moved. But people who left before seven are probably in the clear.'

Silence.

'How about you two?' I tried to sound casual. 'What time did you go home?'

'Between seven and eight I'd say,' said Liz.

'Me too,' said James. 'Hope we don't get arrested, Liz.'

We got back to the office even later than usual. Vicky hadn't hovered at the door with a stopwatch since Nathan's death. There was still no sign of her today and Liz breathed a sigh of relief as she sank into her chair. Laughing as I reached my desk, I glanced down to see a large brown envelope on my keyboard. Unusual. I didn't know anyone in other departments yet, let alone other buildings, and had never got any internal post except for a memorandum about desk ergonomics. Picking it up, I turned it over and realised that it wasn't internal post — it had a stamp.

I sat down, opened the envelope and fished out a Christmas card. Aw, sweet. Or maybe not. Inside, someone had cut out words from a newspaper to form a message:

Stop Interference or you will be Dead

An anonymous letter! Unbelievable.

I examined the envelope. It was standard — A4 business. The postmark was almost illegible. I could just make out 'Moorgate' and that day's date. The stamp was a normal first class stamp.

I stared into space for a moment, then looked behind me. I picked up the card again. This was crazy. I set up a meeting with James and Liz in the games room, pronto.

'Look at this.'

I handed the card to James. He frowned as he took in the threat. Liz read over his shoulder, her eyes widening.

'Who could have sent it?' James asked.

'Anyone?' I replied. 'Anyone who works here. Moorgate is only down the road.'

'Or who doesn't work here, but knows what you're up to,' said James.

'You mean Harold? I suppose it could be him.'

'How can we find out?' Liz asked.

'I don't know,' I told her. 'With an email there are ways to track it. Sometimes you can retrace the jumps or analyse the IP address. Occasionally you can figure out who an anonymous account belongs to. But someone physically took this to a post-box and dropped it in. There's no trail. What a fiendishly clever way to send an anonymous message.'

We all looked down at the card, awestruck by its crude, old-fashioned simplicity.

'Yeah,' said James. 'How can you find out who sent a specific snail-mail letter? There's just no way to do it. Unless…' He looked at me. 'How did they do it in your detective stories, Cynthia? Back in the dawn of time, before the Internet?'

'Um. Postmark. But that's Moorgate, tells us nothing. And fingerprints of course. We're not exactly equipped to test those, though.'

'We should give it to the police, they could analyse the prints and probably get DNA and everything,' said Liz.

'And look delusional?' I asked. 'The Super doesn't think the burglary's relevant, why would he take this seriously? No thanks. Anyway, it's a clue. If we could find the sender we'd have our murderer. If we give it to the police it'll disappear and we'll be none the wiser.'

'The cut-out words seem to have come from headlines. I wonder what newspaper they used,' said James.

'Good question. It looks sort of familiar,' said Liz. Then she added 'Back in a sec,' and ran out of the room.

'James?' I asked.

'Mm?' He picked up the card again, grinning at the glittery robin on a log.

'I was wondering. How come you were here till half seven the night of the murder?' I asked.

'Was I? I dunno. Time ran away with me, I suppose,' he replied, holding the envelope up to the light.

'Liz left around then too.'

'Did she? How do you know?' I had his attention now. 'Did you get hold of the CCTV record or something?'

'Of course not. Just, I happened to hear…'

'Coincidence, Cynthia. You're getting a suspicious mind. I think there might be a way to find out who sent this.'

Liz flew back in through the door, triumphantly waving a copy of *City A.M.*

'I thought I'd seen those clippings before,' she said. 'Look.'

She was pointing to a headline:

'Stop Interfering' Say Top Bankers

'And here,' she pointed to the next page:

Derivatives Trading Not Dead

The typescript in the headlines was identical to the card — the words 'Stop', 'Interfering' and 'Dead' had obviously been taken from the paper. After a short search we found the sources of the other words.

'Right. We're getting somewhere,' I said. 'Our culprit must have picked up *City A.M.*, pasted the text into the card, and sent it. All on time to get here by lunch. We need to find out when they start handing out *City A.M.*, and where. Then figure out who was in the right place at that time this morning.' I groaned. 'It's an impossible task, isn't it?'

'Plus, Cynthia, that's yesterday's paper,' said Liz, apologetically.

'OK, forget all that,' I said. 'We're back to anyone could've done it.'

'Maybe not,' said James. 'What about fingerprints?'

'We've no way of analysing them,' I said. 'We'd have to ask the Super, and then we'd probably never even hear back. Perhaps you're right though, and we should.'

'Hang on a sec,' said James. 'Guess what my niece asked me for for her birthday?'

'What?' How like James to go off at a tangent.

'A *CSI: Miami* fingerprint detection kit. It's a toy, but fairly sophisticated. We could buy one and dust your letter for prints. Then we just have to get samples of everyone's fingerprints and compare them.'

We looked hopefully at the card. It was slightly the worse for wear.

'Good idea, except we've all handled it now and the envelope has also had the attentions of a bunch of Royal Mail employees,' I said.

'Hey, there's something in here,' said Liz, peering into the envelope. She upended it. A piece of glossy white cardboard fell out. We stared at it, mesmerised, as though it was the holy grail.

'One of your business cards, with "RIP" inked in after your name,' said Liz. She picked it up by the edges and tilted it to the light. 'A set of prints!' she shouted with justifiable delight.

'Shall we give it a go?' asked James.

'Be a shame not to,' I replied. 'Is this toy hard to get?'

'No. Most toy shops do it. I should be able to pick one up on the way home from work.'

'We could have a meeting tomorrow and do the testing. So all we need to do is get samples of everyone's fingerprints before then,' I said.

'Let's divide up the suspects,' said Liz.

We sat down and went through the list:

Eugene
Vicky
Archibald
Ronan
Bharathi
Harold
Mrs Boyle
Cecil Howell
Peter

'Peter?' said Liz.

'Ah, we want you to have *some* fun, Liz,' said James. 'I'll take Eugene and Archibald. Cynthia, you work on Harold, Mrs Boyle and Vicky. Liz, that leaves Ronan, Bharathi and Peter.'

'Can't you take Ronan, James?' she asked. 'He's never said a word to me. I'm terrified of him.'

'OK. I'll take him as well as Eugene and Archibald. You've got off lightly, Liz. I'd give you Cecil Howell but I don't see how we can get to him at the moment. We'll have to leave him out of this, I think. We all clear?'

'Yep.' I stood up. 'Thanks, you two. I really feel like we might be getting somewhere at last.'

I spent the afternoon talking Eugene through the automated testing I'd introduced to the project. Of course he annoyed me by coming up with one or two possible improvements. It was worth it, though. Co-ordinating unit testing was the last organisational role I had on my hands. Once I'd offloaded it on Eugene I could focus on finishing the Overflight unit tests. And on my investigation.

I wanted to find out if Peter had any insights for me. The guy at the desk next to his said he was down in the server room so I descended to the ground floor to look for him.

This was where all the test servers and mainframes operated. It was called the server room but it was actually an entire floor devoted to machinery. There were hundreds of computers there, probably worth millions of pounds. Access required a dedicated security pass. I had one because I occasionally had to change test server settings that couldn't be accessed remotely.

The heavy door closed behind me with a thud that was swallowed by the pervasive hum of the assembled machines. Ahead stretched a central passage tiled with echoing metal grids. Labyrinthine, towering stacks of servers darkened the atmosphere. The heat generated by thousands of computer processors couldn't compete with the intensive air-conditioning. It was always chilly.

Normally I loved the busily murmuring machines and the impression of unseen industry, but today I found them spooky. I felt a cold frisson of fear as I walked past group after group of servers whispering to themselves. I peered around in the cool gloom, my footsteps ringing out eerily against the background hum. There were no humans. I was afraid to shout for Peter in case I attracted the attention of all those electronic brains.

Finally, I found him. He had removed one of the metal floor tiles at the end of the room near the back door, and was trying to isolate a network connection in the cavity.

'Are you busy? Would you mind if I asked you a few questions?' I asked, sitting on the floor.

He glanced at me. 'Ask away.'

'Do you have any idea who killed Nathan?'

'Liz tells me you're trying to investigate his murder yourself.' (She does?) 'Do you think that's wise?'

'Why not?'

'Depends who the murderer is,' he said. He separated the end of a wire from a clump and examined its label, then bent it aside. 'What if it's someone with a temper? Zorr over the cheating thing, or…'

'What cheating thing?'

'Didn't you hear?'

'What?'

'It's just a rumour.'

'What?'

'Might not be true.'

'Peter! *What?*'

'Well.' He glanced at me again. 'I heard that Nathan owed Zorr money.'

'He did? And? Zorr wouldn't kill anyone over a few quid.'

'Yeah, I know, but it was a gambling debt. Hugh told me about it.'

'Same. The worst Zorr would do is embarrass Nathan in public until he paid up. Not exactly a motive.'

'Mm. But the thing is, Cynthia, Nathan was refusing to pay.'

'What? Why?'

'Well…' Peter abandoned the tangle of wires and sat back against a server stack. 'Hugh said there were five of them playing, a casual game in the pub after work. The usual, everyone puts a tenner in the pot and winner takes all. The other two were useless, Andy and Den, out in half an hour and they went off home. Hugh hung in there for another hour, then he was out too. He stuck around to watch the end of the game. Thought Zorr would have it sorted in no time.'

'And?' I asked.

'No sign of anyone winning. Pile of chips going one way, then back the other way. One of those games. I'd rather watch paint dry. Nathan was an awful poker player but Hugh said he got fab cards. Zorr was only getting wins 'cos he's such a good bluffer. Then Zorr looked at his watch and said he had to go. Went "all in".'

'So Nathan matched him,' I said. 'One hand, winner takes all.'

'Yep.'

'A bluff I'd say. Zorr knew he had a winning hand but didn't want it to be too obvious. Pretended he had to leave.'

'Yeah,' said Peter. 'But Nathan thought *he* was going to

win. Offered him double or quits for the cash in the pot. He had three Kings and an Ace. And a seven or something.'

'So, three Kings basically. Let me guess, Zorr had three Aces and a King?'

'Better. Full house. Wiped Nathan's eye for him. Game over. Zorr gets the pile of tenners and Nathan has to match it 'cos of the double or quits.

'But Nathan didn't have the cash?' I asked.

'Worse. Nathan says Zorr's getting too cocky, everyone knows he cheats and no way is he paying up.'

'*Cheats*.' *Shit!* 'When was this?'

'Wednesday.'

'But Nathan was still alive on Thursday.'

Peter grinned. 'I know. Hugh says he couldn't believe it when he heard him. He nearly threw himself backwards off the chair in case he got killed by a flying table. Thought Nathan was toast. But Zorr was cool. Said everyone knew Nathan was a stingy fuck who wouldn't pay for his own grandma's broadband connection. Said he'd give him till Monday to cough up. Took Hugh off for a pint in the Dragon.'

'And did Nathan pay up?'

'Don't think so. Hugh says he was bitching at the office party on Friday, saying he's always thought Zorr's a cheat and it's time someone stood up to him.'

'Jesus he was such a bloody idiot. What a stupid thing to say. Everyone knows Zorr's fanatical about fair play.'

'He *says* he is. But are you sure? What if he *was* cheating, and Nathan had proof?'

I looked at him in disbelief. 'Peter, you've got to be joking. Zorr? He's about as likely to cheat at cards as Nathan was to leave the pub during happy hour.'

'He's not one of your suspects, then?'

'No way. Unless…' I grew thoughtful. 'D'you think he could've killed Nathan in a rage, if he heard that Nathan was going round slagging him off and calling him a cheat?'

'Dunno. But I know I wouldn't like to annoy him.'

We chatted some more while Peter traced the wire he needed and replaced the floor tile. We parted at the lift. The lobby seemed deathly silent after the hum of the server room. My conversation with Peter gave me food for thought as I headed through the graveyard to the gym. I nearly fell over a squirrel.

For once I was on time for the six o'clock Step class. Vicky was already in the changing room. Normally we greeted each other politely and went our separate ways. Our lockers were in different sections. After our tumultuous week, though, it seemed natural to fetch my gym clothes from my locker and join her while changing. I had a number of ulterior motives of course, but also I found myself feeling more in sympathy with Vicky than ever before. She looked haggard and withdrawn from the shock of Nathan's death. She was clearly still deeply upset. I felt sorry for her.

My strategy for getting Vicky's fingerprints revolved around this gym visit. She usually bought a bottle of water on her way up to the changing room. I had bought two and I simply swapped one of them with hers while she wasn't looking. I put hers in a freezer bag and slotted it into my kit bag, and brought my second one in to class.

You need water in Step because it's hard work. The principle is simple. You place a plastic step on the floor in front of you. The instructor plays loud, fast music and calls out various routine names. Experienced members of the class and the instructor then perform the routines, none of which are more than a few minutes long. At your first class you mostly just stumble around and stare at everyone else, but eventually you work the routines out. There's a lot of repetition.

The pace is fast and taxing. I'm hot and breathless after five minutes and worn out after ten. I usually get a second wind after a while. I try not to watch the clock, ignoring it for half an hour only to find that a mere two minutes have passed. There've been times when I've been so weak and exhausted, convinced my aching legs wouldn't hold me up for another second, that I've almost grabbed my sweat towel and headed for an early shower. I've seen new girls do just that, making a break for the door when they realise what hard work the class is. (There are rarely any men. I'm not sure why. It's a good workout for anyone but I suppose they think the plastic steps look girly.)

There was always a slight edge of competition between myself and Vicky. Arguably, it had helped me to persevere in the first tough weeks.

'Did you send me a note today?' I asked her, watching the fit instructor adjust his sound system.

'What sort of note?'

'The unfriendly sort.'

She stared at me. 'No.'

'And did you have an argument with Nathan on Friday?'

'No.'

'Are you sure? Someone said you came out of his office crying.'

'"Someone" should mind their own business. We had a small disagreement. Nothing major.'

'What about?'

Music drowned out her reply. Just as well, if my lip-reading skills are to be trusted. We were called to attention by the instructor, and the class began. Occasionally the work rate slowed, but then I lunged for my water, too busy glugging it to interrogate anyone.

By the end of the class I was bright red, as usual. A pleasant glow of virtue spread through my limbs on the way back to the changing room. I caught up with Vicky and repeated my question.

'What did you disagree with Nathan about on Friday?'

'The police already asked me that,' she said. 'It's got nothing to do with his death. I don't see why I should tell anyone.'

'Fair enough.' I raced to my locker and stripped for my shower at lightning speed, wrapped myself in a towel, then came back and sat beside her.

'Have you ever met Nathan's wife?'

'Yes, why?' she looked at me strangely as she thrust her socks and trainers into her locker.

'I wondered if you could tell me anything about her.'

'God, that woman,' she said. 'She's a right bitch.'

'Really?'

'Yeah.' She started to undress. 'She met Nathan at some do-gooder event and she got her claws into him. He fell for her straight away. The money, the clothes, the feeling of power. But she never understood him. She expected him to obey her all the time — she's loaded so she thought she was the boss. She used to go mad if he just went for a few pints after work. She'd ring him in the pub and he'd have to leave and talk to her on his mobile out in the freezing cold. Sometimes she'd make him go home before closing time like a good little boy. She's older than him, and she treated him like her little lap-dog. She even wanted him to give up his job. He told me that, but he said no one was taking away his independence.'

'It wasn't a successful marriage, then?' I asked, studying my toenails. They needed painting.

'God, no. He was going to divorce her. He was just waiting for the right time.'

'Wouldn't he have been skint if he got divorced?'

'He had his salary, didn't he?' Vicky wrapped herself in her towel. She was ready for her shower but she lingered to talk, leaning on her locker. 'I suppose he wouldn't have had a yacht in the Med or an Aston Martin any more, but he didn't care about material things. He said he couldn't live a lie.'

Oh dear, I thought. So the rumours were true.

'When did he start working at Airwolfe?'

'Same day as me — five years ago. I'd just finished secretarial college. On our first day I was his PA.'

'Did he have the same job he has now?'

'No, he came in as a manager in charge of the whole department. It was smaller in those days. When the numbers went up, they split it into four sections and created the UK

Technology Director role for the overall head. Nathan applied for that job but they gave it to an outsider. Nathan said it was all pull, the new guy played golf with the IT VP.'

'The new guy. Would that be Archibald?'

'Yep.'

'Was Nathan upset when Archibald got the job?'

'He said it was what he expected. He's fairly friendly with Archibald though. They were both in Egypt for that company bash. They seemed to get on better afterwards. Archibald's wife died over there. Maybe that brought everyone together.'

'When did he marry Harold's mother?'

'Oh I forgot, you know the son, don't you? He was at the party last week. Right little drip, he is. Nathan said he's never done a day's work in his life. Just swans about spending his mother's money and making sarcastic remarks.'

'They didn't get on too well then?'

'No. Harold did his best to stop his mum marrying Nathan but he hadn't a hope. Laura doesn't listen to *him* either.'

'I'm meeting her tonight, with Harold.'

'You are?' Vicky asked. She stood abruptly, heading for the shower room. I followed her. 'Why?'

'I want to find out if she knows anything about the murder. Maybe she's the killer.'

'She couldn't be. She wouldn't have been able to get into the building, and anyway she wouldn't know about the blind spots.'

'Blind spots?'

'If you use the stairs you can go anywhere in the building without showing up on CCTV. They discussed it in the managers' meeting last week. I was doing the minutes. They were wondering whether to do something about it — I suppose they will now.'

'Did anyone else know? Did you tell anyone?'

'No, but all the security staff probably knew. I suppose Nathan could've told Laura, but why?'

'Good point. Plus, why would she kill him?'

'Oh, well.' Vicky turned away and hung up her towel. 'Maybe if he told her he wanted a divorce. I know that's not a good reason to stab him to death but maybe he said he never loved her or she was crap in bed or something.'

She retreated into her shower cubicle.

'None of it seems very likely,' I said, leaning against the partition between the cubicles with my back to her. 'Killing him in the office would cast suspicion on the staff though, that'd be good from her point of view.'

'I hope it *was* her,' said Vicky venomously. She raised her voice to be heard over the drumming water. 'I'd love if she spent a few years in prison. She wouldn't be so bloody hoity-toity then.'

9 — ENTER HAROLD'S MA

I was meeting Harold and his mum at eight at a Greek restaurant near Hoxton Square. It was nearly a quarter to by the time I'd showered and dressed. After making a big effort the night before and not getting so much as a snog I'd been half-tempted to attend tonight's event in an old tracksuit. Instead, I'd bought a silver sleeveless top (to go with my silver shoes) and a dark red pencil skirt on the way to work, this time from Next. I'd been rushing and hadn't even tried them on. Now that I was about to wear them that seemed like madness.

Fortunately, the skirt didn't bump or bag anywhere and the top was simple enough to survive being silver. I spent a few extra minutes on my make-up, and tried to jazz up my look with sparkling blusher and unaccustomed eye-liner.

I walked to the restaurant through quiet back streets. The night was cold but dry. Step had alleviated the anxiety of the murder and the burglary, leaving me pleasantly relaxed. I strolled along, enjoying the cool-down. Three office workers sped past me, high heels clicking, coats flapping in the breeze. A burst of chatter and music escaped from a pub doorway ahead as they went in. Their perfume lingered on the air. Through the window as I passed, I saw them join a group of men with loose ties and open shirt-collars. The

Thursday build-up to the weekend was under way.

The restaurant was in an old church, with high ceilings, and dedications on the walls funded by long-dead parishioners. Full of light in the daytime, it felt warm and intimate as I entered from the winter night.

I was glad I'd made an effort when I saw Harold's mum. She had luxuriant blonde hair, tied into a neat chignon. She wore a black draped cashmere dress with a soft cerise scarf. She had beautiful, dark, deep-set, serious eyes. Eyes that were difficult to look away from. Harold's presence, usually bright as a searchlight, dimmed in her company as though unable to compete with her compelling aura.

'Cynthia, this is Laura. Laura, Cynthia,' he said.

'Cynthia, how lovely to meet you,' said Laura, rising to kiss me as I approached her chair. She made me feel about fourteen years old. Her cheek against mine was scented and soft. She took my hands in a warm, firm clasp, looking into my eyes. 'My son has been telling me that you found Nathan's body.'

'That's right, Laura. I'm very sorry for your loss,' I said, trying to sound like a grown-up.

'Thank you, my dear.' She squeezed my hands, released them and sat down, holding my gaze. 'I'm sorry you had such a dreadful experience. Poor Nathan, it's difficult to accept that he's been murdered.'

'Yes. Everyone at work is pretty shell-shocked.' What on Earth was I doing here? We had imagined a threatening possible murderer. This was a distraught woman grieving for her dead husband. What had we been thinking?

'I'm sorry for intruding,' I said. 'I'm sure you'd prefer to be alone with your son at a time like this. Perhaps I should join you another time.'

I picked up my bag as I spoke, but she put out a restraining hand.

'No, my dear, please, I'd prefer you to stay,' she said. 'It's comforting to meet someone who worked with poor Nathan. Nothing can bring him back now, but I get pleasure from talking about him.'

'Yes, do stay,' said Harold, who'd been filling a champagne glass. He placed it in front of me and smiled.

Impossible to walk away from that smile. I sat down and picked up a menu, but I couldn't relax. I was a terrible fraud. OK, I had known Nathan, but hello, I had disliked him? What would I say if she asked me stuff about him? I focused on the menu, trying to calm down. Giant beans were still available as a side dish. I love giant beans. I spent ten heavenly days in Greece once and, being a veggie, giant beans and Greek salad were practically all I ate.

When we'd ordered, Laura looked gravely at me.

'Harold says you're investigating Nathan's murder?'

'Yes,' I said, wondering nervously how she felt about it. 'In a way — I'm trying to see if I can find anything out.'

'And have you found anything out? Have you managed to find anyone with a motive?'

'No. Well, yes, but none of the motives are very convincing. Not worth committing murder over, if you know what I mean.'

'I understand, but Nathan *was* murdered. What motive would you consider sufficient?'

'You've put your finger on it,' I smiled. 'I haven't been able to think of any convincing reasons to kill in general, never mind in particular. So many traditional motives have been eradicated by today's liberal society.'

'Possibly,' she said, 'but the primitive still bubbles below the surface of our thin veneer of civilisation. No matter how well-educated we are, how sophisticated we believe ourselves to be, the old emotions remain. Jealousy. Possessiveness. Anger. Hatred, a fury strong enough to force us to destroy another human being. They've been with us since the dawn of time, and they'll always be here.'

'I suppose you're right,' I said slowly. 'I had a bad temper when I was small, but surely people get over that sort of thing as they reach adulthood? I mean, what's worth killing over?'

'Ah, but maybe there's nothing you care about very deeply?' she said. 'Love, the urge to protect, especially one's family, one's child. They can be strong forces too.'

Harold looked embarrassed. 'Mum, you didn't murder Nathan because he said I should get a job, did you?' he joked. She waved at him to stay quiet.

'And probably you have no dark secrets in your past? The urge to save face, to prevent damaging disclosures — that could also trigger a murder. A more calculating, premeditated type of murder. Oh yes, I can think of many reasons why one human would want to eradicate another. You, on the other hand, have a barrier to your attempts to understand this.'

'What's that?'

'You're not the murdering type.' She shrugged and sat back, sipping an orange juice. 'When you encounter a problem, the list of possible solutions that presents itself to you doesn't include "kill the person responsible".'

'It sure doesn't. At least, except maybe as a joke.'

'You see, that's rarer than you might think,' she said. 'After all, why *not* kill the person responsible? You remove the problem. If you do it efficiently there's no reason why you should be discovered or punished. In some circumstances, it's a perfectly logical response to a difficulty.'

'You sound very well-informed, Laura,' said Harold.

'I suppose,' I said, 'I just don't believe in killing people.'

'Conditioning.' She waved her hand. 'Would your tame philosophy survive a real threat? I wonder.'

'I think so, but you're right, without being in the situation who can tell?'

'Yes. It's important not to be complacent,' she said. 'However, my point is this: you must bear in mind that the list of possible solutions for some people *will* automatically include murder. So a motive that you find unconvincing may nevertheless be a decisive one for the killer.'

'I'll try to remember that,' I said. Her penetrating eyes remained fixed on me. I smiled weakly and tried not to fidget. I was in shock. This woman had married Nathan?

What qualities did he have that we'd missed?

Harold seemed ill at ease. I wondered if he thought I might resent his mother's grilling. And then, of course, I'd never heard him stay silent for so long before. He relaxed as they began to chat about the day's news. As they discussed a forthcoming African election it became clear that they were both very well informed. Proud that I could remember the name of the Head of State of the country in question, I found myself abashed as they analysed the merits of his rivals for the position, and the geopolitical implications of the likely result.

It was hard to concentrate. The Mediterranean smells in the restaurant — garlic, olive oil and other delicious things, definitely including olives, that I was enjoying fantasising about — were distracting me and I was beginning to feel faint. I'm always starving after exercise. Every time a waiter appeared with a plate I started salivating, only to watch him approach some other lucky diner.

Even after my stuffed vine leaves arrived, tempting me with their earthy smell of pine nuts and herbs, I had to politely restrain myself while Laura's kebabs and Harold's meatballs were served. When I finally took my first bite I moaned involuntarily. Harold glanced at me. I blushed.

The conversation turned to the plans for Nathan's burial. Airwolfe were having a memorial service the following afternoon. The police hadn't released the body yet so no arrangements could be made for an actual funeral. Laura was philosophical. 'As long as they find out who killed him. I'd like to know that he was avenged,' she said. 'Did Harold tell you that our house has been searched?'

'Not yet,' said Harold, 'I've been meaning to tell you, Cynthia. The police took my mother's house apart yesterday. And they searched my flat today.'

'How awful. Were you there?'

'Yes. They were reasonably polite. They took away my laptop and some CDs. God knows what they expect to find on them.'

'Will they come across anything interesting?' I asked. 'Maybe your unpublished poetry, or Satanic blog?'

'Nothing as exciting as that,' he said, grinning. 'I didn't use the laptop much. I don't like computers. Just surfed the net now and then, it's practically still out of the box. And the CDs have been in that drawer for years so I can't even remember what's on them. I think one's a freeware typing tutor and one's an anti-virus program from around 2002. I didn't like to spoil their fun though. Laura and I were wondering whether you got the same treatment? Being Number One Suspect?'

'No,' I said, thinking that the police wouldn't find much in my gutted flat. 'Unless they didn't tell me. Can they just go and search when you're at work or whatever?'

'They probably have to have a warrant.'

'No danger they'd be turned down for one, considering I've no alibi and was only a few metres away when it happened,' I said gloomily.

Laura turned a reflective gaze upon me.

'I didn't kill him, Laura,' I said, trying not to look shifty.

'Good,' she nodded, and released me from her intense scrutiny.

My plan to get their fingerprints involved handing them each one of my business cards. The idea was to ask them to contact me if they thought of anything useful vis-à-vis the murder. While we waited for the main course, I did this. I hadn't anticipated the fatal flaw in the plan. Laura put the card away in her wallet. Doh!

'It's OK,' said Harold, 'I have your mobile number.'

'Oh yes,' I said, still holding my card out by the edges. I was hoping he'd absent-mindedly take it and then hand it back, but no such luck. 'Maybe you should check that it's the same as on the card.'

He gave me a puzzled look. 'I've been using it to contact you for the past three days.'

'That's true. Yes, you must have the right number. But perhaps you should make a note of my email address.'

'I don't have a computer,' he reminded me, 'but OK, if you insist.' And he took the card and put it in his wallet, which vanished into his jacket. Curses. What a stupid idea that had been. I racked my brains to think of an alternative, then realised that Laura was talking to me.

'Pardon?'

'Do you know Vicky Hubbell? I think she's the office manager now.'

'Oh, yes I do. She is the office manager, that's right, or the Orfuss Mancher we call her,' I sniggered. Laura looked puzzled. Oops. I shouldn't have said that. I didn't want her to think I was an idiot.

'I beg your pardon?' said Laura.

'Oh, just an office joke. Her spelling isn't always all it could be.' I was mortified.

'Yes, I remember that she had some communication problems,' Laura nodded, 'but Nathan felt she had a lot of potential. And do you know Tom Archibald?'

'I do.'

'He was Nathan's boss. Nathan thought he was, what did he say — she looked at Harold — oh yes, "an ignorant fuck". Yes, I'll miss Nathan's unique turn of phrase.'

Harold did all but cast his eyes up to heaven.

'He was a rough diamond, but a diamond all the same,' she sighed. 'It's difficult to accept, Cynthia. I lost my first husband many years ago. I hoped never again to go through something like that. At least this time I don't have a distraught little boy to take care of, always asking me where his Dad is.' She smiled at Harold. 'The most difficult question I've ever had to answer.'

Tears pricked my eyelids at the thought of the adorable, lost little boy looking for his Daddy.

'What happened to your first husband?' I asked.

'He was stabbed in the back of the neck while sitting in his office,' said Harold. 'Sorry, sorry, just trying to lighten the atmosphere. He drowned, didn't he Mum? Out in a storm in a leaky boat.'

'Yes. I knew something was going to happen,' she said. ('The thunder and lightning were a big clue,' muttered Harold.) 'Sure enough, night fell and he didn't come home. They found him months later. Thankfully they didn't ask me to identify the body. I believe little more than a skeleton remained. It was a terrible blow. I'd never stopped hoping. I thought maybe he'd lost his memory or got stranded on an island somewhere.'

My mind was wandering as I wondered what to do about the fingerprints. Harold and I were, inevitably, drinking champagne. The possibility of stealing his glass occurred to me only to be dismissed. It was cut crystal and would not hold useful prints. Laura's plain orange-juice glass might work but I imagined that it'd be better to use something that the suspect had touched only once rather than about a hundred times. Surely the prints would be clearer? And how would I get away with putting two people's glasses in my little handbag, not to mention the fact that any prints would probably be rubbed off in the process? No, I needed an alternative. But what?

'Don't you think so, Cynthia?'

What?

'I beg your pardon?'

'I was saying, cremation is probably a better option. Then I can scatter his ashes in his favourite place. Don't you think?'

'We don't go in for it much in Ireland but I'm sure you're right. Um, where was his favourite place?'

The bookies, I assumed, or perhaps some Soho lap-dancing club.

'He loved the sea around Juan-les-Pins,' said Laura. 'The clear blue Mediterranean below the brilliant white of the Picasso museum. We went yachting there the summer we first met. Scattering ashes in the Med is probably illegal but no one need know. What do you think, Harold?'

'Whatever you want, Mum.'

We were finishing our main course. There was the cutlery,

but again there'd be too many mixed-up fingerprints. Plates? They were huge. Not practical.

'Just a quiet ceremony, ourselves and a few friends. Do you think his work colleagues would want to go, Cynthia?'

Credit card? I could pay for the meal, then show them the card. People often commented on the picture.

I was clutching at straws.

'Oh definitely, they'll want to be there,' I assured Laura. It would be a few hours off work. And there would probably be people who'd want to make sure he was dead.

I had a flash of inspiration. A quick root through my handbag produced a laminated card advertising a seedy London nightclub. Surreptitiously polishing it on my leg, I handed it to Harold and asked him what he thought of the venue. He politely said he hadn't been there. 'Are you thinking of going?' he asked.

'Yes.'

He looked astonished.

'My cousin runs it,' I improvised desperately.

'Really? That's a rough area. If you want to go, maybe I should come with you.'

'That'd be great. I'll let you know. Um, I think he's away at the moment.'

Harold absent-mindedly went to add this card to the collection he had stashed in his wallet. Gritting my teeth, I gestured for it and he handed it back. He was watching me so I couldn't use one of the 'evidence envelopes' (freezer bags) that James's niece had suggested. I crossed my fingers and hoped for the best.

Before we started on dessert I took out my little silver compact mirror and reapplied my lipstick. Casually, I handed the mirror to Laura, saying 'What do you think of my mirror? I got it in Rome for only fifty pounds. And it's so handy.'

In reality I picked it up in Brick Lane for a quid, but I was relying on Laura's innate good manners and she didn't let me down.

'How divine,' she said, adding 'retro is all the rage now' as she handed it back. With a sigh of relief, I replaced it in my handbag.

Harold was giving me his quizzical look and I wondered if he'd rumbled me. I tried reciprocating by gazing at him adoringly but I wasn't convinced that he was taken in.

With the fingerprint debacle over, I relaxed and enjoyed the rest of the evening. We lingered for a long time over Irish coffees, chatting about this and that. I developed enormous respect for Laura. I wouldn't have described her as hysterical with grief, but she was clearly very sad, and trying to deal as best she could with the early death of a second husband.

Harold was taking his mum home. Disappointing, but at least I didn't have to worry about inviting him back to the Holiday Inn. As we ordered taxis and put on our coats he drew me aside.

'Can I see you tomorrow?'

'I was going to ask you that. Could you come with me to meet a guy Nathan was fighting with? I want to find out what it was about, and he might tell you, you're family. I've an appointment just before Nathan's memorial service and it's near our office so…'

Harold looked intrigued. 'I certainly could.'

'I'll text you,' I told him.

Laura had disappeared to the Ladies. Outside the restaurant in the cold moonlight, Harold took my gloved hands, pulled me towards him and kissed me.

'Make sure you do.'

My mind raced as I travelled back to the hotel in a warm glow and a taxi. How on earth had Laura fallen for a boor like Nathan? She had amazing presence. I could believe that he'd be on his best behaviour around her. But surely she could have had any man she wanted. What had made her choose him?

Perhaps in her eyes he'd had a charming recklessness. Maybe she'd never met anyone quite like him. I remembered her comment about his unique turn of phrase. Was he her bit of rough? Could it be that simple?

Whatever the chemistry, she must have known a very different Nathan to the one who'd rendered my working life hideous for several months.

I pondered over what she'd said about motive. Was she telling me that she might be the killer? She'd spoken of the effects of rage and hatred in general terms, but I felt she'd had some particular person in mind. Herself? Vicky? Not Harold, surely?

As I double and triple-checked the lock and tumbled into bed, I thought drowsily that the more I found out the less I understood.

10 — MEMORIAL

Next morning I retrieved my hidden memory stick, attached it to my laptop and steeled myself to plunge back into Nathan's sordid world.

None of the remaining mails from the day he died were interesting so I started on the previous week. The usual dross from Sam. Then I came across this:

To: Nathan Boyle
From: lovybunny@innocent.com
Snuggly bear, why are you been so cold to me? I thought youd be very happy. Meet me tonigt in the place.
Your lovybunny xxxx

I sat still for a few minutes to avoid barfing in the en-suite. When I'd recovered slightly, I read the email again. Who was 'lovybunny'? Nathan hadn't replied, no clue there, but something about the misspelt missive rang a bell. I only knew one person with spelling as bad as that. I scanned the day's remaining mails but didn't find anything that seemed relevant. Sam was Nathan's most prolific correspondent by far. I sighed. I'd have to talk to him again at some point. I tried to be fair and remind myself that his ridiculous photos and off-putting jokes had never been meant for my eyes, but after two days' worth of the inside of his brain, I wished I could avoid him for the rest of my life.

In the meantime, breakfast must be eaten and decisions must be made. If Laura and Harold's places had been raided, a search of my flat and/or hotel room was probably imminent. I had once again removed all traces of Nathan's correspondence from my laptop, but the hiding place I'd devised for my memory stick would never survive a police inspection. Time to figure out something better.

On my way to the office I bought a suit — jacket, skirt and a crisp white blouse. I needed one for the memorial service later, and to visit Cecil Howell with Harold. I didn't own any dark grey suits so it was an investment, really. I put it on straight away. The jeans I'd worn to the shop could join the ever-increasing pile of clothes-bags under my desk.

I picked up an early *Standard* and flicked through it looking for anything about Nathan. The newspapers had been remarkably murder-free, thank goodness, apart from the intriguing article about Nathan's finances. That was one blessing. I shuddered as I imagined being door-stepped by the *News of the World*.

As soon as I arrived at work, Archibald summoned me to his presence.

'Word has it,' he said, fiddling with a pen on the table, 'that you are attempting to investigate the crime yourself, Cynthia.'

'Yes. Well, sort of.'

'May I ask of what your investigation consists?'

'Yes. Well it's not really an investigation really. I've been asking around. Had dinner with Nathan's wife and son last night. That kind of thing.'

'I see. Would that be Laura and…um…Harold?'

'That's right.'

He put down the pen. 'Indeed. I met Laura on our Cairo

trip several years ago. She's a most interesting woman.'

'Did you? Is that the trip your wife…um…?'

I was too embarrassed to continue.

'Yes. She died,' he said with a sigh. 'Poor Janet. Such dreadful pain…she begged me to call a doctor but he arrived too late. Everything was so difficult. We had to return to England immediately. Laura is a remarkable woman.'

'I only met her last night. She has amazing presence.'

'Yes. Janet thought that she had wonderful strength. They often went out on the balcony for a cigarette and they became very friendly. Janet said that Laura and Nathan hoped to have a child, but she had a medical condition that prevented it. I thought myself that she seemed rather possessive of Nathan at times. She's an extraordinarily self-possessed woman, and frightening, in some ways. Her first husband died too, didn't he? Did you enjoy your meal?'

'Yes, I did. Funnily enough, it took my mind off the murder.'

'Ah yes, your investigation. You're the only potential witness. How convenient for the murderer that you're notoriously unobservant. Has anything come back to you?'

'No. I was concentrating too hard, I'm afraid. I've gone over all the work I did that night just in case I remembered anything, but no joy.'

'A pity.' He picked up the pen again and clicked it a few times, then looked up at me.

'I can quite understand your desire to investigate the crime for yourself, but I would prefer if you concentrated on the AirCross project. If you do remember something you can go straight to the police. In the meantime, we should leave matters in their hands. We're a good deal behind schedule already.'

'You're probably right. I haven't found anything out anyway. I'm just worried in case they haul me off to jail.'

'I'm sure that won't happen. I've made it clear that you're necessary to the successful completion of the project.'

Was he joking? Surely not. I couldn't tell.

'In the meantime, please attempt to give your full attention to your work over the coming weeks. Thank you.'

As I left the room, I wondered whether the tight deadline for AirCross might be the only thing separating me from my P45.

Around half eleven I stopped by Vicky's desk.

'Could you spare a few minutes for a chat?'

'Don't you ever get sick of talking?' she asked.

'Come down to Prêt? Please?'

'Oh all right,' she said ungraciously, picking up her shiny black handbag.

We went down in the lift in silence. I was trying to think of a way to broach the subject I wanted to discuss with her. As she bought a fruit juice and I the inevitable tea, I decided to come straight out with it. As soon as we'd sat down, I asked:

'Vicky, are you pregnant?'

The flash of panic I glimpsed in her eyes before she lowered them gave me my answer. She said nothing for a moment, then

'Why do you ask?'

'Just instinct,' I lied. 'I noticed you weren't drinking on Friday night. Thought it might be something like that.'

She sighed, and said. 'Well you're right, Mrs Great Blooming Detective. Hope that makes you happy.'

'Is it Nathan's?'

She shook her head irresolutely, staring at her juice.

'Are you sure, Vicky?'

She looked up at me. 'Oh, well. Yes, it is. If it's got anything to do with you.'

'Was he happy about it?'

'Yes. No. It was a surprise, but I know he would've been thrilled in the end. He just needed time to get used to the idea.'

'What did he say?'

As she blenched, I added quickly, 'Never mind. When did you tell him?'

'On Friday at work. You're right, I was crying. He got a shock, I think. He asked if I was sure it was his and he said "I'm not going to get saddled with a direct debit for someone else's brat".'

Her voice shook slightly.

'You poor thing,' I said. 'You were with him later, on Friday night, though. You left the party with him and Sam.'

'Yes. He rang me and apologised, said we'd sort something out, said he loved me and hadn't meant to hurt me.'

'So everything was OK? Big relief.'

'Yes.' She hesitated. 'Then I didn't see him for a while, though. I got worried.'

'Did you go into his office on Monday?'

She didn't answer.

'Did you ask him what he planned to do?'

'Yes.' A sniff. A tear trembled at the corner of her eye. Her chin began to wobble pathetically. 'He told me he couldn't leave Laura. He said I had to have an a-a-abortion.' She could barely get the word out. I got up, located some napkins, handed them to her, and found myself patting her shoulder. When I heard a stifled sob, I gave her a hug.

The sympathy pitched her into full-blown misery. Prêt was too busy with early lunchers for so much emotion. We went for a walk in the graveyard and sat on one of the benches. The cold winter sunshine seemed to calm her down. Tentatively I asked her:

'What time on Monday? I'm sorry to hassle you, Vicky, but it might be important.'

'About half six, quarter to seven,' she said. 'I ran out crying again. Luckily, you were the only person around. You didn't notice. Of course.'

'What a bastard,' I said.

'He wasn't a bastard!' she spat at me. 'He loved me! He just got a shock! If he hadn't died he'd've left that bitch by now and moved in with me. He'd be coming to the scan and he'd hold my hand and when he saw the heartbeat he'd kiss me and say he loved me.' She wailed. 'Oh God, the scan is on Monday. How am I going to get through it? I can't bear to go on my own. I don't want to see my little tiny baby all by myself. I'll cry the whole time, it'll be so awful. I can't bear it. And…' her voice rose in desperation '…I'm afraid I'm crying so much that I'm going to lose the b-baby.'

She subsided in a pitiful heap of sobs.

'What a bastard,' I thought again, but this time I kept it to myself.

I got back to the office at lunchtime. In the light of Vicky's news, I wanted to know more about Nathan's attitude to the pregnancy so I went looking for Sam. Unusually, he wasn't in the games room. Ronan looked up absently from some car-racing game. He hadn't really seen me.

I dropped over to Sam's section and passed the word round that I was looking for him. Then James, Liz and I headed out for our daily murder conference.

'I rang my sister last night and asked my niece Jasmine about the fingerprinting kit,' said James. 'You have to put prints on slides and use magnifying glasses and all sorts. It sounds terribly technical. Maybe we should just ask Jasmine to do it for us? She's an expert. We could go round to hers at the weekend.'

'Good idea. Did we get samples of everyone's prints?'

'Yep,' said Liz. 'Plastic cups did the trick.'

'Same here,' said James. 'How did you get on last night, Cynthia?'

'You *so* don't want to know. But I got them — I'll give them to you back at the office. Apart from the prints, how are we doing?'

'I've been wondering,' said Liz. 'Are we approaching this whole thing the right way?'

'How do you mean?'

'You know, the traditional stuff. Motive, means and opportunity. Are we looking at all three? Aren't we concentrating a little too hard on motive?'

'Means and opportunity,' said James. 'Aren't they the same thing?'

'No, I think 'means' is access to the dagger, and 'opportunity' is access to the office at the time of the murder,' I said. 'Oh. Yes, they are practically the same thing in this case.'

'Well, who had the means and the opportunity?' asked Liz. 'Do we know?'

'Yes,' I said. 'Anyone in the building at the time would have had both, right?'

'What about the knife?' asked Liz. 'We still haven't figured out how the killer took it without Nathan noticing.'

'They could have taken it earlier in the day when the office was empty,' said James.

'Only if the blinds were closed. When did he close them, Cynthia?'

'Not sure. They were shut by the time I found him, but they were open earlier, I think. Did either of you notice?'

'If the blinds were closed, how did you see he'd been killed?' asked Liz.

'I went into his office to turn the light off,' I said.

'Why was it on?'

'Because he was still there.'

'Yes,' said Liz, 'but I mean why didn't the murderer switch off the light? Did they want the body to be found quickly? Did they have an alibi for the time of death or something?'

'Good question,' said James. 'Maybe they just panicked. They couldn't spend long leaving the room; not with Cynthia right in front of them tearing her hair out over OverFlight.'

'Ha ha,' I said.

'I made a whole list of questions,' said Liz. She was looking serious and going a little pink around the ears. She was applying the dedication she showed in the office to my problem, I thought. Good.

'Here goes:

— Why did Nathan argue with Harold at the office party?

— Why was Vicky crying on Friday?

— What was Nathan doing in his office at 19:30?

— Why was the light on in his office?

— When/how did the murderer get the knife?'

'If this was Agatha, you'd already know the answers to all those questions and who the murderer is, and you'd be toying with us,' I said.

'No such luck,' said Liz.

'Well, I can tell you why Vicky was crying.' I filled them in on the pregnancy. 'She's going to spend the weekend with her parents in Essex. She doesn't want them to know she's been seeing a married man, but she needs help to deal with the baby. She's hoping her mum will go to the scan with her.'

The other two were silent. Then:

'Poor Vicky,' said Liz.

'Yeah. And the poor baby. I hope it doesn't arrive late,' said James.

There was a pause while we all tried not to laugh.

'So what's the plan?' asked Liz. 'Cynthia, have you found out why Nathan argued with Harold?'

'No, but we're having dinner tonight, I'll try to find out. Hey,' I added as they made kissing noises at each other, 'it's only because his step dad's been murdered. Naturally he wants to have dinner with me every day. I'm on the scene, I can give him the gossip.'

'Just be careful,' said Liz. 'We don't want you losing your heart to a murderer.'

After lunch I embarked on one of programming's most tedious tasks — updating the Design Specification to reflect the actual implementation. In theory, we needed it to train our new team-mates. In practice, they probably wouldn't read a word of it. Write-only documentation. Naturally I kept a keen eye on my email.

To: Cynthia
From: Bharathi
Subject: Got a minute?
Hiya,
I want to tell you something. Have you got a minute?
Regards,
Bharathi

I made my way straight to her desk.

'Do you fancy getting a coffee and going for a walk?' she asked. So for the second time that day I found myself sitting on a bench in the graveyard, wrapped up warm in the December sun. There was a smell of wet grass. The people dotted around on benches looked relaxed, happy to be out of the office for a few precious minutes.

'So, what's up?'

'It's difficult to tell you this,' said Bharathi, 'but I heard your flat was broken into and everything was destroyed. Is that true?'

'Yep. The place is wrecked. You should see it, it's terrifying.'

'Then you could be in danger. Whoever is doing this must be stopped. I must tell you something, but I'm afraid you'll despise me when you hear it.'

'Of course I won't. Go ahead.'

'It's Nathan. I found something out about him.'

'What?'

'He'd been embezzling money from Airwolfe.'

I stared at her. 'Are you sure?'

'Certain.'

'Didn't you tell anyone?'

'No. I was going to, but I wasn't positive at first. It was so hard to believe. I thought that most likely my suspicions were wrong, though I couldn't see how. So I went to see him.'

'What did he say?'

'First he tried bluffing, told me not to worry, that I'd made a mistake and everything was fine. So I asked him to show me my error. I'd brought the accounts with me. I'd found items that had been invoiced for by a company I never see except in his budget, and I was pretty sure those items hadn't actually been supplied.'

'Shit.'

'So I kept asking him, I still thought it was OK but I couldn't pin it down, and finally he said, "Look, you…stupid cow, if you just keep your mouth shut everything will be fine".'

Bharathi hesitated over the unfamiliar insult. Once again I seethed with rage against Nathan.

'So what did you do?'

'I said, 'I'm sorry, Nathan, I can't conceal something like this. I'll have to raise it with head office.'

'What did he say?'

'He said "Don't be stupid. You want your brats to stay in school don't you?"'

'What? What did he mean?'

'Lisa and Tony. They go to an expensive school. You know that.'

'Yes.' Bharathi had told me about their public school. Private school? Whatever. She was proud of how well they were doing.

'Nathan's wife is one of the governors. He said if I didn't ignore the accounting problem, he'd arrange for them to be expelled.'

'Oh my God.'

'You don't know what it's like, Cynthia. When we went to check out our local school a few years ago, a little kid, not even a teenager, ran up to us and shouted 'Pakis go home!' and ran away again. His friends were all watching and laughing and making rude signs. I don't want Lisa and Tony exposed to that. That's why we sent them to St. Anthony's, even though it's so expensive. It's worth it to have the peace of mind of knowing they're not treated like aliens in their own country.'

'You're right, Bharathi. Of course you couldn't risk them being expelled.'

'You don't understand. This thing with Nathan only happened on Monday. I talked it over with my husband on Monday night, and we agreed I'd have to report it. We decided to take our chances with the school. I don't know Mrs Boyle, but I couldn't imagine she would want to get two random children expelled, and anyway she probably couldn't do it even if she did want to. But life would've been hell for me once I'd informed on Nathan. I would've been lucky to keep my job.'

'Monday? What time on Monday did you see Nathan?'

'Monday evening. Just before seven o'clock.'

It was difficult to make sense of all this. It didn't seem to supply a motive for anyone, but I wondered if it implicated Archibald. He signed off on Nathan's purchases. If it ever emerged that not only were Nathan's projects all late but he was embezzling to boot, I didn't give much for Archibald's promotion chances.

On the other hand, how would Archibald have found out? Bharathi hadn't told anyone else, and Nathan would hardly have told him. Plus, murdering Nathan might make him feel better but it wouldn't exactly solve the problem. No, it looked as if Bharathi's story wasn't relevant, except to remind me once again what a horrible boss I'd had.

A squirrel scampered past, breaking my reverie.

'Did you tell the police?' I asked Bharathi.

'No. I'm afraid they'll think I have a motive. Nonsense, of course. I'd do nearly anything for my kids, but I wouldn't kill to keep them in school.' She laughed.

I smiled, but thinking of Laura's analysis of what would propel someone towards murder, I wondered suddenly, *wouldn't you*?

'Nice suit,' said Harold, when we met outside the office at half past two. This time he hadn't sent a taxi. 'So what's the story with this guy?'

'Your dad fell out with him over something,' I told him. 'He came to his office and stamped around and shouted before the party on Friday. I just want to cross him off our list of suspects, that's all.'

'Not my dad. Step-dad, remember? You know I still disapprove of your investigation, right?'

'Mm-hmm, but I need your help on this one. Aren't you a tiny bit curious?'

I smiled hopefully up at him.

'Yes, but,' he grinned down at me 'you owe me.'

Cecil Howell was just as pompous as I remembered. He sat behind his desk, toying with a gold pen, surveying us blandly as we explained what we wanted.

'Mr Harold Mansfield here is Mr Nathan Boyle's next-of-kin,' I said. 'On an informal basis, we wish to know the source of your disagreement with Mr Boyle. Our concern is that the value of his estate could be affected.' I'd presented myself as a financial adviser and been confident that he wouldn't recognise me as an Airwolfe employee. He'd mistaken me for a secretary at Airwolfe, and no one looks at secretaries. Seemed I was right.

'That's possible,' said Mr Howell. 'However, if he had allowed our disagreement to go to court he would have incurred substantial legal fees. He would certainly have lost the case; therefore I suspect that his legatees have been saved some considerable depredation of his finances.'

'What was the nature of your disagreement?' I asked.

'It was ridiculous in every way,' he said. 'Mr Boyle's residence before his marriage, which he still owns, is adjacent to a number of dwellings belonging to me. These were purchased by myself in order to develop a commercial property. Specifically, a small shopping centre.'

'A new one?' asked Harold. 'Difficult to get planning.'

'That particular block has been rezoned. Planning is not an issue,' said Mr Howell curtly.

'So the problem was?'

'Mr Boyle claimed squatters' rights over the house next door to his own.'

'Squatters' rights?'

'Yes. Specifically, he claimed that he had been using the bottom floor of the house as a workshop for twenty years, and that he had therefore acquired ownership of same.'

'And had he been using it as a workshop?'

'I believe so,' Mr Howell said grimly. 'However, that would probably not be sufficient to establish ownership in law. Nevertheless, to expedite matters I offered him a reasonable sum to relinquish his claim to the house. He replied that nothing would convince him to sacrifice his right to due process. He said he'd see me in court.

'Delaying tactics, of course. He would have sold in the end. He was merely trying to push up the price. He was difficult to deal with — but one shouldn't speak ill of the dead.'

'Will his death delay your development?' asked Harold. 'I mean, will you have to wait for probate and see if his claim is taken up — or abandoned?'

'No,' said Mr Howell with satisfaction. 'He won't be objecting now. Planning permission has been granted, and we are proceeding imminently.'

'**S**o he didn't really have a motive,' I said as we dodged a taxi, crossing City Road.

'You think?'

'Well, he obviously thought he'd win his case in court. Just a matter of time. Not much point going round killing people.'

'Sweet little innocent,' said Harold. 'Don't you realise he

was certain to play the whole thing down? If he'd suggested that Nathan had a genuine case then I might have decided to pursue it. If Howell was on weak ground we're the last people he'd tell.'

'I suppose you're right.' I felt naive.

'And even if Nathan hadn't a hope of winning, there's no such thing as 'just a matter of time' for developers. Time is money. If they'd gone to court it could've delayed him by a couple of years.'

'Would that have mattered though?

'Yep. He'd be paying interest on the money he's already invested in the scheme. He probably took out mortgages on the properties he purchased. Sounds like he bought them recently so he probably paid fairly hefty prices for them. He'll be paying those mortgages off even if he hasn't started development yet, and, don't forget, interest rates have gone up.'

'Not a pleasant position,' I admitted.

'No. There's also the opportunity cost — tying up capital for years in a scheme that's not progressing. He could earn four per cent in any shitty little savings account instead. Besides, the appetite for retail buildings could be gone by the time his project got the green light.'

'So Nathan's objection was going to cost him a lot of money?'

'Shed-loads,' said Harold, 'not to mention legal fees, and as I was saying, he could even have lost the case. Presumably Nathan's legal advice suggested that was possible. Nathan's death is a total godsend for this guy.'

'So maybe he killed him?'

'Maybe he did. But he's not a member of Airwolfe staff. Surely you would have noticed him wandering around the office?'

He looked down at me.

'No? Well, never mind.'

We parted outside Airwolfe. Harold went off to meet his mother. There was still an hour to kill before the memorial service. Up in the office, Liz wasn't around but I brought James to the games room and told him about the interview with Cecil Howell.

'It's hopeless,' I concluded.

'What is?'

'The whole thing. The whole idea that I'll be able to track down the killer is just so far-fetched. I started off thinking all I needed was someone with a motive. Now I've got people with motives coming out my ears and I still don't know who did it. Every time I talk to someone they tell me some other awful thing Nathan did. He was just asking to get himself killed. I don't know how he got away with only being murdered once. And everyone had the chance to get into the building, and as far as I can gather no one had an alibi, and the weapon was right there waiting to be taken, and—'

'Hold on, hold on,' said James, putting an arm around me and giving me a gentle squeeze. 'Yes, it looks hopeless now, Cynthia, but whoever did it was almost certainly someone we've talked to. We probably have all the information we need if we could only see it. And what about the torn photo? The fingerprints might give us a clue.'

'Yeah, but maybe the burglary *is* unrelated. I wish we knew what the police are thinking. They must have *some* ideas.'

'Wouldn't it be useful to know,' said James. 'Well, maybe we can find out.'

'What we really need now,' I said thoughtfully, 'is another murder.'

Even if I stripped naked and did the can-can I didn't think the Super would give much away. But James said I should try, so try I did. (Without the naked can-can bit though).

'Do you have any leads on my break-in?'

'I gather nothing was taken?'

'No, even though my digital camera was sitting on the coffee table before the burglar kicked it over.'

'A nasty crime, but a lot of burglaries are. However, it's rare to have nothing stolen.'

'Do you think it's related to Nathan's death?'

'Difficult to say, but I shouldn't think so.'

'Have you found any new murder clues?'

'I'm afraid, Cynthia, that you continue to be the most likely suspect.'

'Great.'

'I thought you'd be pleased. How's your own investigation coming along?'

'Stuck. Motives everywhere but how can I tell which one was strong enough for murder?'

'You've found motives?'

'Yes. Haven't you?'

'No. Care to share?'

'I can't. Most of them were told me in confidence.'

'And the rest are people you think are innocent.'

'Yep.'

'We could take you in for questioning.'

'It's all there, if you know where to look.' I was dying to air my superior knowledge, but I didn't like to shaft anyone.

'We've found some intriguing emails from an unidentified source. It would be interesting to discover who sent them.'

'Really?' I said innocently. 'Perhaps you should email them back and ask.'

'Not a bad idea,' said the Super. 'Not a bad idea at all.'

The memorial service that Airwolfe had organised for Nathan was due to start at four o'clock. Normally people bail out as early as possible on Fridays. Management go to play golf, parents go home to their kids and the rest of us hit the pub. So it's hard to organise anything on a Friday afternoon, but it turned out that a memorial service for a staff member stabbed at his own desk does pull in the numbers.

From half three on, a steady trickle of people descended to the basement. The service was to be held in the large meeting-room down there. I suspect the assembled staff of Airwolfe City Road were better disposed towards Nathan that day than they had been for months. Everyone seemed unusually solemn. Although the dress code at Airwolfe was casual — and this was pushed to extremes in our small, previously half-forgotten City Road outpost — most people had made an effort today.

'Hiya,' Ronan greeted me as we arrived in the lobby together. He wore a suit. I didn't even know he owned one. 'How's the investigation going? Any clues?'

'Too many,' I said. 'Haven't been able to pin it on anyone yet though. Where were you at zero hour, Ro?'

'Ha, ha, Hegarty, you're so funny. Have a bit of respect, this is the closest to a funeral he'll be getting for a while.'

'You're heading down early,' I commented.

'Going out first to get some food into me. The speeches at this thing could take forever. Archibald can yak for an hour no bother and the IT VP is supposed to be coming too. We could be there for three hours easy. It'll be worse than a wedding. You should grab something too before they get started.'

'Good idea. I'll see you inside.'

He hadn't mentioned the printer.

Laundry had not been my top priority recently. My grey 'financial advisor' suit would do for the funeral, but I had nothing to wear that evening. I legged it down into shabby, functional Old Street underground, to the trendy shop that always has something divine for twenty quid. Already a flood of City workers were heading home to their loved ones, or off for a night out. The queues at the underground ATM, and the unusual sound of laughter, signalled that the weekend had arrived.

I grabbed a swirly wine-coloured dress to wear for the dinner I was hoping to have with Harold later. Black heels would have to do — silver would never work. I had to fight my way against the fast-flowing hordes to get back up to street level. No time for food. As I approached the office I ran into Zorr.

'You're going to this thing too?' I asked him.

'Yep.'

'I didn't think you were mad about Nathan.'

'No, but he was killed on my watch.'

'Doesn't look good for SwordBlade, you mean?'

He held the outside door open for me and nodded at Hugh in reception. We started down the stairs.

'You're dead right,' he murmured. 'I don't think there was a security breach, I think it was an insider, but I'll be relieved when everything's cleared up. That broken camera on the back door could raise its ugly head if Airwolfe cut up rough. You didn't hear anything about it, did you?'

I nodded. 'Vicky told me, said all the management knew.'

'Yeah, the committee in charge of this building would've all known. Wish this thing was sorted. Do you've any idea who did it, Cynthia?'

'You're the second person to ask me that today.'

'People want this fixed now. The police don't seem to be getting anywhere. Did you see the thing in the paper about unexplained payments? Any ideas on that?'

'I wish. All I've found out so far is that even more people hated him than I thought. I believe you had a fight with him recently.'

'That little toe-rag? I wouldn't fight him if he was the last man on Earth.'

'Maybe a run-in is a better description.'

'Yeah. Everyone had run-ins with him. But shh,' he said, as we reached our destination, 'quiet now.'

The partition between the two large basement meeting-rooms had been thrown open, and the oval tables removed to accommodate chairs for the crowd. There was a funereal hush. One of Ronan's minions was checking the sound. Most of the seats were occupied. James and Liz had kept a spot for me. As I sat down, I saw the back of Harold's blond head in the front row. Laura sat beside him. I took out my phone to turn it off:

Babes don't run away we'll take you out after. H x

'I wonder if his wife's going to speak,' Liz whispered to me.

'Half the management are here,' James said, leaning across her, 'US heads and all. They must be taking this seriously.'

'Well he *was* killed in their office,' Liz pointed out.

Shushing noises. We shut up and turned face forward.

'Mr Nathan Boyle was a model employee…' said Michael Clegg, the UK Vice-President of Operations. Thus began a long eulogy in which Nathan morphed into an unrecognisable paragon of all the virtues. The norm at funerals naturally, and who would grudge it to him?

'…and we've asked his wife Laura to say a few words,' concluded Mr Clegg. Laura stood. She wore heavy, lace-draped black. Slowly, solemnly, she made her way to the microphone. Airwolfe bigwigs sat behind her facing out, giving the room a church-like atmosphere.

'I would like to say two things.' Laura looked gravely down at us.

'The first is that although Nathan had many faults, he was my husband and I loved him. The second is a request. Whoever did this, please come forward.'

The room was still. Slowly, her eyes moved through the crowd. She seemed to examine the innermost being of each person. She paused when she got to me, gave a slight nod and passed on. Surrounded by silence, she continued:

'Murder seems easy, but it becomes a dangerous habit. It will damage you even more than your victim. Please, look inside yourself. Open your heart to truth. You will know what to do. Thank you, all of you.'

She walked back to her seat through stunned silence. I wondered if the murderer was in the room. Would they be inwardly sneering? Laura's authority radiated from her. Far more likely, I thought, that they'd be counting the seconds until they could get out of the slow-moving, guilt-enhancing atmosphere she had created.

Mr Clegg looked uncertainly at his fellow managers. After a moment or two he stood up again.

'Of course, there's no certainty that Nathan Boyle was killed by one of our employees. Far more likely that a lapse in security allowed the attacker to come in from outside,' he said. I winced on Zorr's behalf. He was right; he needed this murder solved now, and he needed an Airwolfe murderer.

Another couple of VPs made speeches. The gist — and here I will spare you hours of tedious, ungrammatical monologue — was that Airwolfe regretted the incident, had upped its security, and didn't expect anything of the kind to happen again.

'What was that all about?' I asked James, when they'd finished.

'The share price, petal,' said James. 'People are asking questions. If someone can hang around the office murdering folk, maybe someone else can drop in and steal some of our valuable intellectual property and flog it to our competitors.'

'Surely our competitors have more sense?' I said.

He grinned at me. 'Arse-covering Cynthia, arse-covering. Look over there.' He nodded towards the wall at the back. Sure enough, a couple of camera-wearing strangers were taking discreet notes.

'It'll be in the business press. *"Airwolfe draws line under office murder"* etcetera,' he said.

'Life goes on, doesn't it?' said Liz sadly.

'Eet certainly does. Zere is free drink.' Pierre made for the door, wielding a glass of wine and fumbling for his Gitanes.

A table at the side, discreetly concealed during the memorial speeches, bore glasses of red and white wine. Harold was already there.

'Probably asking for champagne,' said Liz. 'How are you getting on with him, Cynthia?'

'Could be worse. The fact that he's a murder suspect is

affecting me less than I'd expected. It gives us something in common.'

'Have you found out what Nathan was arguing with him about yet?'

'His affair, I think. Nathan's, I mean. Wonder how long we're expected to hang around?'

'What are you up to later?' Peter asked, joining us with Bharathi. 'We thought we could go in to Chinatown for a meal. What do you think, Liz? James? Cynthia?'

Liz looked thrilled, I saw with amusement. Give that girl some reticence, I thought.

'Cynthia.' Harold had indeed managed to procure champagne. He must have brought some with him.

'Can you come and hang out with us? Laura's feeling glum. She finds these US corporate types deeply depressing.'

'She's not the only one,' I said, following him with an apologetic glance at the others.

Some of the seats had been removed and a few tables brought in. Laura sat at one of them with the corporate boyos. This is a breed I generally avoid. Fortunately, they seemed relieved to be able to withdraw their attention from her on our arrival, and began to talk amongst themselves. They were discussing the effect of Nathan's death on the share price. Harold shot them a disgusted look.

'Nathan was dying to hang out with that crowd. If only he could hear them now,' he muttered.

'Your speech was very moving,' I said to Laura. 'Maybe the murderer will come forward.'

'I hope so,' she said. 'Death has occurred, it's irrevocable, now the net has been cast and the killer will either accept his punishment or try ever more frenziedly to escape. This is the time when he's most dangerous. He may feel that he has nothing to lose. We must hope that the last vestiges of his humanity will bring him into the light.'

'You think he's a man then?' Harold asked her.

'I don't know,' she said thoughtfully.

'Where's Vicky?'

Liz had come up behind me.

'Hi, Harold. Cynthia, Tom Archibald's looking for Vicky. Have you seen her?'

'Haven't seen her at all today,' I replied. 'Wasn't she here for the memorial? It's not like her to miss a big event.'

'No, I thought she'd be here telling us all to shush,' said Liz. 'Maybe she's avoiding people.' And she was off.

Harold suggested dinner in a Vietnamese on Kingsland Road.

'Do they have champagne?' I asked him.

'No, but they let you bring some if you pay corkage. Laura needs something to take her mind off all this. Do come.'

Before I could leave, I had to go up to my desk to set the system tests running over the weekend. It was dark and quiet on the third floor. I rushed through the necessary steps, trying not to look behind me, standing impatiently at the computer banging hot-keys at intervals. I stashed the bag containing my new wine dress under my desk — I wouldn't have time to change.

Just as I was picking up my coat I heard screams from the other end of the building. I ran down the corridor. Liz stumbled towards me, white as a sheet.

'Dead!' she sobbed, throwing herself into my arms. 'Oh, Cynthia, stabbed as well!'

'Who? Vicky?' I asked, putting my arm around her to support her.

'Vicky? No! It's Sam!' And she collapsed against the wall, pulling me off balance so that I fell with her.

He was in the Games Room, in the sofa he always sat in to watch the racing. He still gripped the remote control, but he wouldn't be channel-surfing ever again. Just like Nathan, a dull metal hilt protruded from his neck.

I had a routine this time. I rang reception in Docklands, got security, and deployed my phone camera. Meanwhile, Liz sat slumped at the nearest desk outside, resting her head on her arms. She seemed shell-shocked, shaking and whimpering. I knew the feeling, but I was a veteran. Hugh came straight up to secure the room. Soon it was clear that word of this second tragedy had gone round the memorial service. Lift-loads of people arrived, milling about and asking questions. With a feeling of déjà vu, I saw the same baby-faced PC appear as before. He seemed stunned, looking from me to Hugh to the assembled mourners as though he couldn't believe his eyes.

'He was stabbed in the games room,' said the Superintendent. Gone was my friendly Super. He'd been replaced by a stern, frowning stranger. 'Not long before Elizabeth found him, by the look of things. Cynthia, where were you?'

'At my desk, just down the corridor,' I admitted, 'but I didn't do it, Superintendent. I didn't even see him.'

'What were you doing there at this hour?' he asked.

'Setting off tests to run over the weekend. The weekend is valuable testing time. You can run the servers for seventy-two hours with no interruptions. You get vital information.'

My voice was shaking. I could feel tears behind my eyelids. I swallowed and smiled tentatively at the Super. No response.

'I'm told you were looking for Sam earlier today.'

'Yes, but not to *kill* him. To ask him some more questions about Nathan. I had a feeling he knew more about Nathan's death than he was admitting. Maybe he did. Maybe that's why he got himself murdered. Don't you think?'

'Interesting to find you on the spot again,' said the Super.

'I'm being set up! I thought it was spooky in here. Someone must have been watching me. All your other suspects were in the building too — you need to find out what they were up to.'

'What other suspects?'

That's when I knew I was really in trouble.

'Look, Cynthia, I don't want to arrest you for murder. I like you, and you strike me as far too happy-go-lucky to leave a trail of destruction across the City. The fact remains, however, that I have two dead bodies here, you were on the scene *both times* without an alibi, you could easily have done the deed and I'm running out of excuses to avoid hauling you in for questioning. This doesn't look good for you. Being a suspect in one murder could be misfortune, but being a suspect in two…'

'…looks like carelessness. Yes, but I didn't do it. Anyway, I've no motive!'

'You were overheard stating that you planned to kill Mr Boyle.'

'When?' I demanded. 'Not that it matters! I said that nearly every day but I wasn't actually planning to actually kill him. Just…he was a stressful boss.'

'Our informant seemed to think it was more serious than that.'

'What informant? When?'

'I'm not at liberty to tell you who discussed this with us. We're told that Mr Boyle made an offensive comment to one of your colleagues at the staff party last week. Immediately afterwards you were overheard saying that you were going to kill him.'

'Who told you that?' I tried to remember who'd been around. 'Peter? James?'

'I'm afraid that's classified. Is the story true? Did Mr Boyle offend your colleague?'

'Yes, it's true. He was an oaf — a drunken one — he was extremely unpleasant.' I told him about Nathan insulting Liz, and that she'd been upset. 'I probably did say I'd kill him but not as a statement of intent, honestly. I was furious, that's all.'

'I understand, Cynthia, but you need to understand where I'm coming from. That threat is documented, and my superiors have seen the document. They're already wondering why you're still roaming the streets of London. When they hear that another body has cropped up in your path, my chances of keeping you out of custody will be close to zero. What can you give me to fend them off with?'

'What do you mean?'

'You said you had motives coming out of your ears. What are they? Who do you think might have done it?'

That was putting me on the spot. I thought of all the people who had motive of a kind. Ronan, Zorr, Archibald, Bharathi, Peter. Far more so, Laura, Vicky and Eugene. Pompous Man. Maybe Harold. Was I prepared to land them in trouble to keep myself out of a police cell? Who would I sell down the river to stay out of handcuffs?

'Superintendent, I have no idea who the killer is. There are a number of people with motives that an outsider might miss. I suggest you send an email to the anonymous lover asking her to come forward and be ruled out. Also, check the status of Nathan's projects, bearing in mind he got a 'Best Manager' award at that party. You should be aware that his financial dealings were not always characterised by scrupulous honesty. He had difficulty understanding the concept of honour, which may also have caused a run-in or two here and there.'

The Super glanced at PC Lawson in the corner, to make sure she was taking notes.

'Will I find a motive if I check those things out?'

'You may find several, but none of them seem convincing to me. If I figure out who the killer is, believe me, I'll deliver him straight to you!'

'You said 'he'. You're convinced it's a man, then?'

'No, that was just a figure of speech. I've no idea, I'm afraid.'

'What about Sam? Why was he killed?'

'I don't know, Superintendent, but he seemed to think he knew something about Nathan's murder.' I described Sam's reference to Nathan's mysterious secret. 'If Nathan knew a dark secret about someone, maybe they killed him? Then

Sam let them know that he knew, so he had to die too?'

'Don't you think that's rather far-fetched?' the Super asked me, but I hoped he was secretly intrigued.

He folded his hands.

'As you know,' he said, 'we have, up until now, believed that you were not involved in Boyle's murder. However, the situation is now critical and we must act immediately. I'm afraid we need to search your personal belongings and your multiple residences.'

'You do?' I felt the icy grip of fear.

'It is only because Inspector Gannon and I were convinced of your innocence that we haven't already taken this step. We don't want to waste resources investigating the wrong people, but we can no longer reasonably refrain from conducting a search. We don't need you to agree if we have a warrant, as I'm sure you know. However, I'd prefer if you'd save taxpayers' money and voluntarily consent.'

'Of course I consent! It wouldn't go down well if I didn't, would it?'

He smiled at me. 'Good girl! Don't worry, it's merely a formality. Unless we find something, naturally. I'll have to confiscate your passport for a while.'

'OK. It's in my desk drawer. I'll hand it in.'

'Thanks. You might as well give me your mobile now too.'

My mobile.

I froze.

'I need it.'

'I know. We'll get it back to you as soon as possible.'

He held out his hand, still smiling. I reached into my pocket for my iMate.

Should I tell him now about the photos? But supposing they didn't find them? Yeah right. But supposing they didn't? And what else was on there? Nothing that incriminated anyone but me. As far as I could remember.

I thanked my lucky stars that I'd found a new hiding place for the memory stick.

I put my iMate into the Super's grasp. His large fingers closed over it. It looked tiny all of a sudden, tiny and vulnerable. A metaphor for me.

As I stood up, the Super added:

'By the way, how was dinner?'

'Delicious, thanks. I don't think either of them did it.'

'There's a surprise,' he said. 'Where will you be over the weekend?'

'At the hotel and maybe out and about. If I get it back, I'll keep my mobile with me.'

'Good, and kindly keep it charged, too. We don't want to arrest you, Cynthia, but if you become uncontactable we'll be forced to.'

Not even a farewell smile. He was definitely less friendly than before. Just wait until he saw those photos.

'**S**o let me get this straight,' said James. 'You were on the scene for two — not one but two — murders, and you haven't been arrested yet?'

'Nope.'

'Well, Cynthia, here's to you,' and he raised a glass to me.

We were in a cheap and cheerful Vietnamese on the Kingsland Road, not far from the office. Everyone at the memorial service had been identified, briefly questioned, then allowed to depart. James, Liz and the others had abandoned the idea of going to Chinatown. They'd joined dining forces with Harold and Laura.

I had been kept on ice and interviewed last. My interrogation had taken far longer than most. I wondered if they'd all been half expecting to hear about my arrest. They must have been relieved when I finally arrived to join them.

Except, perhaps, the murderer.

Now I ate a belated dinner while the others drank coffee and finished the wine and champagne. The restaurant was cold but I was starving and my vegetable pho was aromatic and hot, tasting wonderfully of ginger and lime juice.

'Thank goodness you're all right,' said Liz. Pale and shivering, she sat hunched between James and Peter. She was wearing Peter's jacket, and he had a protective arm around her.

'I'm fine. What about you? Are you OK, missus?' I asked her. She nodded forlornly.

'When did it happen?' asked Harold.

'Before, during or just after the memorial service,' I replied. 'Seems like pretty much everyone is a potential suspect. Scary, but nice for me. At least there's more than one of us.'

'I was with people all the time, I think,' said Bharathi, 'from lunch until we realised something was wrong. But they were different groups of people and it'd be nearly impossible to prove it. I suppose we're all in the same boat. Anyone coming in from outside might be OK though.'

'Yes, you two may be in the clear,' I said thoughtfully to Harold and Laura. 'I imagine you stayed together after you arrived in the building?'

'I wish we had,' said Harold. 'I went looking for you, Cynthia. With no success, obviously. I left my mother in one of the basement meeting rooms for ten or fifteen minutes.'

'Were you with anyone?' I asked Laura.

'I'm afraid not,' she said apologetically, as if reluctant to disappoint me. 'I read the paper, and thought about my speech.'

'It was a very good speech,' I said.

'Thank you, my dear,' she said, 'but apparently it wasn't good enough.'

I realised that she was close to tears.

'Now the killer has struck again and no one is safe. We must all be on our guard. It's true what I said earlier, murder is addictive. The interval between crimes tends to shorten. I'm worried. Very, very worried.'

I gulped. 'Who do you think will be targeted next?' I asked her.

'Well, dear, I wouldn't be surprised if you were,' she said

gently.

'Laura thinks that your investigation could seem threatening to the killer, and they might try to terminate it by terminating you,' said Harold. 'She suggested I whisk you away for the weekend. I have the perfect destination in mind. No one will ever find you there, and you'll love it. Can you come after dinner?'

'Um, I'm doing something tomorrow morning,' I said, 'and I can't really get out of it.'

'Tomorrow afternoon then,' he said. 'Four o'clock suit you?'

Conversation waned as the horror of the second murder sank in. We all left when I'd finished my main course. I thought James looked shaken. He offered to put me up again, but the several locks on my door in the Holiday Inn beckoned. Harold flagged a taxi down for me before heading off with his mother. Peter escorted Liz. James and Bharathi walked to the tube together. We were all, as they say at home, a bit shook.

I arrived back in my hotel room as the police searchers were leaving. They were polite. They'd hardly messed the place up at all. It was a hotel room — it had nothing *to* mess up. I didn't go out to check for the memory stick in case I attracted any unwanted attention, but I was optimistic that it was still there.

My flat was a terrible, hideous disaster zone already, so no matter how messily they searched the cops could hardly make it any worse, I thought, trying to look on the bright side.

I wanted to call the Super and confess about the photos before he found them. I doubted that having a dozen photographs each of two murder scenes on my phone would be considered normal behaviour. Even I, now that they were shortly to be discovered, was appalled by my insensitivity, idiocy and general stupidity.

Eventually I made up my mind. I would ring him.

Then I realised that my police contact number was on my mobile.

I climbed into bed and watched an anorexic spider make its leisurely way across the ceiling. I should undress. I turned on the TV and drifted gradually asleep to *Only Fools and Horses* repeats.

In the small hours I jerked awake, terrified, grasping blindly for Sparky.

No Sparky.

This was the worst night yet.

11 — THE FINGERPRINT EXPERT

At barely seven o'clock the next morning I got a call. My hotel phone had never rung before. Still half-asleep, I couldn't identify the sound for a moment. I fumbled for the receiver and knocked it onto the floor. I picked it up, cursing, and nearly fell out of bed. The police. I woke up.

'Superintendent Foster would like to see you.'

No Saturday lie-in, then.

I showered, grabbed a croissant from the breakfast room and went straight to the police station. The Super kept me waiting for ages, and I grew more and more tense. The dull green paint in institutional places is supposed to relax you. It had the opposite effect on me. Finally a policewoman appeared and called me. She escorted me to his office. I sat in the straight-backed wooden chair in front of his desk and folded my hands together, trying to appear calm.

'Please excuse me a moment,' he said, typing on his laptop. I studied him while he worked. He looked rested and alert — recently shaven, freshly laundered shirt — but serious.

He looked up. 'Here's your phone, Cynthia,' he said, sliding it towards me. 'I must say, I was appalled by what I found on it.'

I expected him to start going 'More in sorrow than in anger, I arrest you in the name of the Queen,' or something. I'm out of touch with the current phraseology after all the terrorism stuff.

Instead he said quietly,

'Who's Sparky?'

'Sparky? Oh, Sparky's my ex.'

'Does he often send you abusive texts?'

I stared at him.

'Um. Only when he's drunk. Did he send some?'

'Three. How long has this been going on?'

'Since we split up. About a year, I suppose. Not every day, of course.'

'Most days?' he asked.

I nodded.

'Cynthia, you do realise that you could prosecute him? Take him to court? Force him to desist?'

'Well. It's my fault really. I split up with him without any good reason, you know? I let him down. Naturally he's venting a bit. He'll stop soon.'

'If he's the type to send texts like that, I'd say you probably had good reason to break up with him. Have you tried changing your number?'

'Do you think I should?'

'I'd consider it, if I were you.'

'It's so much trouble though,' I said. 'I'd have to tell everyone I know, and he'd probably just get my new number straight away. We share loads of the same friends. Anyway, it's not like I actually read his texts, I haven't opened one for months. I just delete them.'

'I suggest you start keeping the texts,' said the Super. 'You'll need a record of them if you decide to do something. Come back to me if they're upsetting you, and I'll tell you what steps to take.'

'Thanks,' I said.

Were they really that bad?

'Oh, by the way,' said the Super, eyebrow soaring, 'why

were there two dozen photos of murder scenes on your phone?'

'I thought they might come in handy for my defence lawyer,' I said.

'You're either a young woman who thinks on her feet,' he said, 'or a cold-hearted murderess. Are you sure you weren't planning to sell them on eBay?'

'No. What do you mean "weren't"? Did you take them off?' I asked.

'Afraid so.' He smiled affably at me. 'Can't have you carrying vital evidence around. Your phone has been wiped down and is now clean as a whistle. You may go.'

The Super had taken up most of my morning. I didn't have long before I had to meet James. Then Harold was whisking me away for the weekend. I had to have clothes. I hadn't done any laundry since the wave of murder had swept over my office. My jeans were on their last legs. So I went back to Next once again.

I looked around and was gripped by panic. I had no clue where Harold was taking me. Baronial castle? Friendly B&B? Five-star hotel? Paris? I flicked through the racks feeling increasingly hysterical. I checked my phone. Half an hour. I grabbed a pair of dark skinny jeans. With heels they'd be reasonably dressy. With the trainers I was currently wearing they would be casual. I didn't have time to go back to the Holiday Inn for anything. I found a simple, cheap pair of black heels in my size. I pulled a fitted dark green top off a shelf. It looked like it would show a hint of cleavage. I grabbed a chunky silver chain that would dress it up if necessary.

Then I snatched up some t-shirts, knickers and socks and a very warm wine-coloured jumper. No time for the changing room. Anyway, the very thought of stripping off my coat, gloves, hat, jumper, jeans etc and trying clothes on was exhausting. I would just hope for the best and keep the receipt.

I legged it into Accessorise next door and seized a capacious cloth carryall covered in spangles and embroidery. It was more than I would normally pay for a mere bag, but it'd be worth it if the destination was fancy. I fretted while I waited for my credit-card PIN prompt. I ran to a bus stop and just caught a 75.

I'd be on time. I climbed to the top of the bus and got a front seat. I transferred my new clothes into the spangly cloth bag, giving the dark-green top a little pat. I hoped it'd look good on. I love new clothes. I checked the bottom of the Next bags for receipts, then scrunched them up to chuck away.

Then I relaxed. The sun came out again as we went over Waterloo Bridge. The London Eye sparkled, the river gleamed and rippled, and I remembered why I love London. But I felt disconnected from the world around me, as though I might float away. As I rose to get off the bus, I wondered if I would ever feel normal again.

I was glad the Super had deleted the photos. I'd never have looked at the Sam ones anyway.

It was exactly eleven when I arrived at Waterloo, and I hurried over to where James was waiting, next to the croissant stand. We took the interminable train out West to Martins Heron, near Bracknell. The journey was an hour long, and I do mean long. By the time we got there I could recite a list of every station on the line all the way to Reading, as recounted periodically by the automated announcer. Occasionally he varied his routine by bellowing that we were sitting in a 'quiet carriage', and instructing us to keep the noise down.

The announcements and the unbelievably loud beeping of the train doors at every station set my teeth on edge and my head throbbing.

When we arrived at Martins Heron I nearly fell off the train in my rush to alight.

We crossed a sorry-looking patch of grass leading to an

estate of small, identical modern houses. A group of teenage goths passed us, black coats swinging. No doubt they'd be getting the hourly train to somewhere where their wall-leaning skills would be more appreciated.

'Not much scope for being cool,' I said to James, 'if you live in Martins Heron.'

'You should see Bracknell,' he replied.

James's sister Martha opened the door and brought us up to her daughter's bedroom. Jasmine was tiny, with very long curly brown hair and thick glasses.

'Just wait here, I have to get my stuff,' she said.

James sat at her desk. I pushed a pink net curtain aside to sit gingerly on the edge of her small, very pink four poster bed. The carpet was pink. The walls were pink, with pink bookshelves. The child had hundreds of books. The usual children's classics — Narnia, Artemis Fowl — interspersed with large tomes about space and science.

There was a telescope in the window.

'Christ, James!' I hissed, when Jasmine had left the room.

'What?'

'You never told me she's *six*!'

'Eight. Too old for you? Told you she's my niece didn't I? How old did you expect her to be? I'm still only twenty-nine, remember.'

'For the last five years, I hear. I don't know. I just thought she might, maybe, have all her teeth?'

'Relax. She's an expert at this. Wait and see.'

Jasmine reappeared wearing a white lab coat.

'Did you bring the equipment, Uncle James?'

James delved into his backpack and produced a new *CSI: Miami* fingerprint kit and a box of freezer bags.

'I thought you already had the toy,' I said to Jasmine.

She frowned at me over her glasses.

'I do already own a kit, Cynthia, but I've run out of dusting powder. You don't want me to fail due to inadequate equipment do you?'

'No of course not. Sorry, Jasmine.'

'That's OK.' She flashed me a forgiving gap-toothed grin — probably cute if you weren't relying on her to uncover a vicious murderer. 'Can you give me the things with the suspect fingerprints on, please?'

My skydiving photo made me shudder as James handed it over in its freezer bag. I'd printed and framed it as a reminder of the freedom and fun I'd found in Australia. A burglar ripping it in half seemed like a bad omen.

We'd also brought the business card Liz had found at the bottom of the envelope containing the anonymous note. The one with 'RIP' added in after my name. It didn't inspire me with confidence. I'd peered at it from all angles and the prints looked blurred.

Jasmine solemnly carried both items over to her study table. James jumped up to get out of her way. She slid into her chair, switched on a powerful desk light and picked up the bag with the photo in it.

'You can go and talk to mum now, Uncle James,' she said absently. 'I'll let you know when I have results to report.'

Thus dismissed, we descended to the kitchen to drink a cup of tea. Martha had asked us to lunch, and mouth-watering smells emanated from the oven. I realised I hadn't eaten since the croissant at dawn. Hungry.

I liked Martha. She shared James's wicked sense of humour. She seemed to suspect my concern at Jasmine's extreme youth.

'Don't worry, Cynthia, if there's anything to find she'll find it. I know I'm her mum and all but she's a bit of a little genius,' she said. She opened the oven door, jumped back from the heat, looked happy with whatever was bubbling in there, and added a tray of garlic bread.

After summoning us back up to her bedroom, the little genius swivelled towards us on her chair.

'I've been unable to get fingerprints from the photo.'

'But I saw them. They were clear as day.'

I was panicking. Surely we hadn't come all the way out here for nothing? And had she wrecked our only pieces of evidence? We should have given them to the police.

'I'm afraid not. The prints on the photo are actually thumb prints,' said the little pedant.

'Fingerprints, thumb prints, whatever. Did you manage to get them off?'

'I'm happy to say I obtained prints from the photo for both the right and left thumb. I also obtained prints from the card. However,' she continued seriously, 'the prints on the card don't match those on the photo. I suspect that the prints on the card are not thumb-prints, but it's also possible that the two sets of prints belong to different people.'

'OK,' I said. 'So the prints on the photo and the ones on the card could belong to the same people? In theory?'

'Yes.'

'Wow. That's great. Thanks Jasmine.' said James. 'Can we give you the samples from our suspects for comparison now?'

'Please do,' she said graciously.

James delved in his bag again and produced freezer bags containing a number of plastic cups, the dodgy nightclub card with Harold's fingerprints, Vicky's water bottle and the small mirror that Laura had handled. Each freezer bag had been labelled with marker.

Jasmine sighed. 'Hardly ideal materials,' she said, 'but I'll do what I can. It'll take some time.'

Just then, Martha called us all down for lunch. It was macaroni cheese. Hot, steaming and delicious. Just right for a cold winter's day. James must've told her I was a veggie.

I tried not to fret at the delay — children had to eat, I supposed — but I was happy when Jasmine scoffed her lunch at lightning speed and announced her immediate return to work.

Martha passed me the garlic bread again.

'So, Cynthia, what did you think of Nathan?' she asked. 'James said the murder was the best thing that ever happened to him.'

James gave her an admonishing glance and changed the

subject. He and Martha describing their eccentric upbringing on an organic cheese-making farm made a funny double-act but time passed slowly. I hoped we were on the verge of a major breakthrough. Upstairs, materialising under the hands of our eight-year-old sorcerer, could be the pointer to a vicious murderer. My thoughts racing ahead, I imagined Jasmine in the witness box, standing on tiptoe and leaning forward to peer severely at the jury over her thick glasses.

We were just finishing our coffee when she called us.

'First,' she said, when we'd squeezed together on the little bed, 'your business card. The person who handled it appears to be the owner of the water bottle.'

Vicky.

'The prints on the bottle are fragmentary, as are those on the card. As I'm sure you know, a match of at least twelve of the details of the print — forks, merges and branches and that — is usually required for definite identification. I've managed to match fourteen.'

'Well done, Jasmine,' said James.

'The photo is more difficult. It's not Vicky. I'm afraid I can't find any match for it. All the water cups are smudged, Uncle James. I managed to get prints from some of them but I think they're not thumb prints, and none of them match the thumb prints from the photo. The one marked 'Peter' came out OK, though. I'm pretty sure it's a thumb-print, and it doesn't match the photo.'

'What about the mirror and the nightclub card?' I asked. Laura and Harold. I felt tense. I didn't want them to be involved. Even if whoever had burgled my flat hadn't been responsible for the murder, it was impossible to imagine either of them destroying all my stuff. I crossed my fingers as I waited for the judgement.

'The prints are pretty damaged. You should have put them into evidence bags straight away,' said Jasmine sternly.

'I know, only I forgot to bring the bags.' I couldn't tell her I'd bagged my items furtively under a restaurant table while slightly squiffy on champagne. She was supposed to think the whole thing was just a game.

'I'm pretty sure they don't match.'

'Jasmine,' said James, 'you're a star. You're getting the best Christmas present ever.'

'Make that two presents. And thanks, Jasmine.'

'Did I get it right?' Jasmine asked shyly, finally behaving like the eight-year-old she was.

'You sure did, darling,' said James. I smiled at her too, and solemnly shook her hand. I was disappointed that we hadn't found out more, but at least Laura and Harold seemed to be off the hook for the burglary.

'**S**o what have we learned for sure?' asked James as the beeping of the doors died down on the train back to London.

'Peter, Harold and Laura didn't trash my flat,' I replied.

'And Vicky wrote the letter,' said James. 'But why? What a crazy thing to do. What's that about?'

I rang Vicky.

'Vicky, why did you write me that anonymous letter?'

'What?'

'The letter. I've had it fingerprinted. I know you wrote it.'

A gasp at the other end of the line.

'Cynthia. You told the police!'

'No.'

'Are you going to?'

'Not if you tell me why.'

'Because of the baby. Because I was afraid you'd find out about it…and you did.'

'What's the big deal? Why does it matter whether I know?'

'I was afraid you'd tell the police and they'd arrest me for murder. They'll definitely suspect me if they find out I was sleeping with him. And then there's the baby. And they say Nathan died around seven, and I didn't leave work until ages after that.'

'Why *did* you stay at work so late? You usually don't.'

'No. Well. I had some things to do.'

'You did?'

'OK, if you must know, Cynthia, I was sitting on the loo crying.'

'Oh, Vicky.'

'I was just being stupid. Anyway, I've told my parents now and they're going to help me. It's not so bad.'

'That's brilliant news.'

'So, will you tell the police?'

'No, but I think you should tell them yourself. It'd look better. I mean, the police are certain to hear sooner or later.'

'I'm not telling them, and if you keep your mouth shut too, Cynthia, they'll never find out. If they do I'll know it was you who told them.'

'Charming,' I said to James, 'and to think I'd started to like Vicky!'

I hadn't forgotten Harold's promise to whisk me away for the weekend. I'd to meet him at Pudding Mill Lane tube station at four, so when we finally got back into London James and I parted ways. My head ringing from the announcer and the loudly beeping doors, I vowed never again to take the Reading-bound train. If I walked instead it'd probably only take a day or two. It'd be worth it.

I arrived at Pudding Mill Lane a couple of minutes early. My first reaction was to get straight back on the tube and hightail it out of there. I was used to colleagues saying my beloved Shoreditch was seedy but this was something else. It seemed to be an industrial area. The only visible exit route from the tube station was a narrow path between tall graffiti-covered hoardings. There was no way to avoid anyone you met walking along it. At the other end, judging by the noise, was a major arterial road. My sense of direction is shaky but I thought it might be the feeder road for one of the tunnels under the Thames that take you out of London.

Harold arrived on the next tube, thank goodness. He carried a backpack that sloshed suggestively as we walked.

'Champagne?'

'No, not this time.' He opened his bag to reveal a couple of flagons of cider. Not a fancy destination then.

'Where are we going?'

'Wait and see.'

As I'd suspected, the path terminated at a multi-lane highway. I could smell fumes on the breeze of the passing traffic. The narrow pavement vibrated underfoot as cars and lorries thundered down into a huge tunnel to our left. Around us crouched barren, dilapidated, graffiti-covered warehouses.

Fortunately, we didn't have to cross the death-trap road. Harold turned left and led me along the pavement to a gate in a chain-link fence. It seemed to be securely fastened, but he fiddled around for a moment and it swung open.

'Hey, where are we?' I asked him as he led me into a spacious yard.

'A friend of mine lives here.'

It dawned on me that I'd been incredibly stupid. What if Harold was the killer? What was I doing in this post-industrial wilderness? Yeah, I know, I should have seen it coming, right? He was so cute, though.

Then I remembered that James and Liz and everyone knew I was meeting him. Even his mum. That was kind of a protection.

We crossed the yard and stopped at a steel door. No sign of a doorbell. Not surprising, considering Harold's friend's gaff was a warehouse. Harold got his phone out. I looked around. There were heaps of household electronics along one wall. A clapped-out-looking white Transit with a single fluorescent pink flower painted on it lurked in a corner.

As I peered through a window of the van, the front door opened. A beautiful, casually-rumpled blonde woman stood framed in the doorway. She threw her arms around Harold, kissed him, then grabbed his hand and pulled him up the stairs, calling out 'come in, darlings.'

The stairs opened on to an airport-length corridor with several doors on either side. The blonde beauty brought us into a kitchen. It was the size of my whole flat and smelled faintly of cement dust.

'This is Alexandra,' said Harold, grinning. 'Alexandra, this is Cynthia, the girl I was telling you about.'

'I belieff you 'ave been 'aving a 'ard time,' said Alexandra in a sexy Eastern European accent. Wow. This must be a stunning girlfriend whose existence Harold had kept under wraps. She was slim and artistic-looking, with long butter-coloured curls tumbling down her back. She seemed friendly and kind as well. Double whammy.

'Are all the rooms this big?' I asked her, to avoid saying 'Are you sleeping with Harold?'

'This is the smallest.' Clocking my expression, she laughed. 'I am a sculptor. The space is useful. Come and 'ave a look.'

She opened the door into a room apparently acres long. Far away I could just make out a double mattress on the floor, surrounded by a small pile of clothes. A few other items were scattered around the space — an old bicycle frame with the pedals missing, a shiny new upside-down men's urinal, a utilitarian-looking greenhouse. A Van-Goghian boot containing a vigorous-looking trailing plant stood on the windowsill. A skeleton of dubious lineage was suspended from the ceiling. 'My bedroom,' said Alexandra.

Setting off down the corridor she waved at doors on the left: 'Other bedrooms.' A single door on the right led into an enormous sun-filled space that must have run the length of the building. It was full of intriguing power tools. I recognised a chainsaw and a drill. At the distant other end, a slender woman with cropped black hair worked at an easel. Around her were propped canvases of varying sizes, abstract experiments with colour and shape.

'Aferdite,' said Alexandra, indicating the artist, who probably didn't even hear her.

Dotted about the place were half-finished sculptures. In fact maybe they were finished — I don't know much about art — but most were surrounded by heaps of tools and objects that I felt might end up being added to them. Some were of beautiful, lustrous wood, others apparently assembled from bits and pieces of commercial waste — old computers, fridge doors, broken typewriters, scaffolding poles.

The room itself was a piece of art, a positive space radiating possibilities. In spite of my worries about Alexandra, I felt optimistic for the first time in days. Maybe I would be able to figure everything out after all.

'I didn't think there was anywhere like this left in London,' I said.

'Zere isn't,' said Alexandra, 've are sinking that the landlord will sell it at any moment.'

I had no idea why Harold had brought me here, except that this was obviously the sort of place to which people ought to be brought. Alexandra ushered us back to the kitchen and made tea. She made three extra mugs, glancing occasionally at the wall as she wielded milk and sugar. She disappeared with these and I went to see what she'd been reading. In a fine script written directly on the wall was a simple table with 'tea', 'coffee', 'sugar', 'milk' along the top and 'Barnaby', 'Aferdite', 'Alexandra', 'Shahid', 'Harold' down the side.

In each square there was a tick — or not. At the end of the list of tea-making ingredients someone had added 'lemon' in a new hand — the only tick was for 'Harold'. I studied Harold. A slice of lemon floated incriminatingly in his tea.

'You live here?'

'I wish.'

'Oh.'

'No, I hang out. My own place is one of those new apartments overlooking the river. Very now, but this is more relaxed.'

'It couldn't be much more relaxed or it'd fall over,' I

agreed.

'Alexandra and Aferdite will be glad. They like to create a welcoming family atmosphere.'

'It's cool, but what am I doing here? Apart from absorbing rays of artistic energy, obviously.'

'Apart from that, they're lending us their van.'

'Their van? You mean the flowery wreck outside?'

'It's highly reliable. Transits nearly always are.'

'I belieff zey are known as Dagenham Dustbins.' Alexandra had reappeared.

'Why are we borrowing it?' I asked baldly. Shit, I sounded like I was agreeing already.

'Rainbow festival in Kent,' replied Harold. 'Hippies sitting around vibing. Remember I told you about it? You said you'd love to go.'

'Yes, but I meant hypothetically, if I wasn't a murder suspect,' I said. 'I have other things on my mind right now, and I'm not supposed to leave London without telling the police.'

'You can tell zem,' Alexandra shrugged. 'I 'ave ze address of ze festival 'ere.'

'Farmer Giles's Field, Upper Gristle, Kent,' I read. 'Is this a joke?'

'We'll check out the van in a bit,' said Harold. 'If you don't fancy it we'll have dinner somewhere nice instead.'

I've never driven a van, but I've always wanted to. Like a child, I hopped up into the cab and played with the steering wheel. I surveyed the yard below from my regal height. It'd be like driving a tank.

'It has open insurance,' said Harold enticingly.

I jumped down and he unlocked the sliding side door. There was an interior light. The compact space was fitted up comfortably with a large double mattress, spotless duvet and Aferdite's artwork on the walls. There was even a sparkling antique chamber pot in a specially-constructed frame, discreetly tucked into a corner.

'I'll sleep beside the van in a tent,' said Harold.

Not if I had anything to do with it.

'Won't Alexandra mind us going off together?' I asked him. He looked puzzled, then laughed.

'No. She's not interested in what I get up to — as long as I don't try to seduce Aferdite,' he said.

'Oh.' I felt embarrassed. Now he was going to think I liked him.

'Hang on,' he said, 'I forgot the cider. Just hop up and have a poke around.'

I climbed in. Harold was right, this would be perfect. I'd ring the Super and tell him about Farmer Giles and his field. I'd done all the investigating I reasonably could for the weekend. And this was one brilliant van. Was that a gas stove?

As I investigated the cooking facilities, the sliding door slid shut with a clunk.

'OK, it's cool, I'll come,' I said, turning round, but I was alone. Harold must have thought I'd got out.

'Hang on, I'm still in here,' I shouted.

There was a click. I grabbed the handle of the sliding door. It was locked. The driver's door slammed, the engine started, and the van reversed, took off and braked hard, precipitating me backwards onto the mattress. OK, some joke. I sprang up to bang on the wooden partition between me and the driver, but with a screeching turn we sped off so fast that I was thrown back to the floor again.

As I struggled to stand we stopped, presumably at lights. I jumped up and started banging, calling out 'Harold! Stop, this isn't funny!'

No reply. Then, chillingly, Radio One was switched on. The driver turned it up full blast, drowning out my cries.

It couldn't be Harold in the driver's seat. I was sure he'd never listen to Radio One. But…if not Harold, who was it?

Was I being abducted?

The van took off, flinging me onto the mattress again.

There was no point trying to stand up when it was moving.

My phone.

I slapped my pockets. Nothing. It must be in my handbag, but where had I left that?

In the cab of the van? I hoped it wasn't lying in Alexandra's yard.

I remembered that I'd promised to ring the Super if leaving town. There was no way I could do that now. Maybe he'd put out an alert for me.

Initially I wasn't frightened. I lay on the mattress, jolted continuously, flung to one side or the other whenever the van turned, and furious. But as we sped along I felt the first twinges of fear. I was sure the mystery driver would crash. If he didn't, what would happen when we stopped? Panic gripped me and I began to feel hysterical. That wouldn't help. I tried to lie still, breathing deeply, pretending I was in yoga class.

The van lurched round a corner. Something slid along a shelf, dropped, and gouged me in the forehead. I picked it up. *The Little Book of Calm*, in hardback.

I had an abrupt fierce longing to be at home in my cosy flat, watching *Black Books* DVDs and drinking beer with Alice. You don't really need to know this, but I started to cry.

When the van finally stopped there was a merciful reprieve from Radio One. I leaped to my feet and yelled at my captor to let me out. The driver's door slammed. Footsteps receded. I banged on the double back doors, shouting at the top of my voice, but nothing happened except I hurt my hand. I pulled off a trainer and hammered at the sliding side door with it. No reaction. Time passed and I shouted and shouted until my voice was ragged and my throat too sore to continue. I would just be left here. I couldn't believe it.

I was hungry and I wanted to go to the loo, and gradually I was forced to accept that the antique chamber pot would have to be deployed. Gross. I'm a hippy at heart, but not this much of one, I reflected, thanking my lucky stars for the packet of tissues in my pocket.

The only food I could find was an old but still edible banana in a cupboard beside the stove. I'd already devoured it when I realised that I should have eked it out. How long would I be here? I remembered a Dick Francis where the hero is stuck in a van, in the dark, with nothing to eat but cheese for weeks on end.

That wouldn't happen to me, though. I had a light.

As the hours passed, I began to truly believe I'd been abandoned. Then fear took over. Had Harold kidnapped me? Knowing he could be the murderer, I'd still trusted him. Fool, fool, fool. No wonder he was so bloody charming. They say all killers are charming.

I went back to beating my fists on the doors, shouting and screaming, but my throat was already in agony and soon my voice had completely gone.

I could feel myself losing control, slipping into hysteria. That way madness lay. I had to get a grip. Leaning on the doors, I breathed deeply, releasing each breath over ten seconds to centre myself. At first I kept panicking, gulping for air, losing count, dislocating. Gradually the rhythm of the even breathing took over and I began to feel calmer.

I forced myself to lie down on the mattress. I needed to rest.

I knew I should turn the light out to conserve it, but I absolutely couldn't choose to be in the dark. My thoughts flew wildly in every direction. I reined them in, and trudged slowly towards sleep by forcing myself to methodically think through every detail of both murders.

Had Harold really committed them? Who else could the killer be?

12 — A RIVER TRIP

I slept uneasily at first, tossing and turning, occasionally half waking. But I must have slid into deep sleep eventually, because when I woke up the back doors were open on a woodland scene, with daylight pouring in.

'Right,' I thought, 'I'll kill him!'

I picked up a discarded trainer and held it like a weapon. It was better than nothing. I jumped down from the back of the van and shouted 'Oy!'

There was a sickening crash. I stumbled, dizzy and stunned. Blackness.

When I came to again I was cold, wet and confused.

I sensed a slight rise and fall beneath me. Everything was green. I turned my head. Narrow planks. I seemed to be in the bottom of a wooden boat. Beautiful, ancient foliage formed a canopy overhead. River then, not sea. A light rain fell. It had soaked through my thin clothes, chilling me down to the bone. My jeans and shirt clung icily to me; coat, hat and gloves were gone. My whole body shook with cold. I thought it was probably the chattering of my teeth that had woken me.

I managed to sit up, leaning back against the side of the boat. By the way the trees glided by overhead, I guessed it was drifting.

Oh well, at least the lunatic is gone, I thought. I'm bound to wash up somewhere sooner or later.

My head ached and roared. I rested it between my legs, closing my eyes. I remembered jumping out of the van. Then nothing. Had someone hit me?

The roaring grew louder, drumming through my thoughts. Was I going to pass out again? I felt myself lurch and spin. Too much. I lay back down on my side, wondering if I'd be sick. Only when the boat tilted crazily, and seemed to jump, did I realise that the roaring was coming from the river.

I didn't care.

Until the boat disappeared, flinging me underwater. I had never felt such cold. I surfaced and struggled to breathe. My frozen throat made a frightening whooping sound as it refused to co-operate. My lungs felt constricted with cold. I gasped for air, panicking, trying to keep my head out. I couldn't swim against the strong current. It yanked me under.

I surfaced, breathing in desperately. The pressure on my lungs eased. I gulped precious oxygen while the water attacked me with savage intent. It was only a few feet deep, but it pummelled and shoved and pushed me, forcing me under the surface, dragging me over sharp stones and boulders like a toy. Terrified, I used my hands, my feet, my torn knees, anything with purchase, to advance towards the bank an inch at a time. As I got closer the river fought back, propelling me sideways, tumbling me against rocks. I kept lunging, stumbling, flinging myself onward. I could touch land but the river swept me along. Rocks and branches ripped at my legs and tore agonisingly at my frozen, grasping hands. I couldn't get a grip on anything. I was losing the fight for air. I was freezing. I was getting weaker. I would never survive.

Mercifully a tree snagged me, whirling me to a tumultuous halt, giving me precious seconds to embrace a protruding branch.

Adrenalin got me over tree roots and foliage, out of the water and on to the bank. I lay prone, throbbing, aching and shivering. Now I had to find help. But it was so very very cold, and I was so very very sore and tired. I would just have a little rest.

The darkness retreated.

When I saw Harold's eyes looking into mine, I thought I was dreaming.

'Cynthia,' he said. 'Are you OK?'

'Why did you leave me?'

'Why did you steal Alexandra's van?'

'That piece of shit?'

The darkness returned.

'**Y**ou may or may not be surprised to hear,' said the Super, taking a seat by my hospital bed, 'that some of my colleagues thought you'd fled the country to avoid being prosecuted for a double murder.'

Lovely. The Super was the first visitor I'd had since I'd woken up. Doctors had been in and out, and a nice nurse had given me tea and toast, but no visitors. Good job I liked him.

'What about you? Did you think I'd done it?' I asked.

'The suspicion in my section was that you had been detained by the murderer. Involuntarily. A view, you'll be relieved to hear, that is now confirmed.'

'You don't think I knocked myself out and left myself drifting down a river in a punt then?'

'No. We investigated the possibility, of course. It was dangerous — you came quite close to death — but you could have been suicidal due to remorse.'

His eyes glinted back at the scorn in mine. 'However, an examination of your injuries has established that it would have been difficult, if not impossible, for you to hit yourself on the back of the head in that precise fashion. And the doctors believe that, had you sustained that injury while in the river, you would have lost consciousness and drowned.'

'So that's what happened. He hit me and I blacked out,' I said, pulling at my pillow and trying to get comfortable. The back of my head throbbed. 'I was on dry land at the time though. It was just after I'd jumped out of the van. That's how the killer got me into the boat, I suppose. But why didn't anyone see him? And why didn't he just finish me off instead? I've been thinking and thinking about it and the only explanation that makes sense is that he wanted my death to look like suicide.'

'We believe so,' said the Superintendent. 'We think the murderer calculated that we'd attribute the head injury to your passage through the river. Indeed, we might have done so, if you'd completed the journey he'd planned for you and drowned. You're lucky you woke up when you did.'

'I don't feel lucky. I feel sick, and my head hurts, and everything smells funny. But I'm in the clear?'

'Apparently. It is, of course, possible that there are two vicious murderers in this case — you and your attacker — but we incline to the statistically more likely theory that there is only one and that you were one of their intended victims.'

'Oh. Right. Cheers.'

'And you know I think you're far too cute to be a murderer,' he added, 'although that's not a thing I would ever say.'

I noticed PC Lawson, taking notes in the corner of my hospital room, smile slightly and cross something out.

Alice rushed in, full of sisterly concern.

'I flew over to make sure you're all right,' she said, kissing me, nodding at the Super and drawing a chair up to my bed without pausing for breath. 'When I landed and couldn't contact you, I wasn't too worried. I thought you'd be out sleuthing. I just headed into town and kept trying your mobile. But when your phone rang out and went to voice mail for the gazillionth time, I started thinking about the burglary. I got freaked out. I spent the night at your Holiday Inn and got up practically at dawn and checked but they still had your key in reception. So I rang the police and asked for the Superintendent in charge of the Airwolfe murders, and told him you were missing.'

'How did they know where to find me?' I asked.

'Your mobile. It was in your handbag under the passenger seat of the van. They tracked it. I've no idea why your kidnapper didn't turn it off, everyone knows about being able to trace mobiles these days.'

'I mean, how did they know *exactly* where to find me?' I was getting agitated.

'Weren't you told not to upset her?' asked the Super. 'I'd like to talk to you alone, Cynthia. Would you mind if Alice left us?'

'Yes, I would, and there's no point anyway because whatever you say to me I'll just tell her as soon as you've gone,' I said. 'You might as well let her stay here and save me the effort. I'm too sick for complicated talking.'

'But what I'm going to tell you is confidential. We're still in the middle of a murder investigation, remember?'

'Oh *come* on, Alice isn't the murderer, she doesn't even live in this country, and she hasn't met any of the suspects so she's got no one to blab stuff to,' I said.

'Oh, all right,' said the Super. I thought he probably didn't mind much. Alice really is very pretty. 'Did you see anyone on the riverbank?'

'No.' I hated lying to him, but what about Harold? If they knew he'd been there they might get the wrong end of the stick. Obviously, if he'd wanted to kill me he could have pushed me back in the river and gone off. So he had to be innocent. But supposing the police didn't work that out?

'Strange. Harold thought you'd regained consciousness briefly,' said the Superintendent.

'*Harold* was there?' asked Alice, providing a welcome distraction.

'Yes.' I sensed the Super watching me thoughtfully.

'How come? Is he the murderer?' asked Alice.

Why did everyone always jump to the conclusion that Harold was the murderer?

'Probably not,' said the Super. '*He* reported Miss Hegarty missing too.'

'Did he? When?' I asked. Turning my head from one of them to the other was making the bruise on the back of it throb even more. I tried pulling myself into a sitting position. The Super got up and started rooting through a nearby cupboard.

'When it became clear that you weren't coming back with the van,' he said, producing a pillow and pushing it in behind my shoulders. He sat back down. 'Unfortunately he spoke to the nearest police station who advised him that he should wait twenty-four hours to see if you returned. They asked if he'd like to report the theft of the van, which would get things moving, but he said he wouldn't. He didn't realise you hadn't taken it yourself.'

'Oh my God. So what happened next?' I asked.

'You didn't respond to repeated phone calls and Harold became concerned. He had my card. He rang me this morning and asked me to run a search on your mobile. I told him I already had. Your sister having been previously in touch.'

'My phone was probably on silent,' I said. 'It's a habit of mine, from work. So you told him where I was? I mean, where my phone was?'

'It would not be ethical for a police officer to pass on personal information,' the Super said sternly. 'I informed him of that fact, and added that if he wished to discuss it further he could meet me at Oxford boat yard, where I was investigating the theft of a boat.'

Alice looked wonderingly at him. 'You're right, he *is* attractive,' she said, plunging me into confusion.

'So I've been told,' said the Super, thinking (luckily) that she meant Harold. I'm sure PC Lawson blushed. She must have told him Harold was cute.

'He walked along the river bank and found me,' I said.

'He rang me and you were rushed to hospital,' said the Super. 'Any later and you'd have hypothermia. You're lucky, Cynthia. You have Harold to thank for your rescue.'

'How do you know it's not all an elaborate double-bluff to make sure you don't suspect him?' asked Alice.

'Nothing is ever certain,' said the Superintendent. 'However, we have another reason to think he's probably innocent. We've been informed that he's a corporate private investigator, hired to investigate embezzlement at Airwolfe.'

About to tell him acerbically that I was ill and in no mood for jokes, I realised it made sense.

'So *that's* why he wanted to go to the party with you,' said Alice, rather tactlessly I thought. 'He wanted to pick up the office gossip.'

'Yes, his investigation only began a few weeks ago,' said the Super. 'Apparently he was chosen for the Airwolfe job because he had the entrée through his stepfather, although Mr Boyle was not informed. No compelling conflict-of-interest concerns arose as long as Harold himself had no objection. The Airwolfe financial director initiated the probe.'

'Harold told me he didn't have a job,' I said.

'Well that was a big fat lie,' said Alice.

I closed my eyes. I was so tired. If she reminded me that she'd told me not to trust Harold, I would…I would…get even tireder.

'I gather his work is intermittent and undercover,' said the Superintendent.

'So he's off the hook for the murders,' I said.

'It would seem so,' said the Super. 'However, we've decided to allow the impression to emerge that he's our main suspect. We want to lull the killer into a false sense of security. Harold has agreed to disappear for a few days. We'll allow people to think that the investigation's winding down. Meanwhile, we'll be pursuing various avenues of inquiry.'

'Do you mind my asking what they are?' I asked him.

'Not at all, but I'm afraid I can't answer you,' he replied, smiling faintly down at me. 'Now, I must be off. Here's my card in case you want me. Alice, I'm glad you're here. Cynthia needs someone she can trust. Cynthia, did you tell Alice about Sparky's texts?'

And on that bombshell, he left.

'What's this about Sparky's texts?' asked Alice.

'Oh, it's nothing,' I said. 'I'll tell you later. Where's my handbag?'

I was dying to talk to Harold, but my phone was still missing.

'I think the police took it in for questioning,' she replied. 'What do you mean, nothing? Why's the Super asking you about Sparky's texts? What texts? How does he know about them, anyway?'

'He took my mobile in as part of a search,' I said. 'Sparky sent me a few messages while he had it.'

'And?' said Alice.

'And they weren't very polite, apparently.'

'Haven't you read them?'

'No.'

'Why not?'

'Well, after we split up, you know how jealous he could be, he started sending me messages asking who I was seeing and that sort of thing. So I replied to a few of them and said no one and so on, but they kept coming, and then they got a bit nasty. So I started deleting them without reading them.'

'That toe-rag. Why didn't you just block him?'

'I don't know,' I said, squirming into a more comfortable position. Now the Super had gone, I could keep the back of my head off the pillow by lying facing her. 'I blocked his emails all right, I filtered them to my delete folder. With the phone, I meant to, but I just didn't get around to it. He was so lovely when we were first going out, I just couldn't block him, it would've made me feel like he was a psycho.'

'He *was* a psycho, sis. *Is* one, if he's still texting you. How long since you broke up? A year?'

'Yeah. Roughly.'

'You never told me about the break-up. One minute you're all loved up in Vientiane, next minute you're single in Bangkok. What happened?'

I sighed and closed my eyes again. I'd always avoided talking about it and Alice, most uncharacteristically, hadn't probed, but I'd known this moment would come. Only I wished it hadn't come when I was hospitalised, exhausted and battered and bruised. Both physically and otherwise.

'Cynthia?'

She reached out and took my hand. I blinked back a tear.

'Come on. It's time. Tell me.'

So I told her.

There was very little to the story, after all. It's happened to a million people before me, and it'll happen to a million people after me. I just found myself in love with someone who didn't love me back.

Oh, he said he did. Especially in the beginning. He was all flattery, all attention. He and I were both working for a bank in Dublin. He was a business analyst. One day he asked me out. I was dead chuffed. He was good-looking and fun, blond with a cheeky expression, an intriguing English accent and hair that begged to be ruffled.

Things moved fast. He sent me a rose a day — which became a bit of a running joke at the office — and we saw each other all the time, and after a couple of months he asked me to move in with him. It seemed kind of soon, but my landlord wanted to sell my house and I had to move somewhere. Sparky could be very persuasive.

Alice knew all that.

Then things started to change, slowly. Sparky thought some of my skirts were too short. He thought maybe it'd be better if I didn't stay out late unless he was with me. He began to slag off my friends. Since I was a programmer, a lot of the colleagues I hung out with at work were blokes. Bless them, you couldn't meet a lovelier bunch of fellas, but according to Sparky they were all arseholes. He didn't believe you could have a friend of the opposite gender, he thought sex would inevitably get in the way. It got so any time I went for coffee with a man there was a long, boring scene later.

He was always popping up at lunch-time. Soon we were having lunch together every day, and Sparky was sullen and unwelcoming to anyone who joined us.

Then there was a desk re-org in the office. He had been on a different floor. Now he sat a few metres away. I found he was hovering even if I went for a glass of water. I only escaped from him when I went to the Ladies, and if I stayed in there gossiping with one of the girls I could feel his eyes bore through me when I came out.

It began to occur to me that maybe he was a bit controlling.

Alice, by this stage, was dissing him every chance she got. He guessed, of course, and lost no opportunity to put her down to me, remarking thoughtfully that she was obviously jealous of our closeness and our strong bond. I began to tell him I was doing something else whenever I met her. I don't like to lie, but it was worth it to avoid the sulk.

By this time there were fewer nights of passion and more fights. He didn't like it when I went out without him but I put my foot down. He didn't like that either.

A few weeks after the desk re-org a work friend of mine, Joyce, stopped me in the Ladies to tell me she was pregnant. I was thrilled for her. I knew she'd been trying for a long time and she'd had a few disappointments. We stayed in there for ages chatting, and then I suggested going for coffee. As soon as we left the Ladies, Sparky came up and said he needed to discuss the functional spec for the project we were working on. I told him I wanted to have coffee with Joyce. He said his work issue couldn't wait.

Joyce backed off immediately, not wanting to cause a row. She said it was fine. But I will never forget the glance she gave me before she turned away.

A look of frustration and pity.

I said nothing to Sparky. Luckily I had marketable skills and financial independence. I researched the Australian working holiday visa. I handed in my notice, and asked my boss to keep it quiet. I think she knew why — anyway, she did.

One day at work I told Sparky I was going for a smear test. I went to the Australian embassy and applied for my visa instead. It arrived by email a few weeks later. I went straight online and booked my flights.

That night, I told him that I couldn't handle living with him anymore, that he was too controlling and that I was leaving for Australia in four days, travelling via South-East Asia.

Immediately, Sparky the First reappeared. He was shell-shocked, he hadn't realised how I felt, he was so sorry, he never meant to hurt me etc etc etc. He turned the charm back on, he said he just loved me so much, and working in the same office had been a disaster.

Looking back, his interest in me was renewed when it looked like I might get away.

He told me he'd love to come on the trip too. He would join me in Vietnam. We were loved up. I rang Alice and told her our travel plans. She said 'Don't take Sparky, Cynthia, he won't let you have any fun.'

'Ah, he's changed,' I told her. 'He's as thrilled about this as I am.'

Sparky tried to get me to change my flights so that we could leave together, but I was too excited.

That saved me.

When he arrived in Vietnam I'd been there a month. A whole month of doing what I liked, wearing what I liked, talking to who I liked. I'd hooked up with three Irish women in the first hostel I stayed in, and we'd travelled together since. By the time Sparky was due to arrive they were heading for Thailand. As I said goodbye to them and headed to Ho Chi Minh City (previously Saigon) to meet Sparky, I realised that my heart had sunk to my boots.

OK. Maybe it was over, after all.

But…he was still pretty sexy. The day he arrived we had a passionate reunion. (No details, sorry, my parents might read this.) We lay awake nearly all night, planning the details of our trip. Next day I had fun showing him around Saigon and telling him about my adventures. We were headed to Thailand ourselves, via Cambodia and Laos, and I was looking forward to hooking up with my new friends again. I figured we'd meet them somewhere along the way.

All went smoothly for a couple of weeks. Then in a café in Vientiane in Laos (where I had the most perfect *croissant au beurre* I have ever tasted in my life) I got chatting to a guy who looked bored and lonely, sitting at the table next to us on his own. He cheered up. We all went and had a few beers together and it turned into a lovely evening. Or so I thought.

Much later, back in our room, Sparky informed me that I was a slut, and couldn't keep it to myself. I would not like to repeat the things he said about that poor sad, lonely guy.

'That's it!' I said, and started packing.

'I didn't mean it, please forgive me,' he begged, back in over-apology mode. 'I love you so much blah, blah, blah.'

I made sure I finished packing before I forgave him.

At the crack of dawn I let myself out of the room while he was sleeping, took my bag, walked to the bus station and got a ticket for the next bus, which happened to be going to Bangkok.

That was the last I saw of him.

I never realised he'd got so bad,' said Alice.

'I thought it was all *my* fault. I should have tried harder,' I said. 'But it seemed like nothing I could do was ever enough, you know? I was worn out, I couldn't do it any more. Then after the month in Vietnam I started thinking maybe it was him who had a problem, not me. Leaving was hard and it took me a few months to get over it, but then I was delighted to be rid of him.'

'*I* should have tried harder, to get you to dump him early on,' said Alice.

'I'm a big girl, Alice,' I said, grinning. 'I wouldn't have taken too kindly to any interference.'

'I wonder what was in his texts,' she said.

'We'll read them when I get my phone back. It's bound to turn up sooner or later. Now let's forget him. I'm wrecked. And I want to talk to Harold.'

I didn't have Harold's phone number or his card. I considered ringing the Super and asking him for his number, for about minus zero seconds. The thoughtful pause at the other end of the line was too much to contemplate. I asked Alice to try directory enquiries but she had no success. Harold was probably ex-directory. Pretentious sod.

Meanwhile, the hospital wouldn't let me out of bed. There was little in the way of medical care, as I kept pointing out to Alice. No doctors, just people taking my temperature and checking my blood pressure and random strangers wandering in to ask me how I felt.

'Sure, we could do that at home,' I told her. Then they said I'd have to stay until a doctor released me. That was the last straw.

'Give me my clothes.'

'Cynthia,' Alice said, 'I really think you should wait until you get the all clear. You might still be in danger, you nearly got hypothermia, what if you collapse?'

'You can take me to A&E,' I said. 'Give me my clothes!'

I was wearing a hideous hospital gown. I didn't want to be in it for another second.

'I can't. I don't know where they are.'

'Go and buy me some then.'

'Honestly, I think you should wait.'

'You heard what they said. I'll be here till midday tomorrow at least if I've to wait for a doctor. I can't stand it, Alice. Go and buy me some clothes or I'll go out and flag down a taxi in this thing. And leave your make-up bag.'

She gave in suspiciously easily. Alice loves shopping.

While she was gone, I had a rudimentary shower, thinking about my adventures. Who'd tried to kill me? Two deaths and an attempted murder — who would be next?

And why try to kill *me* in particular? OK, people might dislike me or find me annoying, but it seemed more probable that the attempt was linked to Nathan's and Sam's murders. Was it because I'd been on the scene when Nathan died? Was the killer afraid, as I'd suggested to the police, that I'd seen or heard something and would eventually remember it? Or was I in possession of some piece of information of which, in classic Christie tradition, I didn't understand the significance? Was I in effect the adenoidal housemaid of this story?

No, I decided, trying to revive my pale complexion with some foundation. I was still alive and hadn't been brutally strangled and left with a clothes-peg on my nose, so I was probably the heroine. So did that make Harold the hero? Or would the Super get a look-in at the end?

These possibilities kept me pleasantly distracted until Alice got back half an hour later, all smiles.

'Are you going to work tomorrow?' she asked.

'On a Sunday?' I looked at her pityingly.

'*Hello* Cynthia, today's Monday,' she said. 'By the way, you are *not* supposed to leave. I met that nice nurse in the corridor and asked if you could go home. She said definitely not, you've to wait until the doctor comes in tomorrow to give you the all-clear. She seemed quite annoyed.'

'Best to sneak out quietly then. What did you get me to wear?'

She produced a pair of red stilettos, a seductive black dress into which I could barely fit, and out of which I spilled in, admittedly, all the right places, and a red pashmina.

'How delightfully unobtrusive. Alice, this is so not a suitable outfit for breaking out of hospital.'

'Yes, but, Cynthia, I didn't want to waste money on horrible clothes that you'd never be seen dead in afterwards. Tell you what, let's swap. You can wear my skirt.'

'No way. This dress is to die for.'

Fifteen minutes later I strutted into the hospital reception area. I flinched inwardly as the nice nurse bustled towards us, but Alice's unlikely choice of garments served as a fabulous bluff. I looked more like someone who'd got lost looking for a nightclub than a fugitive patient. The nurse walked straight past me and we made it outside. No way would I admit to Alice that the short walk had just about wiped me out. Luckily, she'd insisted on ringing a taxi before we left. I climbed thankfully into it.

'Sorry, miss, don't do London,' said the cab driver, when I gave him the address of the Holiday Inn.

'You don't? Where are we?'

'Oxford, you goon. Take us to the station please,' said Alice.

On the way to London on the train we argued about where to stay. Alice thought we should go back to my apartment. She said she could start the clean-up and get the bedroom done by bed time while I rested on the sofa.

I came up with lots of logical and unembarrassing reasons why this was a bad idea, but she had no truck with any of them.

'I can't,' I admitted at last, 'I'm too scared, Alice. Someone tried to kill me, they nearly managed it, and I'm sure they did the burglary so they know where I live. Let's just go to the Holiday Inn. You can share my room, or I'll book you in next door. I want to feel safe tonight.'

'You should have stayed in the hospital then, you eejit. OK, Holiday Inn it is.'

'I'm going to ask James and Liz to call round,' I told her.

'As long as you're sure neither of them is the murderer,' Alice laughed.

'I'd like you to meet them.'

'Oh, Cynthia, we were frantic with worry,' said Liz, when she arrived. Should I believe her?

'Are you really living here?' she asked.

'Yes, but please don't tell anyone. And I mean anyone,' I said. 'You already know Alice. James is on his way.'

James gave me a big hug when I opened the door to him. 'What have you been up to now?' he asked.

I told them, leaving out Harold's job. Liz gasped when she heard about the van and by the end of my story she was drawn and quiet. James said:

'You were supposed to warn us if you poked at snakes with a stick. I wonder if Harold did do a double-bluff?'

'I don't think so,' I said, 'some aspects of the case just don't add up if it was him.'

'Like?'

'Like why would he abduct me at a time when everyone knew I was with him? He'd be the top suspect. And why would he kill Sam at a time when everyone knew he was in the office? And doesn't the motive for the original murder seem a bit weak — would anyone really kill their stepfather just for having an affair?'

'Yeah, much more likely the wife would do it,' said James.

'Not Laura, though,' I said, 'it's too banal.'

James and Liz nodded. They'd met Laura.

'Maybe Harold has another motive that we don't know about yet,' said Liz.

'Maybe. Or maybe he just didn't do it.'

'Yes but aren't you biased?' asked James. 'You have a crush on him, Cynthia.'

'Yes, and that's another thing. I can't believe that my judgement could be so bad. But I've been wondering recently.' I looked thoughtfully at James. 'Did you get home OK on Saturday? Were you out Saturday night?'

'Yeah I got home but I was wrecked. I stayed in and watched DVDs.'

'What about you, Liz? Did you go out on Saturday night?'

'No, I stayed in too.'

'With your mum?'

'No, she's away.'

'So you were alone?'

'Um, yeah. A bit of peace for once.'

'Can anyone confirm that? And you, James? Anyone to back up your story?'

'Cynthia.' James rose slowly, staring at me. 'Are you saying you think one of us kidnapped you?'

'One or both. You know, you and Liz never really explained why you worked late the night Nathan died, and why you left at the same time.'

'I don't believe this,' said Liz hotly. 'We've been helping you all along, trying to watch your back—'

'You were on the spot when Sam was killed, weren't you Liz? Do you know the percentage of people who find bodies who turn out to be the murderer?'

'No.'

'Maybe we should google it.'

Alice chose this moment to intervene. 'What are you saying, Cynthia? I thought James and Liz were friends of yours.'

'So did I.' I hated the wobble I heard in my voice.

James sat back down. 'OK. You've had a pretty awful couple of days. People trying to kill you etcetera. I can see why you'd stop trusting everyone. And, of course, we haven't been friends all that long. I stayed late the night of Nathan's murder because I was playing Second Life in the games room. Slightly embarrassing and nerdy. I didn't leave at the same time as Liz, though. At least I don't think so. I don't know when she left.'

'You left within a minute or two of each other,' I said.

'Liz, what's your excuse?'

Liz had gone a deep red. I began to feel curious. 'Well? Would you prefer to tell me in private?'

'No, it's OK.' She put up her chin. 'The reason I stayed so late is I was snogging Peter.'

'You were?' Someone please give me back my jaw. 'In the office? Where?'

'Gurbledyburbledygook.'

'Speak up Liz, we can't hear you,' said James with delight.

'In the photocopying room.'

No one could keep a straight face after that. James nipped out for a couple of bottles of wine and we settled down for a good gossip.

'I didn't really suspect the two of you, but I needed to be sure,' I said. 'As you say, James, I've been through a lot and trust is a commodity I'm running low on.'

'If it helps, I had Peter round Saturday night so really I do have an alibi,' said Liz.

'I've a pretty good one too,' said James. 'I can't drive.'

'So who are your suspects?' asked Alice.

'We drew up a list,' I told her, 'but it's probably shorter after all this.'

'You know, with the back door open for the delivery it could be a person we've never even heard of,' said Liz. 'A total stranger who Nathan looked sideways at on the tube.'

'Not now, though,' said James. 'Now Sam's dead and Cynthia's been abducted we've more to go on. It must be someone who was at the memorial service. That's no help, though, all our suspects were. Of course it could be someone else in the office who we haven't even thought of.'

'So who are your suspects?' asked Alice again.

'Peter's in the clear. He really was with me on Saturday,' said Liz. 'We hooked up at five o'clock and he spent the night.' She looked shy.

'OK, so that leaves the following. Alice, take note,' I said.

'Harold — OK we know all about that.

'Laura — still possible, but I think she'd come forward if she thought Harold would be blamed for her crime.

'Archibald — maybe he discovered Nathan's incompetence and lost it.

'Cecil Howell — stood to lose a lot of money if Nathan hadn't been killed, but would he know Sam?

'Vicky — Nathan shafted her. But would she have killed Sam or kidnapped me? I don't fancy Vicky,' I said. 'I think the kidnapper was a man.'

Liz nodded.

'Why?' asked James. 'Did you hear him talking?'

'No,' I shook my head uncertainly, thinking back. 'I heard his footsteps when he left the van. Not heels. It could have been a woman in sensible shoes, but they sounded heavier and more masculine to me.'

'OK,' said James, 'we'll concentrate on the men.'

'Eugene,' I continued, '— to keep his job;

Ronan — to prevent outsourcing;

Zorr — to defend his honour.'

'The last three don't seem very convincing,' said Alice, when we'd explained the reasoning behind them. 'Nor does that Archibald guy. I'd say Cecil Howell is your best bet, if it wasn't Harold.'

'It wasn't Harold,' I insisted, 'but Cecil Howell doesn't even know who I am. I'm sure he didn't recognise me when we went to his office, but he would have done if he'd trashed my flat a few days before.'

'So that leaves, basically, no one,' said Alice, 'except Harold. Maybe you should accept that it was Harold, Cynthia.'

'Eugene,' I said, but James and Liz were shaking their heads, and even I had to admit that the thought of Eugene knifing not one, but two people seemed very unlikely. Plus there's the fact that fathers of triplets are rarely free for several hours on a Saturday evening/Sunday morning.

'Hang on,' said James, 'aren't we forgetting something?

How did the killer know you were visiting a dilapidated warehouse in an obscure part of the city?'

'He'd know all right if it was Harold,' said Alice, irritatingly, 'because he brought her.'

'You'd have known if you'd followed me,' I said to James, to annoy him.

'Darling, I'd seen quite enough of you for one day. It *must* be Harold, unless he told someone where he was taking you. His mum, perhaps.'

'How did the police find out you were in Oxford?' Liz asked.

'My mobile. It's not Harold. I just know it isn't.'

'Maybe the killer used your phone to track you to the warehouse,' said Liz.

'So now you're saying it was a policeman. The Super, perhaps?' I scowled at her.

'No, but there's a service, isn't there? Some type of online thing where you can track people down?' she asked. 'I read an article. You can stalk your boyfriend or girlfriend. Pretends to be for monitoring your kids, but of course it's a magnet for weirdos.'

She picked up my laptop. 'I'll check it out.'

After a few minutes she looked up. 'Yep, it's do-able. You have to apply for a code though. It's sent out by snail-mail. Takes a few days, which our killer didn't have in this case.'

'They might have the code already, though,' argued James. 'Obviously the murderer is an unsavoury character. He or she might be spying on someone else already. Or maybe there's a different site that doesn't need a code.'

'You need access to the phone of the person you're stalking, as well,' said Liz. 'The company sends out a text telling them they're being tracked when it starts tracking them. You'd need to be able to delete the text before your stalkee saw it. That could be a clue, Cynthia. Has anyone borrowed your phone in a suspicious manner in the past few weeks?'

'No, but it's always on my desk at work. Anybody could

"borrow" it for a few minutes. How does the stalker find out where I am afterwards?'

'Types your number into an Internet site. Spooky. I wonder if they're still tracking you? Where's your mobile?'

'With her handbag, I suppose. In a police station somewhere in London. The killer will think she's under arrest,' said Alice.

'Phew, I might have a few attack-free hours then. This is ridiculous. Let's get more wine.'

We talked desultorily about the murders. Eventually the others realised that I was exhausted and in desperate need of some murder-free time.

'I was talking to Martha today,' James told me. 'Apparently Jasmine thinks that's the coolest game anyone's ever thought up for her. She's planning to get a DNA testing kit next Christmas, she's hoping you'll get involved. Only joking,' he added as I bent astonished eyes on him.

James and Liz finally picked themselves up and stumbled off to get the last tube. I was wiped out but I didn't want to be alone. I was too embarrassed to tell Alice that, though. She'd booked a room nearby. She was preparing to turn in when someone knocked loudly on my door.

'Don't get it,' I said, feeling frightened.

'Nonsense. *I'm* here,' said Alice, and flung the door open. The Super walked in and dropped my handbag and my Accessorise bag of weekend-away clothes inside the door. Yay, clothes! But he didn't look happy.

'What the hell are you doing? Do you *want* to be killed? What did you mean by slipping out of the hospital? I thought they'd got you at last!'

'Er, hi. Would you like a glass of wine?'

'What I'd like, Hegarty, is to put you over my knee and give you a good spanking.'

'Oo, you never said he was kinky,' said Alice.

The Super glared at her — I thought he would order her out of the room. Then the anger died out of his eyes and he started to laugh.

'Cynthia, what were you thinking? I had a man watching your room, you were safe in the hospital.'

'He wasn't watching it very well then, was he? He never appeared when I came out.'

'I told him to be unobtrusive. He didn't see you but he says he had the door under observation at all times. He says the only people around were your two glamorous sisters.'

Alice and I exchanged looks.

'Well done, sis,' I said.

I turned to the Super. 'I'm sorry. I didn't mean to worry you, but I hated the hospital. The food was appalling and everything smelled funny and people kept coming in and poking me and asking me stupid questions. I didn't know I was supposed to be under guard and I was afraid whoever has it in for me would come back and finish me off. And I was homesick.'

'For a *Holiday Inn*?'

'Did you *see* that hospital?'

'No harm done, Cynthia, but please don't do anything like that again. I've arranged for a guard here instead. *Kate*,' he raised his voice. PC Lawson appeared in the doorway. 'PC Lawson here will be outside your door for the next while. Don't try to slip away, and don't go anywhere without telling her. You got that? Someone will replace her when her shift is over.'

'How long for?' I asked. 'You can't keep that up for ever. It must cost a fortune.'

'Until we find the killer,' he replied. 'Don't worry, we'll get him soon. The murderer's made several mistakes now. The more people he kills, the easier it is to track him down.'

'Is that so? Maybe I should tie a target round my neck and go outside.'

'Don't be bitter,' he said, grinning at me. 'I'm trying to protect you, aren't I? If you're killed I'll be very sad even in spite of all the extra clues I'll get. Now I'm off. Alice, take care of your sister and stop encouraging her to flout police authority.'

He gave Alice a severe look as he left the room.

'I see what you mean,' Alice said. 'There *is* something comforting about him. He's like a big rugged teddy-bear in a rumpled suit.'

'I wish he was staying here,' I moaned tipsily. Then I wondered whether PC Lawson was stationed close enough to hear.

That night I tossed and turned, hot, sore and restless. I got up at about two am feeling thirsty. Alice had gone to her room nearby. I poured a glass of water in the bathroom. The hotel was silent and still. I stood near the door for a minute. I couldn't resist opening it quietly and peeking out. PC Lawson met my eye.

'Is everything OK miss?'

I nodded, embarrassed, and went back to bed. I slept like a log after that.

13 — BACK TO WORK

My head.

Ow.

The throbbing that pounded me next morning could have been caused by the killer's knock-out blow or by the wine. I decided it wasn't the wine. I made myself a cup of tea and felt marginally better.

Meanwhile, I had a new worry. I'd hidden my memory stick in the most cunning place I could think of before my room got searched. The cleaning cupboard in the hall outside. The cleaning cupboard beside which PC…(I opened the door and introduced myself)…Blake was currently ensconced in an uncomfortable-looking chair.

Over breakfast, I explained the problem to Alice. She promised to locate the stick once PC Blake had followed me away.

'So you are going in to work?'

'Yep. I'm dying to find out what's happening. Can't resist. Can you meet me at lunchtime?'

'I'm on it.'

I told PC Blake where I was off to.

'I've been instructed to accompany you, miss.'

We set off on the ten-minute journey. After a moment I

turned round and asked 'Constable Blake, why don't you walk beside me? You're making me nervous back there.'

'My view of possible threats is better from here, miss.'

'Oh.'

Surely any threat was going to come from the office. PC Blake, to my disappointment, seemed to think I was safe once he'd guided me through the few reporters hanging around outside the building. In the lobby, he gave me a mobile number, telling me to ring him when I was ready to leave.

The first thing I did was head straight to Archibald's office, figuring that he might have used his boss-man powers to pick up some bits and pieces of gossip. According to James he'd been concerned about me, asking how badly I was hurt. I still hadn't finished the Overflight unit tests, I remembered cynically.

'Cynthia! Good to see you're OK.' Archibald got up from his desk and came round to shake my hand. 'Very brave of you to come in. Sit down. Do you feel up to doing some work? Er…I believe the Overflight unit testing isn't quite finished.'

'Oh yes, I'm good to go,' I told him. 'I see we're back on the third floor? Is the investigation into Sam's death winding down?'

'Yes. The perpetrator is known and no further on-site inquiries are required. The police have moved their centre of operations to Scotland Yard.'

The perpetrator? I stiffened. Did he mean Harold? Pompous git.

'I gather you're acquainted with the young man in question, Cynthia. It must have been a harrowing experience for you. You have all my sympathy.'

'Thanks.' I remembered the Super saying he'd prefer if everyone suspected Harold. I had a short battle with myself. I lost. 'I'm not sure he's guilty, though.'

'You're not?' His eyes narrowed. 'I understood you saw him during your river attack?'

'On the riverbank, yes. But I was totally vulnerable at that moment and he didn't finish me off. I've been wondering why. I don't think he could be the killer.'

'It's December, Cynthia. Exposure would have done the job pretty quickly. You were very lucky, from what the Superintendent tells me. I hope you'll be more cautious in future. We can't afford to lose you before the project finishes,' he ended with a heavy attempt at humour.

'Are there any new developments?' I asked him.

'Airwolfe issued a statement yesterday to reassure customers, but frankly, it'll take considerably more than a statement. It's unlucky that your story got into the papers.'

'It certainly is. Just as well I'm not living in my flat at the moment. I'd be besieged by reporters.'

'Really?' He seemed interested. 'How sensible. Where are you staying?'

'I could tell you but I'd have to kill you,' I laughed. 'Let's just say I'm safe enough. The police know where I am, and they've given me an armed guard. The killer won't get near me a second time.'

'**K**idnapper steal your watch then?' asked Vicky as I passed her on the way to my desk. I rolled my eyes in disbelief. She was back to her former self.

It was good to sit at my desk again — like coming home. Work didn't seem appealing though. As usual, I eased myself in via my email Inbox. I had plenty of mails to catch up on. I started at the most recent and worked backwards.

To: Cynthia
From: James
Subject: Lateness!
Yoo apier too haf takin adffantidge ov reesint eventts to cum in lait. This sinnikul bid for simpathee is nott akseptabull.
Yors stirnly,
The Orfiss Muncher

To: James
From: Cynthia
Subject: Re: Lateness!
Itt haz bin scientiffcly diturminned that murrders shud onli afekt efishienssy wen dere arr more than tree debts. Pleez remayne att yore deskks untyl then.
Yurrs Optimistiklly,
Teh Awestruck Minger

Apparently, flu had been ravaging the Airwolfe ranks. Or perhaps most of the staff were taking the sensible view that their risk of being murdered in the office would be substantially diminished if they weren't there. Numbers were decimated. Liz, Peter and James had come in, though, as had Ronan and Bharathi.

To: All Staff
From: Ann Dilger
Subject: Fwd: Tragic Events
By now you will have heard about the tragic death on Friday of Mr Samuel Babcock.
Mr Babcock was a long-standing and well-respected member of the Airwolfe IT Department based at City Road. He was found dead in a communal area of the office on Friday afternoon.
We are shocked and saddened by Mr Babcock's death, following so closely on the death of Mr Nathan Boyle last week.
Airwolfe Management would like to assure all staff based at City Road that security has been reinforced at the site and an arrest is expected shortly in connection with the two deaths. There is no need for concern. In the meantime, staff should continue to work as normal and do their best to meet agreed deadlines. Please also refrain from communicating with media representatives present at the site.
With the Q3 results to be announced shortly, this is a crucial period for Airwolfe. Let's all pull together! Let's make it

happen!
Regards,
Jim Dawson
CEO

My phone rang at 12.30, Ronan's name flashing up.

'Andy's?'

'Why not? Who's going?'

'Everyone.' He gave a snort of laughter. 'All six of us.'

Andy's was a nearby pub that housed a Thai restaurant of legendary cheapness and goodness. Friday group lunches tended to take place there. Occasionally they marked the beginning of the weekend for some of the less rigorous timekeepers in the office. A Tuesday visit was unusual. Things really were topsy turvy.

'But you'd better disguise yourself, missus,' added Ronan. 'The reporters outside are after you since yesterday morning. If they recognise you we'll have an extra thirty for lunch.'

Liz and I debated our best course of action. I grabbed my gym-bag from under my desk, went to the Ladies and changed into a jogging outfit, trainers and all. I added my tiny iPod to give myself an air of busy abstraction. I planned to borrow Liz's large shades, but she pointed out that this would instantly attract suspicion. I scraped my curly hair back into a tight pony tail instead and rang PC Blake, warning him to be unobtrusive.

Liz borrowed my jacket and left at the head of the gang, wearing her shades and trying to walk like me but succeeding only in looking highly suspicious. I slipped out a second later, chewing gum and adjusting the volume on the Shuffle, letting my eyes wander uninterestedly over the assembled paparazzi. Liz and the others stopped to answer some questions. I could hear Liz as I headed off, saying 'Cynthia? You missed her. She sneaked out the back door.'

I jogged off through the graveyard — followed at a discreet distance by the unfortunate PC Blake — and made my way circuitously to Andy's. In spite of the tortuous route I got there first.

''Allo love, still alive then?' Andy is the friendliest barman in London. Possibly in the world.

'Just. Could I have your largest pint of cold lager please?'

Andy grinned. 'Tough few days, eh? Coming up.'

As he poured he expressed his sympathy for my recent body-finding experiences. PC Blake sat himself at a small table from which he could survey the restaurant, the bar and the door.

The others arrived, clamouring for drinks and distracting Andy.

'Any hassle?' I asked Liz, picking up my pint.

'No. They totally fell for it. I told them you're suffering from stress and you've gone to an undisclosed location for a holiday. Wouldn't blame you if you did. You must be wrecked.'

When everyone had bought their drinks and caught up with Andy's news, we moved to the restaurant section at the back. I dropped by PC Blake on the way and recommended the fish. We sat at one of the long wooden tables and took our orders from the tiny Thai waitress. I started with corn cakes. Round and yellow and just moist enough. Yum.

In the middle of the starters, Alice arrived. She slipped me the memory stick and squeezed in at the end of the table beside Ronan. I watched him give her an appreciative once-over, returned with enthusiasm. Great. Ronan, dark-haired and skinny with a cheeky grin, was certainly attractive. He was also single, and for a reason…no sooner did he captivate someone than he lost interest and moved on. A male Alice, in other words. If they got together it'd be the shortest relationship in history. Possibly so brief that they'd spontaneously combust.

Bharathi sat beside me. 'You poor thing. What was it like?' she asked. 'Tell me all the details.'

'Nasty.' I proceeded to describe nearly everything I'd been through since Saturday afternoon. Her eyes got wider and wider.

'And you're sure it was a guy?'

'As sure as I can be. So female suspects are in the clear,' I smiled.

'Well that's a relief.'

Pool?' asked Ronan laconically as we waited for our main courses.

'We really are short of staff if I'm the best you can come up with,' I joked, following him into the pool room. I stifled my guilt at PC Blake having to temporarily abandon his meal to keep an eye on me.

'Wanted to talk to you,' Ronan said. 'Cynthia, I'm worried about these bleedin' murders. Are you sure Nathan's youngfella did them?'

'No.'

'Me neither. It's stupid. How would he know about the games room? Even if he did, there's still no way he'd know that Sam was never out of the place.'

'Yeah. I don't like it either but I can't figure out who else it could be. Any ideas?'

'If I did I'd tell the cops before I end up on a kebab myself. Here. I was poking around Boyle's machine and I came across some stuff you might find interesting.' He handed me a sheet of paper listing a load of websites I'd never heard of. They looked like financial sites.

'What are they?' I asked.

'Embezzlement sites. Howtos. Top fifteen embezzlement techniques — how to do them, how to spot them, how to get away with them. That sort of thing. He could've been on the take.'

I put the list in my pocket. It confirmed what Bharathi had already told me. Nathan had had an unhealthy interest in scams.

'How about your sister? Is she single?'

'Very,' I said. 'But watch it, Ronan. She's scary. She'll rip your guts out and make you eat them in front of her.'

He seemed intrigued. I sighed. This was all I needed. Could life get any more complicated?

Zorr came in as we were finishing our meals. He missed a beat when he saw Alice.

'Andy told me you were here,' he said, drawing me aside. 'He knows I'm looking for you. How are you?'

'Not too bad. Maybe I should give you my mobile number?'

'No need, you're fairly easy to find,' he said.

Lovely.

'Zorr, I'm making a point of being the opposite,' I told him. 'I'm even in disguise.'

'You look the same.'

'Zorr, I'm in a gym kit looking like a sporty person. I've a whole different persona! Different shoes, different jacket, different—'

'Yeah, Cynthia, whatever. Listen. Don't think Harold did it. Cops've made a mistake. Just hope no one else is killed while they're barking up the wrong tree. See you've got Plod with you.'

He jerked his head at self-consciously plain-clothed PC Blake.

'Hope he's up to the job. Take this.'

He pressed a small device into my hand. It looked like a key fob.

'What is it?'

'Attack alarm. Press the buttons on both sides. Very loud, don't test it. Who's the redhead?'

'My sister.'

'Oh?' He scrutinised me with new interest. 'Not much like you, is she?'

'Do you want an introduction?' I asked him sweetly.

'Later,' and he was gone.

Back at the office I still found it impossible to concentrate. I wrote a test, and fixed the code when it broke. Checked the code into source. Had a look at the *Irish Examiner* online (Countdown to Christmas. Queues in A&E). Opened my mail. Ton the travelling Dutchman had moved on to Cambodia and was spending his time dodging a Swiss couple on the same tourist — sorry, backpacker — trail. He'd attached a photograph of himself hiding behind a temple in Angkor Wat.

The memory stick with Nathan's mail seemed to glow through my handbag. I couldn't resist. If I didn't copy the contents onto my hard drive, I should be able to examine them without putting Ronan at risk. I had to find out more. And I wanted to get rid of that nagging doubt about Harold's innocence.

I struggled through another day's worth of soft porn and office minutiae. It took nearly twenty minutes, and I'd still only waded through Nathan's Inbox for less than a week before his death. The only email of interest I'd found had been the one firing Eugene.

Abruptly it dawned on me. I'd been doing things all wrong, looking at the Inbox. The useful Eugene mail had been in Nathan's Sent box. That was where I should be focusing my efforts. There I would discover what Nathan had been saying to people in the hours and days before his murder.

Opening the Sent folder, I felt the twinge of excitement that you get when you tweak the last line of code and a program finally runs. Progress at last. Nathan hadn't been an 'auto-forwarder'. The stupid jokes and round-robin emails he'd been sent by various friends had been killed stone dead in his Inbox. He'd never sent them on. Probably too lazy.

He certainly hadn't been the world's hardest worker. His Sent messages averaged only twenty or thirty a day. But nearly every one was a gem. From the day he died I found the following mails:

– One inviting Vicky to his office at 6:30 that evening.
– The one to Eugene.
– One to Bharathi containing a veiled threat which, after my conversation with her, I had no difficulty in interpreting.
– One to Archibald about the latest AirCross delay.
– One to a mutual poker acquaintance hinting that Zorr had cheated and he, Nathan, would soon be able to prove it.
– One to a company I'd never heard of, arranging to meet to discuss outsourcing software development. (He'd given up on SysAdmin, I thought, and started targeting us instead.)

I went down to Prêt to fetch a decent cup of tea and a chocolate slice. Now for the previous week. This was going to be fun.

I wasn't so happy when I got to Thursday morning. A mail to security jumped out at me:

To: City Rd Security
From: Nathan Boyle
Subject: Visitors to the Office
I have just recieved an unexpected visit from my step-son, Mr Harold Mansfield. Please note that no one should be permited to enter the building except employees and people with appointments.
Do not admit Mr Mansfield again.
Regards,
Nathan Boyle

Why had Nathan objected to Harold's visit to his office? I remembered that it had begun peacefully but had ended with Nathan shouting for a good five minutes. We hadn't taken too much notice at the time. Shouting was Nathan's preferred method of communication. But why would he invite Harold to the office party if he was so angry with him? Maybe he hadn't. Harold had come with me. He'd had an invitation, but he might have got one in his investigator role.

What had made Nathan so furious? This was ridiculous, I had to talk to Harold. When I'd got my mobile back with my handbag the night before it'd had a flat battery, and I'd been too exhausted to do anything more than plug it in.

Now I whipped it out and rang Harold. No reply. I left a voice mail.

'Harold, hi, it's me, Cynthia. Look, I need to talk to you. If you're free, I mean if you're around. Just give me a shout.'

I left my number, in case he'd lost it. I couldn't think of anything else to do. I'd just have to wait.

My headache intensified in the afternoon. I didn't do any overtime. For the first time in ages I left work without a Harold date to look forward to. I went straight home to the Holiday Inn.

'So who's the hot Northsider? Is he the guy who gave you the emails?' asked Alice over a quiet dinner. PC Blake sat nearby. I hoped he was out of earshot.

'Yes, but it's a secret. Don't tell anyone,' I hissed, 'and don't tell him you know.'

'OK, OK, don't get your knickers in a twist. I won't say a word. As long as you set me up on a date with him.'

'*Me* set you up on a date? Haven't you organised one already? You're slowing down.'

She gave me one of her Looks. 'And was that Zorr, that dramatic-looking fella who came in? He's cute too.'

'One at a time, sis.'

'Why? You have Harold and the Super. I should get two as well, it's only fair.'

I buried my head in my hands. 'Are you never going home?'

'No. I took a week off. Look, Cynthia, I'm only joking about the blokes but you are in deep shit. Someone's still out to get you and you need your big sister to take care of you.'

'And London has a lot of shops.'

'True,' she said innocently. 'Handy for killing time while you're at work.'

After dinner, we both went to my room. I picked up the

TV remote.

'Hang on,' said Alice, 'aren't you forgetting something?'

'What?'

'Sparky's texts. Have you checked them yet?'

'No.'

She folded her arms, waiting.

'Shite,' I said, resigned. 'Will you do it?'

I rooted my mobile out of my handbag, handed it over, and collapsed onto my bed. There was silence for a moment or two.

'Well, the little toe rag!' she said.

'What?'

'Cynthia, why didn't you block him? You really should have blocked him. Listen to this:

'who are you fucking now you little tramp that blond dickhead

'sorry about my last text i was drunk

'i know you still want me bitch and im not far away

'What a tosser,' said Alice. 'Terrible punctuation, too.'

'They weren't as bad as that a few months ago, when I stopped reading them,' I said. 'He must be trying to get a reaction. It's kind of sad.'

'Sad? It's pathetic! And nasty. So poisonous. You poor thing,' said Alice.

'I'm just glad we split up,' I said. 'He's got nothing to do with me now. All that stuff, it doesn't seem real. Like he's playing some kind of game with himself.'

'I think you should take the Super's advice and complain to the police,' said Alice. 'Now, Cynthia, I know you don't want to do anything about your flat but it's time to tackle it. I bought loads of cleaning stuff earlier and I've ordered a taxi. Let's go over there. Just for an hour.'

Just climbing into bed seemed like a daunting prospect. An hour's cleaning was out of the question.

'I'm still injured,' I said, 'and I'm tired. I need to take it easy.'

'An hour,' she said. 'You can lie on the sofa while I'm working. Then we'll have a glass of wine and an early night.'

PC Blake asked where we were going. I'd forgotten about PC Blake. I cheered up a bit. I could get used to this police protection business.

We had to swing by Alice's room. She wanted to change and we had to pick up all the cleaning materials she'd bought.

'Housework is fun if you have everything you need,' she said.

She'd certainly changed her tune since we were kids.

She handed me a plastic bag containing several packets of black sacks and bottles of lethal-looking detergents, a second bag bulging with cream and spray cleaners, green scourers and J-cloths, and a mop-bucket.

'Alice, I don't think we'll be polishing floors for a while,' I said, as a tin of beeswax fell out and rolled away. I rescued it, jammed one of the bags into the mop-bucket and picked up the other one.

'It'll come in handy at the end,' she said, grabbing a mop and her own bunch of bags. A set of washing-up brushes poked out of the top of one of them. Green rubber gloves were visible in another. Alice was taking this seriously.

The short taxi journey ended too quickly. I dreaded seeing my flat again, especially the bathroom. All that spiteful broken glass and the stench of spilled toiletries. The kitchen would stink as well now, I realised, with food rotting on the floor and the bins unemptied for a week.

I couldn't face the slashed duvet in the bedroom. I planned to ask Alice to clear that away before I went in.

It took us a few minutes to get out of the cab with all our gear. I didn't like to ask PC Blake to help. He had to watch for villains. Anyway, I was in no hurry. I approached the door, put down my bags and pulled my keys out of my pocket. My hand shook. I fumbled the keys and dropped them. I picked them up and tried again. Finally, the lock turned.

'Me first!' said Alice, barging past me, bashing me on the shin with the mop.

'Charming,' I muttered.

I pulled myself up the stairs behind her. In spite of my tension and throbbing head, I began to feel amused. She looked so un-Alice-like, clad in the slick black tracksuit and brand new yellow runners that were her idea of trendy cleaning gear, her glorious red hair confined in a neat bun. Her mop and a sweeping brush, clamped under her arm, waved wildly back and forth as she climbed. I kept my distance.

I grinned down at PC Blake, stolidly following us. He gave me a rueful smile.

Alice stopped outside my flat, put down her bags and reached behind her for the key. I put it into her hand. She opened the door.

Silence.

'Jesus, Cynthia.'

'Awful, isn't it?'

She turned to look at me. I couldn't interpret her expression. I had expected horror, not wonder and a kind of dawning pity.

'Go on in, then,' I said.

Instead, she stepped aside and pulled me forward. I looked in.

My living-room was immaculate.

No clothes on the sofa.

No books on the floor.

The standard lamp stood innocently behind the armchair, its bulb apparently intact, its shade neatly straightened.

The coffee table gleamed with polish. There was a fresh bunch of roses in the vase. I could smell them from the door.

Cushions were plumped invitingly on the sofa.

It was so creepy.

In the hall behind me, PC Blake's phone rang. He moved

away.

'Cynthia, it seems OK to me,' said Alice. 'Maybe you were just a bit stressed last time you came here.'

'Stressed? The place was totally destroyed!' I said.

'So. In that case, unlikely as it may seem, someone has tidied up,' said Alice. 'And cleaned up, too. I was looking forward to some hard work but there's nothing left to do.'

'It's weird,' I said.

'Do you think…?' said Alice, 'I mean, is it possible that with the tension of the murder and everything you could have…well…imagined it?

'No,' I said.

PC Blake came back.

'I'm off.'

'No!' I said. 'I've been burgled again. You can't go.'

'Place looks all right to me, miss,' he said, glancing through the door. 'Anyway, Kate's here. See you tomorrow.'

PC Lawson appeared as he vanished.

As we stared in at my impeccably tidy flat, over to the left, barely in my line of vision, something moved. The handle of the bathroom door turned, breaking the silence.

The door began to open.

I froze. Behind me, I felt a tiny start from Alice. I sensed PC Lawson tense for action.

A slim, well-built guy emerged, tanned and lithe.

Naked.

Rubbing his tousled hair with a towel, he strolled across the living room to the bedroom on the right.

My bedroom.

He went in, shutting the door behind him.

Although his face had been hidden, I'd recognised him by his…by certain features.

'Sparky!' I said.

'OK. At last, I see the attraction,' said Alice.

'Sparky. Is that the gentleman who sends you nuisance texts?' asked PC Lawson.

'Yes.'

'What's he doing in your flat? Have you got back together?'

'I don't know. And no, definitely not.'

She looked thoughtfully at me.

'Did you give him keys?'

'No. He must've broken in.'

She examined the edge of the door.

'No damage,' she said.

It dawned on me then what had happened. The rat.

'Scratch that, I think I know where he got the keys. And I'm going in there right now and I'm going to kill him,' I said.

'Hey, hey, hey.' PC Lawson grabbed my arm. 'I'm not authorised to permit you to commit manslaughter, however obnoxious the victim might be.'

'It's my flat,' I said. 'He shouldn't be in there. He must be committing some crime. Can't you arrest him, Constable Lawson?'

'Call me Kate. Now, here's what I suggest,' she said.

When Sparky emerged from my bedroom — clothed, thankfully — I was sitting on the couch.

'Cynthia!' he said.

'Sparky?' I replied. 'What are you doing here?'

'Waiting for you,' he smiled, and waved at the table. 'I got you flowers.'

'Yeah, I saw. How did you get in?'

'I spotted an open window. I climbed in and the place was wrecked. So I tidied up.'

He looked cool and sexy, hair ruffled, dressed in a red hoody and trendy jeans. His eyes shone blue in his perfect, tanned face. He sat down beside me and took my hand, raising it meaningfully to his lips, gazing soulfully at me.

'You tidied up?' I said, pulling my hand away. 'No way. You've never even picked a pen up off the floor.'

The hint of a frown.

'Aren't you happy to see me, darling?'

'No.'

His frown deepened. This wasn't going according to the Sparky script. He looked even sexier when he was pissed off, but these days I was immune. At last.

'But I've gone to so much trouble to find you. And look at all the work I did. Your place was a mess.'

'Not before you found it.'

'I'm sorry, darling?'

'You wrecked it, didn't you? You trashed my lovely flat and you pocketed my spare keys on the way out. Then you couldn't resist coming back. Why did you clean up? Guilty conscience?'

'I cleaned up because I love you. You're right, I did trash the place. I saw you in Camden with that blond tosser and tailed your cab home. I…' he hesitated '…I couldn't handle seeing you with someone else. I planned to come and tell you how much I miss you but that cow Alice was here all the time. I thought she'd blooming moved in or something. Then she went off with a suitcase on Monday morning. I hung around till night-time but you didn't show. I figured you were with him. I just couldn't take it. I lost it. So, yeah, I broke in and wrecked the gaff. I couldn't help it, Cynthia. I miss you so much.'

He tried to take my hand again, moving in to kiss me. I rose from the sofa and looked down at him, shaking.

'You're crazy, Sparky. I never realised how mad you are. Get out of here right now, and don't come near me again. And if you send me any more of your messages I'm going to report you to the police.'

'If you do that you'll be sorry,' he said, 'you little bitch. Do you think you can come in here and boss me around? I'm sick of your games. I still love you and I want you back.'

He stood up and moved towards me. I backed against the wall beside the bathroom. There wasn't much space left between us.

'Sparky, if you really do love me, please, just go away and

leave me alone.'

'And let you go off with some wanker? I'll kill you first!'

He lunged at me, his eyes glittering.

The bathroom door opened. Alice and PC Lawson — Kate — came out.

'You!' said Sparky, glaring at Alice.

'Hey, Sparky,' said Alice with a smile.

Sparky looked from her to me.

'I'll get you yet,' he said. He spun and ran towards the stairs.

He was too late. Kate stood solidly in front of the closed door.

'No. You won't,' she said. 'Sit down. We're going to sort this out now.'

Sparky advanced towards her. She pulled out a truncheon type thing. She seemed businesslike. Sparky sat down.

'Your phone, Alice,' said Kate, holding out her hand.

Alice's new Nokia had video capabilities. Positioned on the bookcase, it had faithfully recorded the brief scene between Sparky and myself. Kate played it back.

Sparky began to look worried.

'Lest there be any doubt,' said Kate, 'I also got it on my Sony Ericsson. Superintendent Foster will be delighted. He's been keen to prosecute you since he read your texts to Cynthia.'

'Superintendent?' said Sparky. He sneered. 'You're lying. No Superintendent would be interested in a few drunk messages.'

'When a murder investigation is underway,' said Kate, 'any suspicious behaviour becomes a matter of considerable interest. Very considerable interest.'

Sparky seemed to shrink. Like all bullies, he didn't want to play with the big boys.

'I'd advise you to make a formal complaint, Cynthia,' said Kate. 'With those videos as evidence — not to mention his texts if you haven't deleted them — and my personal account of this evening's events, he'll probably get several years in jail.

Long enough to work out that you simply don't want to see him anymore.'

Sparky looked wildly at her.

'I've just got an Australian visa. What about if I go back there?' he asked.

'That,' said Kate, 'would be highly satisfactory.'

'**G**od, I need a drink,' said Alice half an hour later, sinking into a red sofa with blue cushions. We'd decamped to one of Brick Lane's many cafés. The low seating and dim lighting, a faint smell of sheesha and background sitar music gave the place an Eastern feel. There was space for about twenty customers but for the moment we were alone. Kate sat on a nearby sofa, as alert as its squashy comfort would allow. I'd asked her to join us but apparently it was against police rules.

'I don't think they serve alcohol,' I told Alice, 'but we can try.'

'Do you sell beer?' I asked the waiter when he arrived.

'Yes we do. What type would you like?'

'Tiger beer?'

He nodded.

'Could we have two large bottles of it please, and two plates of vegetable samosas?'

I slumped back in my seat, banging the bruise on the back of my head. I'd forgotten about it. I slid a plump embroidered cushion behind my shoulders and closed my eyes.

'Are you OK?' asked Alice.

'Fine. I'm just glad to be rid of Sparky once and for all.'

'Forget Sparky. He's gone. Let's talk the killings through again,' said Alice. 'Every detail.'

So we did.

I hadn't thought about Jasmine's fingerprint analysis for ages. The river incident had wiped it from my mind. I described her to Alice, giving her a chuckle. I told her that Jasmine had excluded Peter, Harold and Laura from the list of potential burglars. She'd got that right, since it had been Sparky all along. And she'd been right about Vicky sending the note too. None of that helped with Nathan's and Sam's deaths, though. I wished I'd had something from one of the crime scenes for her to test.

I hardly noticed the waiter arriving at our table with the beer and samosas.

When it came to the murders, Alice refused to believe that either Zorr or Ronan could be guilty. She said that the killings seemed premeditated. And neither of them had the calculating temperament required. I kind of agreed with her about that. On the other hand, who would plan a murder with a computer programmer working nearby? Despite my reputation for concentration, surely it was too great a risk?

'Another beer?' asked Alice.

I shook my head, then winced. I'd have liked one, but my stiff and tired limbs and my pounding head said no. It was time to go to bed. We signalled for the bill. The waiter came over to us.

'How much would you usually pay for a beer?' he asked.

'What?'

'How much would you normally pay for a beer? You see,' he smiled shyly, 'I got my licence to serve beer only today and you are my first customers to order it. I don't know how much to charge.'

I laughed. 'Where did you buy it from? The corner shop?' I asked, remembering that I'd seen him come in earlier with a plastic bag.

'Yes,' he said.

'Then why don't you charge us what you paid, and add on a pound a bottle?'

I had no idea whether this was a fair price or not, but it seemed reasonable.

'I will give a discount because you are my first customers to drink beer,' he said.

'You see why I love this area?' I said to Alice after we'd wished him luck with his new business venture and left. The episode cheered us up, and I started to think things might not be so bad. Maybe it would all work out OK.

When we got back to the hotel, Kate went into my room ahead of me and checked the wardrobe and bathroom for villains. Although I felt I should pretend to be brave I was delighted not to have to do it myself. Kate's calm presence was reassuring.

'Join us for a chat?' I asked her.

'I can't. Have to stay on guard,' she said. 'Thanks, though.'

Alice turned on the TV. I still had to lie on my side to watch it. The bruise on the back of my head protested if it touched anything.

My mobile rang.

'Your tame gorilless won't let me in.'

Harold! I opened the door and told Kate that he was welcome.

'All right, Cynthia, but you need some sleep,' she said.

'**H**ow are you, Cynthia? Still meddling, I suppose?' Harold asked.

'Yes, and I hear you're a meddler too. A very good one.'

'I have my moments,' he said softly. 'Who's this?'

I introduced him to Alice. He smiled at her and said:

'I hope you're here to take care of Cynthia? She's been having a rough time. Rougher than I realised. Cynthia, why didn't you tell me someone burgled your apartment?'

'Oh, well, I…I was too embarrassed, to be honest. Kind of upset. Plus I didn't want anyone to know I'm living here. I still don't, it's a secret. It just was all a bit…much. And you've had your mum with you whenever I've seen you recently and I thought it might worry her.'

'That's kind of you. She's tired. Very tired, somewhat depressed. She wanted to visit you in the hospital but you'd gone. I figured it was just as well. She might have had a shock. You looked so fragile when I saw you last. I've been worried about you.'

'I believe I have to thank you for saving my life,' I said.

'The Superintendent tracked you down, really,' said Harold. 'When the van disappeared I assumed you were just test-driving it for a laugh so I hung out at Alexandra's for a while. I rang you a few times but there was no answer. Alexandra pointed out that you could have got lost, so I went up to the tube station and walked around looking for you.

'Then it dawned on me that you might be in danger. I tried to get the police going but with no luck until I got hold of the Superintendent next morning. He'd set things moving already. Once I knew you'd been in an Oxford boat yard I was afraid you'd end up in the river. I studied in Oxford — I'm familiar with the territory. So I went up and hired a bicycle and took to the paths.'

'I'm glad you did.'

'Finally I found you. I thought for a minute that I was too late.' He looked away, his mouth hardening. 'But then you opened your eyes,' he finished lightly. 'Alexandra says hi by the way.'

'Oh, say hi back. Harold, will you tell me what you and Nathan fought about the time you visited the office?'

'Yes. I'm sure you've already guessed though. I'd discovered his affair with Vicky, and I told him so. I also said I'd tell my mother about it and advise her to get a divorce. He was furious. He warned me not to interfere.'

'Is it true you've been investigating embezzlement at Airwolfe?'

'Yup.'

'Have you found any?'

'Not yet,' he said, without meeting my eyes.

'Is that why you came to the party with us?'

'It was the initial plan,' he said. He glanced at Alice, who totally didn't make herself scarce. 'Then I…I enjoyed myself.'

'So did I.' I was too shy to tell Alice to bugger off. He

might get the wrong idea.

'I wish you'd brought me, it sounded fab,' said Alice. I sighed.

'You're still tired. I'll be off,' said Harold.

'Do you know who the Superintendent suspects?' I asked him.

'No.'

'Neither do I. I hope it's not anyone I like.'

I struggled out of bed. Lucky I hadn't undressed yet. I planned to show him out of the room and share a private word. Or something. I'd forgotten about Kate, smiling benignly at us from her chair in the corridor.

'I'll see you soon,' said Harold, giving me a peck on the cheek.

'Yes. Soon.'

There was a lot I wanted to say to him but not with Kate there. And so many questions I wanted to ask. Had he really not discovered that Nathan was the embezzler? Had he truly spent Saturday night searching for me? And what had he wanted to say or do, but couldn't because of Alice?

At around one in the morning the fire alarm went off. I grabbed my dressing-gown and opened the door. Kate.

'Standard distraction tactic, miss. Take a jacket, it's freezing. Don't go out of my sight.'

A cold half-hour outside followed. Alice joined us. Other guests milled about in dressing-gowns and pyjamas while the staff came and went, looking alert and enviably well-dressed. We made small-talk. Kate had two kids, three and five, and liked the night shift as she could spend time with them during the day. She planned to visit Kerry for her holidays. We recommended Cahersiveen as the most beautiful place in Ireland.

There was, of course, no fire, and soon afterwards we set off back inside. 'You know what this fire alarm means?' I asked Kate.

'He's found out where you're staying.'
I nodded.
'We'll move tomorrow,' said Alice.

I lay awake for a while afterwards, trying to imagine ways the killer could get rid of Kate. She seemed pretty tenacious.

A woman's scream, heard from afar? That would require an accomplice, and anyway I suspected Kate would just pull out her police radio thingy and report a possible crime.

Hit her on the back of the head? I gently prodded my own bruise. An effective technique, but she had her back to the wall and seemed immovable. But what about 'answering calls of nature' as Gulliver would say? I decided to go out and tell her she could use my loo if required.

I started thinking about the murder instead, and drifted back to sleep.

14 — CYNTHIA WORKS IT OUT

When I awoke, the solution lay neatly docketed in my brain as though dictated by my subconscious. Only one person made sense as the murderer. I knew that something must be done.

Breakfast was subdued. Alice ate in uncharacteristic silence and I felt, nonsensically, on the verge of betrayal. Foolishness. Two stabbings in five days justified extreme measures.

After breakfast I rang the Super and arranged to meet him at his office. I had to get the tube, which made me even more depressed. I told Alice where I was going, but not why. She would be happier not knowing, I thought.

Excerpt from the *Metro*, Wednesday

Airwolfe's stock price plunged another 10% yesterday, in the second day's trading after the discovery of a second body at the company's small City Road office.

'Security at all Airwolfe offices has been tightened. Police are investigating a clear lead and an arrest is expected shortly. There's no cause for concern,' said Michael Clegg, Airwolfe's UK vice-president of operations, yesterday.

The markets don't agree, however, and Airwolfe shares are in

free-fall on both sides of the Atlantic.
Jim Dawson, Airwolfe's CEO, flew into London last night for crisis talks with UK management. 'We are deeply saddened by the news of Babcock's death, and would like to convey our sympathy to his family and friends,' he said on landing at Heathrow. 'We would also like to emphasise to our customers that it's business as usual at Airwolfe. The murder suspect is not an Airwolfe employee and no longer has access to our buildings. We would ask all Airwolfe staff to return to work as soon as possible.'
Adam Dowling, a top London recruitment consultant, says he is currently having difficulty attracting applicants for Airwolfe vacancies. 'Until last week people were falling over themselves to apply for jobs at Airwolfe,' he said. 'Now I can't find anyone who's willing to work there. Let's face it,' he added, glancing behind him, 'who wants to be murdered at their desk?'

The Super greeted me politely. He had a video camera going and a PC taking notes.

'So you think you've discovered who committed these murders?' he said.

'Yes,' I said. I felt awful. I could still change my mind, I thought. But despite my doubts and fears, I had no alternative.

'Tell me,' said the Super.

It was difficult to go in to work as though nothing had happened. What would all these people think if they knew what I was up to? Vicky shot me a filthy look as I appeared at midday. Properly back to her old form then. I chuckled to myself. No matter how bad things got, winding Vicky up by being late never lost its appeal. I went in to see Archibald.

'The Superintendent asked me if you could arrange a meeting of the AirCross team at three in the basement,' I told him. He looked startled.

'Did he say why?'

'No. He said he'd like to talk to us.' I shrugged. 'He asked me to invite Ronan, Vicky and Bharathi along too — I'll tell them myself.'

'What does he want me for? I hope you haven't been getting me into any trouble,' said Ronan.

'Relax, Ro, I'm silent as the grave,' I said. 'Just show up. I think he needs bodies to make things interesting.'

'There've been enough bodies in this building already. OK, OK, Hegarty, I'll come.'

Bharathi looked worried. There were dark circles around her eyes and a new strain on her face. I tried to reassure her but my efforts were at best half-hearted. I was feeling pretty tense too.

I went down to the basement a few minutes early.

I glanced at the printer as I passed. No flashing lights. It was fixed. Great. That was all I needed.

I felt tense and wired. We were assembling in the meeting room we'd all been jammed into for a week after Nathan's death. I hated every inch of it from the unnecessarily huge, heavy oval mahogany table to the whiteboard and ill-connected phones. The rest of the team probably felt the same way, but the Super had insisted. Maybe he wanted to unsettle us, cramming us all in there again.

He sure knew how to make an appearance. The Airwolfe staff all arrived bang on time, due to nerves no doubt. He turned up at three oh five, resplendent in a suit and tie. You'd think he was one of the management brass from head office. My gloom deepened when I saw him. He looked so serious. PC Blake came in from wherever he put himself while I worked. Another uniformed bobby accompanied him.

'It's like being in one of those Poirot-style showdowns,' said James, 'except today's hard-boiled policeman wouldn't dream of such a thing.'

I gave him a slow wink.

Zorr came in, nodded at everyone and stood leaning his shoulder against the wall near the door. He looked impassive, but then he always did.

'We're here today,' said the Super, 'to discuss the two recent deaths at Airwolfe. This office is on my patch. I don't take kindly to people who mess with my patch.'

James tried to meet my eye but for once I didn't feel inclined to scoff.

'Certain facts have come to my attention, that lead me to believe we may be close to finding a solution to these murders,' continued the Super, looking at me. I felt the eyes of everyone in the room trained on me. They had nearly all of them told me something. Now they were probably wishing they hadn't. My face was burning, like my bridges. Too late for regrets.

'When this investigation began, there was no obvious motive for Mr Boyle's murder,' said the Super. 'There seemed to be no opportunity, either, for anyone except Ms Hegarty. The person who finds the body is always an initial suspect. They can explain away most forensic evidence by saying that they touched the victim when they found them. Statistically, a large proportion of body-finders turn out to be the actual murderers.

'In this case, if Ms Hegarty wasn't the killer then the murderer's job would have been difficult, perhaps impossible.

'On the other hand, Ms Hegarty had no obvious motive. She was new at Airwolfe; she hadn't been here long enough to develop a deep emotional involvement with Nathan Boyle or anyone else. A thorough trawl through Mr Boyle's past and hers indicated that they almost certainly had never crossed paths before.'

What thorough trawl? I hadn't heard anything about this.

I imagined the Irish Gardaí (police) visiting my many previous flats, interviewing landlords and fellow tenants and coming up with nothing. Not to mention that I'd had at least twelve jobs at varying levels, each with an associated bunch of workmates who were now dispersed around Ireland and the world. The Garda assigned to my past must be fantasising about throwing it all up to teach scuba-diving in Cambodia.

'Ms Hegarty might, of course, be unbalanced but she showed few signs of mental illness.' (Hello? Don't you mean none?) 'The fact that she set up an 'investigation' of her own, while irritating, also seemed to point to her innocence. She may, of course, have been trying an elaborate double-bluff, but we're not in the pages of a Dorothy Sayers.

'If Ms Hegarty was innocent, we needed to find someone prepared not only to kill the victim, but to kill him while Ms Hegarty sat nearby. Someone prepared to take the risk that the killing would either be silent or wouldn't attract Ms Hegarty's attention. Someone reckless, careless and arrogant.'

Everyone looked at Ronan, except for the people who looked at Zorr.

'Or someone desperate,' said the Super.

'Mrs Rai.'

Bharathi jumped.

'You discovered that Mr Boyle had embezzled Airwolfe funds. When you told him you were going to report him, he threatened to get your children expelled from school. He probably couldn't have carried out that threat, but he made a worse one. He threatened to frame you for the embezzlement, didn't he?'

Bharathi looked him straight in the eye. 'Yes, Superintendent, he did.'

'Could he have succeeded?'

'I hoped not, but he'd been clever with the paperwork. His higher rank in the company might have influenced the investigation.'

'Really,' interjected Archibald. 'I'm shocked. Shocked!

How could he behave in such a way?'

'Fairly typical behaviour for Mr Boyle, I think,' said the Superintendent wryly. 'There was only one way out of the situation, Mrs Rai, wasn't there? If Mr Boyle ceased to exist, so would your problems. If he remained alive, even if he failed to frame you for the embezzlement, your card would be marked and your days at Airwolfe would be numbered. No one likes a whistle-blower. Without references, getting another job would be difficult. He was causing a lot of trouble for you, wasn't he?'

'Yes,' said Bharathi calmly. 'If I'd thought of killing him maybe it would have seemed like an attractive solution, in my private fantasy world, but I didn't.'

She turned from the Super to me. 'I really don't know why I didn't tell you about Nathan threatening to fire me, Cynthia,' she said. 'I think perhaps I worried that it'd make you think I was the killer. I can see that that was silly. I look much more guilty now.' She turned back to the Super. 'He was an unpleasant man. Even an evil man. But none of us may take a life. Superintendent, I didn't kill him.'

Silence hung over the room. I knew Bharathi had told the truth, and I hoped the Superintendent did too. After a moment he nodded.

'I believe you, Mrs Rai,' he said.

Bharathi closed her eyes for a second. Then her shoulders fell and she seemed to relax.

'A trawl through Mr Boyle's communications threw up other interesting possibilities,' resumed the Super, in a conversational tone. 'For example, Mr Reaney, Mr Boyle fired you the day he died, didn't he?'

'Yes,' said Eugene, blinking.

'Would you have got another job easily?'

Eugene glanced at me. 'No,' he said.

'We didn't grasp the huge differences in employability between programmers for some time,' said the Super, 'because no one in here mentioned them. Eventually a colleague with IT experience filled us in.'

Phew. Eugene would know that I hadn't split on him.

'Your sacking gave you a motive on the very day of Mr Boyle's death and—'

'I didn't kill him though,' interrupted Eugene.

'The trouble is,' said the Super, his eyes sweeping the room, 'once we started finding motives they multiplied like fruit flies. For example, Mr Boyle was having an affair. Enter two new suspects: his wife, and his mistress.'

Now Vicky turned to glare at me. Nothing new, nevertheless my heart began to pound.

'We found out after a while who his mistress was,' said the Super. 'There are no secrets in an office like this. Several people told us. We also discovered that he planned to finish the relationship.'

'No he didn't,' said Vicky, then bit her lip.

'He worried about losing his wife,' said the Super, very gently. 'He knew she'd be told about you if he kept seeing you.'

'But he loved me.' Vicky's poise disintegrated. Her chin wobbled and I felt sorry for her again. I was getting totally mixed up.

'Not as much as he loved his wife,' said the Super, nodding at PC Blake who was standing by the door. PC Blake opened the door. Laura and Harold came in, Harold giving me an apologetic look.

Ronan stood up and gave Laura his chair. He, Zorr and Harold leaned against the wall like a bunch of neighbourhood layabouts. Laura, composed, surveyed the room, taking in all the bodies. Then she looked up at the Super.

'Is this the final scene?' she asked.

'I hope so,' he said, smiling down at her. 'Thank you for coming, Mrs Boyle. Mr Mansfield, I invited you along today because I believe that somewhere in this room is…the murderer.'

The tension mounted. It was getting warmer. The air-conditioning never worked properly in that room. Archibald took out a hankie and mopped his bald pate. James shifted in his chair. Liz smiled weakly at me.

'Vicky, you had a motive, and you had the means. The same goes for you Ronan, you Bharathi and you, Eugene. You, Cynthia, threatened to kill Mr Boyle on the Friday before his death. Liz, he belittled you. James, although you had no obvious motive, you had the opportunity.

'Which leads me to the next point. The murder must have been premeditated. No one could have taken the dagger down to stab Mr Boyle in his presence. It must have been removed from the room in advance. On the other hand, the murderer walked straight past Cynthia, both on the way in and on the way out. It doesn't make any sense. Cynthia's powers of concentration are infamous, but what if she took a tea break or stood up to leave?

He paused.

'The killer took a huge gamble and only one explanation makes sense. They had to have been someone who didn't know that Cynthia usually works late, and who didn't notice her when they hurried past to kill Mr Boyle.'

Silence. The Superintendent's gaze moved from face to glistening face. It was growing even hotter. The room had started to smell.

'We exclude anyone who worked with Cynthia on a daily basis. So we won't look for the killer amongst you three,' he smiled gravely at James, Liz and Eugene, sitting together at one end of the table. 'We also exclude anyone who worked on the same floor as Cynthia, dealt with her often or socialised with her. Bharathi, Peter, Vicky and Ronan, you're off the hook too.

'But what about suspects unconnected with Airwolfe? Enemies made outside these walls? Cecil Howell of CityRich, for example? We've ruled them out because they wouldn't be aware of the security issues in this building.

'So we exclude total outsiders. We also omit everyone who was signed in to the building at the time of Nathan's death. The murder only makes sense if the killer thought their presence would go undetected. In other words, we need to look for the murderer in the list of people who didn't work with Cynthia, who weren't known to be in the office, who had a motive, who had no alibi, and who were aware of the broken camera and the CCTV blind spots.'

I was slightly dizzy from tension and the heat. The smell of stress and sweat was becoming overpowering. I wished he'd hurry up. I wanted the awful moment to be over, I wanted to get on with my life.

'That list,' he said, 'includes you, Mr Zappatone.' Zorr started. 'You're head of security, you certainly know how to get into the building undiscovered. You don't work with Cynthia and wouldn't be aware of her antisocial hours.'

'What?' said Zorr, 'I had no motive.'

'Ah,' said the Super. 'You're wrong there. Mr Boyle had been pushing to get your firm replaced with a bigger company. He'd been trying to get rid of you, and you knew it. How many clients does SwordBlade have, Mr Zappatone?'

'Several,' said Zorr, looking strained.

'But only one big, flagship client, I believe. Lose Airwolfe and you lose half your turnover and all your credibility. A motive, wouldn't you say?'

'Ha. Nathan had no credibility himself,' said Zorr. 'No one would've listened to him if he'd said security wasn't up to scratch.'

'No — until the back door camera broke, and remained broken for three days,' said the Super. 'Why didn't you replace it, Mr Zappatone? Did you hope that a useless camera would come in handy?'

'I replaced the bloody camera as soon as we could source an alternative,' said Zorr. 'This is ridiculous. Of course I wouldn't kill someone to keep my security business. Especially not in a building I do the security *for*. Come *on*, Superintendent. These murders have probably cost me my company. They've certainly cost me the Airwolfe contract. I'm going to lose that as soon as they can get anyone else to take this place on. No one will, though, while a killer's rampaging through the corridors. Security guards like to feel secure.'

'You're right. You do seem an unlikely killer,' said the Super, 'but someone else also fits our profile.'

You could have heard a pin drop, even though the floor was carpeted, as he turned his head and locked eyes with Harold. My heart sank. This would be even worse than I'd thought.

Harold grinned.

'I gather you've put everyone else on the rack, Superintendent,' he said, 'so I suppose my turn has come. Do your worst.'

'Airwolfe hired you to investigate suspected embezzlement,' said the Super. I felt a stillness enter the room. No one had known this. I wondered what James and Liz made of it, but I couldn't take my eyes off the unfolding drama.

'You found more than you'd bargained for,' continued the Super. 'You discovered Miss Hubbell's affair with your father-in-law. You knew your mother would be devastated.'

Laura stared down at her hands. I hoped Harold had already told her.

'You argued with Nathan, trying to get him to end the illicit relationship. He agreed. The affair seemed to be over.'

I'd never seen Harold look so grim. He put a hand on the back of Laura's chair. It clenched, the knuckles standing out sharply under his skin.

'Then you saw Mr Boyle with Miss Hubbell again at the office party. Worse, you found out that he was responsible for the embezzlement you'd been asked to investigate.'

'Nonsense,' said Harold.

'And then the final straw. Your mother tried everything to have another child when she married Mr Boyle. Without success. Now Mr Boyle was going ahead without her, having a child with his mistress.'

Laura turned her head towards Vicky and gave her a long stare, difficult to interpret. Rather her than me. Harold moved his hand to Laura's shoulder and clasped it. My heart thumped. I felt breathless.

'You knew about the knife, you knew where Mr Boyle's office was, you'd heard him complain about the inadequate security. You pilfered the dagger during your Monday-morning visit, waited for someone to leave the back door open, and made your way into the building. You'd already assessed the CCTV and discovered how to dodge the blind spots. You went into Mr Boyle's office and killed your stepfather. Intent on your task, you didn't even notice Cynthia, quietly bent over her computer, until you left Boyle's office. Then it was too late, and you did the only thing you could — walked confidently past her desk and back out of the building.'

The Super painted such a clear picture that I could almost see Harold in action, until he looked at me, his mouth twisting as if in pain. I dropped my eyes.

'Harold Stanislaus Mansfield, I arrest you on suspicion of the murder of Mr Nathan Boyle—'

'No!' cried Laura.

'It's all right, mother,' said Harold softly, 'I'll be OK, I didn't do it. Get me a good lawyer.' He bent and kissed her cheek. Then he turned to the Super, extending his wrists. 'Take me away,' he said. PC Blake took him by the arm and they left the room. Harold never looked back at any of us.

Archibald was the first to move after Harold had gone. 'Laura—' he said.

'We need to ask Mrs Boyle some questions,' said the Superintendent. 'She'll be taken care of.' He helped Laura up and guided her towards the door. She could barely walk, she was so shocked. I longed to go and help them but my guilty conscience wouldn't let me. Without me the Super could never have found enough evidence to arrest Harold. I told myself that the murders couldn't be allowed to continue. Cold comfort. I ached all over. My bruises throbbed. I was dizzy. I thought about going back to the hotel, but I had work to do.

The door closed behind Laura and the Super. Nobody moved, we all sat glued to our seats, everyone still taking things in.

'Cynthia,' Bharathi said, 'are you OK?'

'Mm. Yes.'

'Thank God it's over. Funny though, I wouldn't have thought Nathan's little embezzlement would've been large-scale enough to get the company to launch an investigation. I didn't think it'd even been noticed yet. A few hundred pounds here and there. Still,' she grimaced, 'reassuring to find out we're in good accounting hands, eh?'

'Oh. Yes,' I said.

Was she mad? Who cared about the stupid accountants?

'I'm sorry. You must be upset. Did you still, um, like him?'

I nodded.

'Oh, Cynthia.'

She squeezed my hand gently.

'I always thought that if I'd looked up and seen who killed Nathan,' I said, smiling tearfully at her, 'I'd be able to wait until the fuss died down, then blackmail them and go and live in the Bahamas. But now I think I'd clear Harold's name, instead.'

'It's all so awful, Cynthia,' Liz said. 'Come to Prêt for a cup of tea and a chocolate slice.'

'I can't. I'm going back to the Holiday Inn to pack,' I said. 'I just decided Alice and I are going to Dublin tonight.'

On the way to my desk for my coat and handbag, I had to detour to the Ladies. I spent a few minutes getting a red nose and then covering it up.

As I walked back to my desk, Liz stopped me. 'The Super wants to see you in the server room,' she said.

I was surprised. I was expecting to see him, but why down in that floor of servers and mainframes, computers old and new? I ran down the stairs and let myself in with my security pass. The space was cool and restful after the recent heat and intensity. Surrounded by busy computers, I began to relax. I couldn't see anyone, though. 'Superintendent Foster?' I called, as I walked down the central aisle past ranks of forgotten, humming machinery, my feet tapping on the metal floor tiles.

'Over here,' came a voice from the other end somewhere. I continued towards it. I wanted to check the AirCross test machines, but I could do that on my way out.

Ahead of me, a figure stepped out from behind a server stack.

Archibald.

'Hello, Cynthia.'

'Hello, Tom. What are you doing here?'

'I need to speak to you urgently about some worrying AirCross developments.'

'Like what?' I asked, trying to step around him towards the service door at the other end of the building.

'We may have a problem completing the project,' he replied, moving to block me.

'Why?'

'Because one of the key developers will be dead,' he said blandly, pulling a length of clothes-line out of his pocket.

He advanced towards me, never taking his glittering eyes from my face. I edged backwards, about to turn and run back to the main door. But he lunged towards me, grabbed my arm, kicked my legs from under me and pushed and dragged me into one of the aisles of computers. I reached my head up and bit his hand. He yelped and kicked me in the stomach. I cramped up, winded. He kicked me again and pulled me into a corner, hidden from the main aisle by a server stack. I knew I was finished. No one walking through the room would see us.

'What the fuck are you doing, Archibald?' I shouted, desperately hoping to attract someone's attention, even though I knew hardly anyone came down here, and anyway I'd be drowned out by the rumble of computers.

'What do you think, Cynthia?' he hissed, pulling me up and forcing my arm up behind me. 'I'm getting rid of the last bit of evidence against me.'

'What evidence? I never saw anything!'

'So you say, Cynthia, so you say. But I know what you're up to. I've known all along. Wait until the hue-and-cry dies down and then come to me with the begging bowl. You made it very clear this afternoon. Oh yes, I've been through it all before you see. I know how you people think.'

'What do you mean?' I lurched forward but he was too strong for me. 'Did Sam blackmail you?'

'Oh no, no, no, no, no, no, no. No, because he didn't get a chance. I finished him off same as I finished Nathan off, and now I'm getting rid of you too.'

When people chase you in nightmares there's never any pain. Right now his grip on my arm was excruciating. Everything was red. I lurched and squirmed but he jerked my arm further up.

Agony. I groaned.

'This time I'm finishing you off properly. I'll stay here until you're well and truly dead. I should never have tried the suicide-on-the-river thing, too complicated. I won't make that mistake again.'

I believed him. Where was PC Blake? The Super? Harold? Alice? Would they all arrive too late? Would I be an undignified blue heap on the floor with my tongue sticking out?

'HELP!' I yelled. He put his arm over my mouth. I couldn't bite through his thick sheepskin coat.

'It'll be easier if you don't struggle,' he said.

'Easier for who?' I thought.

I looked around desperately for something to hit him with. Nothing. Just computers. Most of them didn't even have keyboards or mice.

'For me.' He released my arm. It fell to my side, helpless with pain. He fumbled, trying to get the clothes-line around my neck.

Once he succeeded he'd be able to stay out of my reach while it choked me.

Wouldn't anyone come to help me?

I tried to lunge past him, but there was no space. His huge bulk blocked the only way out. He grabbed me again, swinging me round with my back to him, getting the line in position at my neck. I fended it off with my hands, keeping my chin clamped to my chest. Trying to remember my self-defence classes, I stamped down backwards hard on his foot. But my boots had flat heels and he just grunted and kicked me viciously in the back of the leg, knocking me forward. I bent even further suddenly, throwing all my weight downwards, but he clamped his arm tighter around me, still manoeuvring to get the clothes-line under my chin. Those bloody self-defence classes didn't cater for fighting a fifteen-stone murderer. I gouged backwards at his eyes but couldn't reach him. I was weakening, already exhausted from the nightmare on the river. He punched my nose and my head jerked back, giving him a chance to get the clothes-line round my neck. I forced my hand inside it but the tight cord bit into my fingers. I was suffocating myself with the back of my own hand. I couldn't breathe. He wrestled me down and sat on top of me, pinning me to the floor.

Zorr's personal alarm!

Where was it?

In my handbag.

On my desk.

On the third floor.

The row of murmuring servers darkened. Frantically scrabbling and kicking at the metal tiles, I raged at having to leave the world so soon.

Abruptly the weight vanished. Footsteps, thumps and shouts. Someone cursed and dug at my neck. A second later the pressure on the clothes-line eased.

Gentle hands turned me onto my back, and I was raised on a powerful arm. I found myself looking into the Super's eyes.

'I'm so sorry, Cynthia,' he said.

'Thank you,' I croaked, and hid my face against his shirt so he wouldn't see me cry.

15 — CONCLUSION

'You were right this morning, Cynthia. Boyle discovered that Archibald had embezzled Airwolfe funds,' said the Super a while later.

I lay propped up on a sofa in someone's office. I'd seen a doctor, who'd tutted over my various cuts and bruises but said there was nothing seriously wrong with me but shock. A cup of tea and a chocolate slice had miraculously appeared. The Super had got an initial confession from Archibald, who had blurted out everything when caught red-handed, as I'd hoped he would.

Now the Super and PC Blake had taken my statement, and the Super was giving me the lowdown on Archibald's admission. It was probably highly irregular, but I didn't plan to object.

'Boyle noticed certain irregularities, put two and two together and made four. Payments of ten thousand pounds each. Archibald was the source of the unexplained payments to Boyle's account.'

'Blackmail, just like I thought,' I said.

'Exactly. Archibald purloined the stiletto some time on Monday. He left at about six as he usually did. He went to the gym, changed into a casual tracksuit with a hood and put on a pair of gloves. He jogged back to the office with the hood up, so he couldn't be recognised on external CCTV. He arrived about the time the stationery delivery was due, and walked into the building while the door was open. He got to Boyle's office just before seven o'clock. He argued with Boyle, said he wouldn't make any more payments. That's when you overheard Boyle say 'You'll have to if you want to keep me quiet.'

'Archibald felt he'd been given the go-ahead. You know how Boyle died. Archibald must have got a shock when he saw you afterwards. He left the office light on to avoid attracting your attention. Frankly, I think that if he'd still had the stiletto he'd have killed you too.'

I shuddered.

'He took a chance and walked straight out, but thinking things over afterwards he grew convinced that you'd seen him. You had to be lying. After his experience with Boyle, he believed you'd try to blackmail him as soon as the hue-and-cry died down. He decided that you had to go, but he had someone else to see to first.'

'So Sam did mention the blackmail to him?'

'Yes. You were right about that too. Sam Babcock was an unsavoury character,' said the Super. 'I suspect he got drunk and told Archibald what he knew. Maybe even taunted him with the knowledge. And probably didn't even remember afterwards.'

'So Archibald had to do it all over again.'

'Yes. He was acquiring a taste for murder,' said the Super. 'He was unlucky that his first attempt on you at the river didn't work. He might have left you alone afterwards if you hadn't insisted on setting a trap for him. He snapped completely. We think he's done it before. We're going to open an investigation into his wife's death in Egypt.

'Will you mind testifying in court, Cynthia? I'm sure you've had enough drama already, but it's a few months away.'

'I'll manage.'

He stood up and walked to the window.

'Will you stay in London?'

I wondered if he had more than a professional interest. He had his back to me.

'Probably.'

'I'll hope to see you around, then.'

He turned. I could detect nothing in his face except mild concern.

'You know where I am,' I said.

'Feckless.' Alice had arrived at last and was dissing the Superintendent. 'Unreliable, Cynthia. How *could* he have let Archibald attack you? Why didn't he stick to you like glue? I'll never forgive him.'

'We wouldn't have got Archibald's confession if he hadn't been caught red-handed,' I pointed out.

'Confession shmonfession,' said Alice confusedly. 'Oh Cynthia, it was awful. When Liz asked the Super where you'd gone, and we realised that nutter must've got to you, I thought you were dead. Why didn't you tell me what you were planning? I'd've looked after you.'

There were tears in her eyes. Alice! It brought home how close I'd come.

'I couldn't,' I said. 'I knew it'd freak you out. You were happier not knowing. Anyway, cheer up. It's almost five o'clock, let's get the others and go for a drink in the Lighthouse. This is definitely Grade A gossip.'

In the Lighthouse with Alice, surrounded by my friends, I finally started to relax. Instead of my habitual barstool at a high table I had chosen a comfortable chair at a normal table, where I could slump a little and rest all my aches and pains. Vicky was missing and there was no sign of Harold. He probably never wanted to see me again after what I'd put him through. I couldn't blame him, I thought with a stifled sigh.

Everyone had plenty of questions.

'So it was all a set-up? The whole denouement in the basement?' asked James.

'Yes. We wanted to pile on the pressure, so that Harold's arrest would come as an enormous relief. Then, just when Archibald thought everything was over and he was in the clear, I dropped the blackmail hint. We hoped it'd spur him into action. You helped, Bharathi.'

'You mean, when I commented on how trivial Nathan's embezzlement had been?'

'Yes. You were right, of course. A few hundred pounds is chickenfeed. I think Nathan suspected Archibald and started poking around, checking out embezzlement websites on the internet. He stumbled across a small, easy fraud and put that into operation himself. I suppose it made him feel like a player.'

'Archibald thought he hadn't been sussed yet, then, when Harold was fingered,' said Ronan. 'He probably thought he'd have time to do a runner. No wonder he went mental after you hinted you'd seen him.'

'He turned into a totally different person, really violent and fast and terrifying.' I shuddered. I hadn't enjoyed my brush with the dark side. 'No one knew I was down there, and I was afraid that by the time the Super found out it'd be too late.'

'Good job he didn't have a gun,' said Peter.

'Yeah,' I said. 'Dumb really, but I thought if he believed someone else had been charged, and then I hinted that I knew he'd done it, he might snap. I didn't think he'd act so fast. I thought he'd try to fake a suicide again. After all, if I died suspiciously then Harold would be off the hook for the murders. I was supposed to meet the Super outside the building to organise my wire and my bodyguard. But Archibald got in first with the fake message he gave you, Liz.'

Liz winced. 'I can't believe I just passed it on without mentioning him,' she said. 'I fell straight into his trap. God

Cynthia, you might've given us a hint. What made you suspect him in the first place?'

'I discovered,' I said, carefully not meeting Ronan's eye, 'that Nathan had been keeping Archibald informed via email about the delays on the AirCross project. Yet Archibald told James and myself that he'd never been notified of any problems. I wondered why. It only made sense if he'd been unable to fire or reprimand Nathan, for some reason.

'Some reason like blackmail. Once I started thinking on those lines, everything fell into place. Archibald didn't know my work habits. He could very well have missed seeing me when he went in to kill Nathan. As a manager he was kept informed about security issues at City Road, including the broken camera. He could have found out that a stationery delivery was due on Monday evening. He would've had access to my personal information as a matter of routine, so he could easily have got my address and burgled my flat. Although, as it happens, he didn't. He was the only person who ticked every single box, but I couldn't think how to prove it, so I went to the Super and asked him to try a set up.'

'I still can't believe you didn't tell us,' said James, putting his arm around me and giving me a squeeze. 'Liz and I were supposed to be minding your back. How do you think we'd have felt if anything had happened to you?'

'I'm sorry.' I looked from him to Liz. 'I feel terrible, honestly. But we needed you all to believe in the set up. Archibald would have sensed if everyone was acting. I wish Laura hadn't come with Harold, though. I didn't want her to find out about Vicky's baby. That was cruel.'

'I think she already knew,' said Bharathi. 'She's planning to set up a trust fund for the baby, on Nathan's behalf.'

'Ha. He would probably have just walked away,' I said. 'But she's an honourable woman. He was a lucky man.'

'I think, deep down, maybe he knew it,' said Bharathi.

'And I'm lucky too,' I said. 'Thanks all of you, especially you, James and Liz. And you Alice.'

Alice playfully slapped Ronan's hand away from her phone, where she was entering his number, and glanced up at me.

'Any time, Sis,' she said.

We'd been in the Lighthouse for about an hour when a glass of champagne arrived in front of me. I looked at it, my heart in my mouth.

'Compliments of the gentleman at the bar,' said the waitress, nodding at a location behind me. I turned. Harold raised a lazy eyebrow. I nearly fell out of my chair getting over to him.

'I'm so sorry. I'm *so* sorry. Are you OK?'

'No. I was put through extreme psychological torture,' said Harold.

'But the Super *promised* he'd tell you as soon as he got you out of the building,' I said.

Harold looked at me with what might have been wry amusement or exasperation. It was hard to gauge.

'He did. He told us I wasn't in any danger, which I knew already because I didn't do it, but that you were putting your head in the lion's mouth and offering yourself up for bait. How do you think I felt?'

I didn't know, but *I* felt shy. I smiled at him.

'Relieved matters were in such good hands?'

'No, you little fool, terrified. That lunatic could have killed you.'

He stopped, took a deep breath, and said 'Promise me you'll never do anything like that again!'

'Why, Mr Mansfield,' I said, 'are you concerning yourself with my welfare?'

'Of course I am,' he said. He looked around impatiently. Half of Airwolfe looked back at him. 'Come with me.'

It was freezing outside, but when he slid an arm behind my back and gathered me inside his coat it got a lot warmer. I was glued to the laughter in his eyes.

'Little investigating girl, I'll be sticking around,' he said, bringing up a hand to trace a deep cut on my cheek. 'You need someone to stop you getting into mischief.'

'Do you think you'll manage it?' I asked, grinning.

'I hope so.' He looked consideringly at me. His eyes darkened, and he bent his head.

We'd exchanged a few pecks before, but this was a proper first kiss. Full of curiosity, promise and delight. I was swept away on a wave of pleasure, deaf and blind to everything but Harold.

Until the door of the Lighthouse banged shut beside us.

'Forsooth, fair damsel, hast thou found thy prince?' asked Ronan, and wandered off, chuckling, into the night.

ABOUT THE AUTHOR

Ita Ryan works in IT and spent several years toiling in the City in London. She lives with her family in Kerry in Ireland.

Ita also gives classes in creative writing and has had her work broadcast on Irish national radio.

If you enjoyed reading this book and would like to hear about new work, you can join Ita's mailing list on www.itaryan.com. If you prefer, you can follow her on Twitter (@itaryan).

Happy reading!